The Year of Passages

Edited by

Sandra Buckley

Brian Massumi

Michael Hardt

Theory out of Bounds

...UNCONTAINED

BY

THE

DISCIPLINES,

INSUBORDINATE

PRACTICES OF RESISTANCE

...Inventing,

excessively,

in the between...

PROCESSES

OF

HYBRIDIZATION

The Year of Passages

Réda Bensmaïa

Translated and with an
afterword by Tom Conley

Theory out of Bounds *Volume 5*

University of Minnesota Press

Minneapolis • London

Herein any resemblance to living beings is coincidental. If, contrary to all expectations, a living being happens to be recognized in any of the characters, he or she is advised to write the narrators of this story. They will rectify as required.

Published by the University of Minnesota Press
111 Third Avenue South, Suite 290,
Minneapolis, MN 55401-2520
Printed in the United States of America on acid-free paper

LIBRARY OF CONGRESS CATALOGING-IN-PUBLICATION DATA
Bensmaïa, Réda.
The year of passages / Réda Bensmaïa ; translated and with an
afterword by Tom Conley.
p.   cm. — (Theory out of bounds ; v. 5)
ISBN 0-8166-2393-7
1. Algeria—Intellectual life—20th century—Fiction.
2. Algerians—Travel—Foreign countries—Fiction.   I. Conley, Tom.
II. Title.   III. Series.
PQ3989.2.B4317Y43   1995
843—dc20
94-36615

The University of Minnesota
is an equal-opportunity educator and employer.

To Slimane, Djamel, and Siria

Youth, you're in despair! Maaaster! You misjudge France with its rich resources and

Algeria, the Academy, and their principles!

Louis-Ferdinand Céline, *Rigodon*

"You speak French admirably," Madame N. was telling him ... Then he paused a bit and

softly, with a modest air: "Oh! Madame, I don't speak ... *I stamph her!*"

André Gide, *Journal*

For more than twenty centuries we have been bearing on our shoulders the weight of

magnificent civilizations that all originate elsewhere; none has sprouted on our soil, we

have set the tone for none. We are whites no less than you, Chevalley, no less than the

queen of England, and yet, for the last two thousand five hundred years we still remain a

colony.

Tomasi Lampedus, *The Leopard*

O N E

(1962–64, Algiers, 1964–71, Aix-en-Provence, August 1968, Switzerland [the Lenk Valley], 1971–88, Algiers, Aix-en-Provence, Algiers, San Francisco, London, Minneapolis, Lyons, Minneapolis, Paris *at all times*)

"Dancing pain, dancing dervish, dancing idiot!
*I'm prospering, prospering!"**

Songs, dwellings, worries, memory gaps, stagnations, orgasms, spasms, and the same old runaround! Will he dance? Will he eat? Will he go crazy? Will he sleep? Will he get on with it? Why the hell do we have so many machines to do the crap we do? I'm finally done with my *Dead Letters*. I threw in what stinks along with everything else! I published them! I threw them up, and publicly! *And you have nothing to do with it!* Will this be my last book? To dance on a tightrope! To murmur, whisper, think in hiding, deform my thoughts, conceal my thoughts, steal away, bury myself like a mole, write like a living corpse!

@ Compare man to an instrument panel with a thousand light bulbs; some go out before others are turned on. W. B.

During my quick visit we had scarcely settled at the back of the studio, the only spot where he had let us bring in two skinny chairs, Francisco told me, "Since I never liked the paintings I saw, I decided to do my own paintings. My friend Raimondo, do you understand what I'm saying? *Tu me suis cher Mourad? Tu piges?* No concessions! No correspondences! No love! No subject! No history! No story! No fabulosities! Only relations! Only transitions! Only passages! Only networks! Skeins of nerves! Nerves, nerves, and nothing but nerves! Modern painters have painted everything, yes, everything, *except for nerves!* They missed the nerves, botched the nerves of our age! They lacked nerve! They opted for plain type! Straight people! I conclude they've opted for the bourgeoisie! Whence I conclude that *they are* bourgeois! Fat bourgeois monsters who gobble up petty bourgeois flesh! Bourgeois nourished, supplied with food in the petty bourgeois charnel house *among heaps of bones, magma, grigris, metastases, estates, states, loma, and schamasch, and kheter, and mufti and the pope, the bishop, and the nun, the imam, and the rabbi and his son, and the Bible and its fruits, and Monday, Tuesday, Wednesday, Thursday, Friday, and Saturday, I mean states, folds, clothing, an organism, a physiology, this side of the finished organ they stuff with their I-who-am-not-finished-the-father-who-knows-best, there's the problem!*[1] As for me, I don't paint the picture of flesh the way, as imbeciles say, who are authorized to speak of my painting as if it were fated for them. I don't paint meat, as idiots say, I paint neither meat nor flesh, flesh, *good flesh* — why that's for the bourgeois — just as this new *religion of the body* is for the petty bourgeois. I paint nerves, my dear friend, *what nobody can stand!* The bourgeois can't stomach nerves! Nerves, nerves drive them *crazy!* I paint *stimulation,* I paint passage! In other words, everything the bourgeois think is utterly *superficial! Because flesh,* my friend Raimondo, is nothing more than the *idiotic edulcoration of a black force underfoot, in the lower intestine, in the right buttocks, in the right earlobe, in the spleen, the bumgut, with bombs!* a fear of *anal-mality!* I think that, well, skin is *superficial!* The nerve-screen! *Olivier, would you please be quiet! What stung you? Would you please stop jumping around like a louse? My dear lady, this boy is driving me crazy!* The greatest and most remarkable work of art always winds up weighing *on* our minds, but *no rectification* please! Like a huge piece of mendacity and vulgarity, *like a fat piece of meat stuffed in our stomach!* I therefore paint what passes through our brains bruised by the modern world, not the *substantific, but the prickly marrow!* I paint what neither the bourgeois nor the modern petty bourgeois want to talk about or even hear! What they've tossed into the dungeons! into the nettles! Gotta write for nerves, Mourad, ya gotta write with your nerves, not with your guts! Leave the guts for the Franks, leave your guts as

---

[1]Francisco, he knew his Mommy by heart! whom he injected with his jaculations every time death happened to speak its fat mouth, to risk its fat mouth in the time of life!

collateral! *Potlatch!* You'll do your best with your nerves! With all the war being waged in your guts, you've got enough tripes the way it is! Don't puke'em with that! That's what they're waiting for, *mon cher ami!* They filled your insides and now they want you to vomit the stuff right back at them, all predigested! They want you to do their work for them! Yeah, even to bear their grief for them! They've crammed you chock-full of mental feed while you, well, you just pour out fertilizer around the clock! And *to order!* They've stuffed your grammar school and high school brains, and now they want you to restore and put in their hands the right *percentage* of key Francophone literature! *Usura!* You extend your arms, and they put you in handcuffs! The only things they can't take away from you are your nerves! Your nerve factory! Maghrebian *pride*, that's what they call it! Yeah, they call it *temperament!* It's *atavism*, that's what they're betting on! That's the way they got you: by *psychologizing nervousness!* Verbosity of nerves! Diverting verbal plops! Ploppy de Vega! A verbal summons! A verbalization of nerves! You've been *verbalized*, Francophoneyed! C'mon, fess up, fess up to mommy France, my little baby boy! Write her your great love letter! Tell mommy how much you've suffered! Tell her what makes you grieve! Tell her where it hurts! Say Sartre, Gide, Camus, Proust, or you'll be cuffed! Say Freud, Marx, Lenin, Jean-Jaurès in French, or you'll flunk! Freud, Marx, but not Fanon, you *dumb idiot! Repeat your Marxist line to mommy and ask to be excused!* The only one who really understood that was Fanon! He began with nerves, with Kris, with Doukdouk, with Fondouk, at least he knew that above all it was about nervousness! But he clearly saw that nerves, well, they've got nothing to do with guts! *Nothing clinical!* Pure nerve! The clinic came later! The clinic, that was a way of taming the *Maghrebian lion!* The clinic? That Dinet! Delacroix! Fromentin! Gide! Daudet and Tartarin de Tarascon! Flaubert! Gérôme, the dirty old man! *Gérôme and his gentilities!* All these *-atalists* of the East! All these *Algerian Women in Their Apartment!* All these odalisques! All these Returns from the Orient! All these Lamartinades! All these Napoleooneries! All these *Turkish Baths!* All these other Turkeries! All these turkeys and everything they're trucking! Everybody went to see! Everyone went with their antiphonies! Antiquities, my friend! Antiquity, that's truth! Make way for the ancients! O beauteous land of ancient monuments! O Paris of the past of my Persian loves! Sweete Olde Fraunce! O the luster of my old colonies! O Arabesse! O Arabeast! Everybody fascinated one like the other by lions and tigers that prowled along the borders of the Sahel! And still *unfazed by our gaze!* All wild, all the while they can't be domesticated! They can't let these animals go public! This is pure nerve! Nerves on the edge! Raw nerves! The women in the Harem, the Fantasia and the lions on the savannah! They got you! All your nerves! All your lions!

All your tigers! All your gazelles! All your Saharas! All your deserts! All your camels! Your disorder, Armando! Your disorder! Ligatured! Trilatured! All your nerves in the whorehouse of the botanical gardens! All in a rush! All your nerves in the windows of the Botanical Gardens in Paris! *<North African Tiger! Sahelian Lion! Desert Fox!>* All your nervousness in the drawers of the Museum of Natural History in Paris. And your *brains* between the Museum of African Arts and the archives of Aix-en-Provence! *Archives du Sud!* Duped! Skinned and quartered! Decerebrated, Dis-enervated, Decorticated! Verbalization without further ado! Fears that one among you might be thinking of revealing their *notorious little secret!* That one of you might be *enervated* again and strictify literature! Triturate the littered ratures wiped off the bed of their ligatures! Ligature their strictures! That's to be avoided at all cost! No, that's not underdevelopment, *it's becoming undertreatment!* They treat you like dogs! You say *Amenokal!* Before and after, no matter! Dogs in the shit! Nigger Trash! *Ratons! Khorotos!* Beurs! Robbeurs! Railers! Bicos! Assholes! Stinkers! Arabs! Rilers! Rattlers! Only Rrrr's remain! There's only growls! There's only growling arabs! grrarabs up for grabs! *We can help them if they want!* Arabuggers! Arababblers! Ara-bums! Aracrybabies! Arabrats! Slobberers! Muzzling Muslims! Moslemouseshits! And even before you had time enough to get over your independence, *Congratula-tions for your big fat baby, Madame Algeria bedecked in flowers!* Even before you've gotten up from your bedtime frolics, they throw a caricature of Louis-Ferdinand in our face! *All nerves are forbidden!* Le Pen blocks your passage with his fat mouth! If you snivel, even if you begin to snivel, you're an accomplice to the Holocaust! *Farewell to Arms! Good Riddance to nerves! The Berezina! No Nerves! A fat mouth, but please no nerves for these guys! They're all faggots! They'll fuck like rabbits! I told you so! I knew it all from the beginning! See, I'm smart!* Flaubert, sure, Zola, sure, Chombart de Lauwe, okay, Dély, fine, Gide, no problem, Sartre, yes, Rimbaud, check, Simone de Beauvoir, why not, Camus, for sure, Breton, right on, *Céline, hell no! No way, José!* Louis-Ferdinand Céline, no! *Too delicate! C'est trop fin pour toi, cher ami! Too sophis-ticated!* National patrimony! Patronal matrimony! National literature! National slop! Patriotistic ligature! Posted property! No Trespassing! All entry foreclosed! National folklore! Literary foreclosure! No one can give a damn if the whole B. N. passes through, provided you don't somehow dig up the only ally you've got there, Louis-Ferdinand, the fascist for the nerve, the sculptor of the nerves, the person they trans-formed into a fascist in order to be done with his nervousness, the person they scape-goated so that you wouldn't go poking around the nervous center of the French ligature, so that you wouldn't find something in the ancestral factory of nerve, so that you wouldn't venture into the *zone, because as long as they don't have any nervous* *fuel there's nothing to be afraid of! As long as they don't dig up Céline, there's nothing to worry about. They'll fight each other, screw themselves over, gobble themselves up! Let'em be! But one thing has to be avoided: a pocketbook copy of Destouches!* Provide them with entertainment: throw Le Pen in their way. *I hope that I'm talking Le Pen with you, my dear friend, and not chagrin!* Make sure they only see fire! A good neurosis for a bundle of nerves! Just the way it is for our horde! As it is for our own ants! The way it is for our masses! for our hill of termites! Scare them! Intimidate them! Cause a blackout! We couldn't care less about Camus, but uh oh, not Céline! Okay for Jean-Saul Tartre, but Céline, in no way! It's too much *for you!* Too dangerous for you! Too refined! Too vulgar! Even *we* don't know how to handle it yet! Suck off a little, Süsse! Even *we* don't quite yet know what to do with it! *Cépa kôatro enfer!* Even *ourselves,* whom he still doesn't allow to have a good night's sleep! If, I say, with him they *want to tamper, in that dead of winter they'll be pitched in a hamper!* Hands off our literary *winterdrome!* Don't touch! Des Touches! Touch-him-not! He's our big boy, so lay off! Verboten! Our literary yellow star, *no visa allowed!* Our *infamous little literary secret!* Interdit! Destouches? An eminently French *matter,* so who would ever want to let it go? *Everything that is national belongs to us!* Cacophony! If we deprive them of the taste for nerves, then we'll turn them into skirtchasers, libidinals! Neutralize their nerves in order to have their libido *surge up!* A marginalization! *Je veux dire, a marginal theory of literary value!* The less nerves there are the more the *demand* for the libido increases! *A great libidinal demand of psychological theory!* If the market lacks nerve, then they'll jump on the libidinals! Marginalize'em! With the libido! Anesthetize them! Hey, with francophone literature! Use the libido to get them *addicted!* Bully them with narrative! Transform literature into cultural anesthesia! Transform their *innately genital* taste for thermoliterature into intellectual *antifreeze* and *politics!* Transform the libidinal novel into an addiction! Transform the nerve factory into a collective neurosis! By means of interposing the libido! *If I can't get a libido fix I'll suffocate! Without libido I'll go crazy! Without francophone literature I'll die!* Lead them to the threshold, and from the threshold to paradise! And a few others into the galleys, with the most *enervating* going to the gallimards! The most *enervated* go off to Dédé-Noël! The *borderline cases* can go to the fairy Morgana or to Sinbad of a thousand and one nights! No matter how, my friend, they're all *overrated!* Underwhelming! Flops! Flunkies! Floozies with all their fantasy! *No rectasy! Bring up the sludge! Fill their nostrils with the smell of farts and garlic! There's always plenty of time to poeticize afterward!* We've got to organize festivals for these asses and the others, for Algeria, for the Maghreb! Saturnalia! Organize fairs! Cultural celebrations! Bookfairs! Francophone festivals! Festivals of order! Bowelfairs! Af-fairs of *sensitivity!* Fairs of the great literary libido! And then, squeeze out the culture, squeeze out the books! Squeeze out the order, squeeze out the bowels, squeeze out the sensitivity and turn yourselves into libidinal squeezos! Become the new squeeze-outs of culture of the Mediterranean basin! You can dip yourself into their cultural squeezings to the point of *puking!* Until you cry *Amen! Amenoka!! That's enough!* Until you show that your tootsies are white! Until you sparkle with the pleasures of a nerveless body! It'll make you appreciate the pleasures of the libidinal consensual consumer society! It'll get you out of your cultural underdevelopment by means of undertreatment! Through specialization in detachable parts! By way of *detached prose!* By directing you toward the zone! By transforming you into zonophiles! By *zonifying* you! Shaming you! Tearing your nerves out! One by one! Beginning with your enteroceptives! *Clean Job!* Turning you into *mummies* of French literature! *A literature for married celibates with libidinal children!* And until it becomes completely unreal! When it becomes unreal, everything'll be unreal! Francophony: *An annual closing of the literary faire dedicated to the labor of grief and to the inventory of cacophony!*

the narrator a little stomached <*Lampedusic*>: *what you have to understand, Francesco, is that we're old, we're terribly old. For at least twenty centuries we have been bearing on our shoulders the weight of magnificent civilizations that all originate elsewhere; none has sprouted on our soil! We are whites no less than you, dear Francesco, no less than the queen of England, and yet, for two thousand five hundred years, we still remain a colony!*

O Eternal Forms, here am I
I am a living Mummy in the country of Life where a Sovereign
reigns,
the Lady with the soft eyes. I am the steward in the Gods'
studio. Everywhere I have sought the Infinite. I have put the Infinite into
all things ...
For Becoming is the great event
Becoming is the great event.
And eternity is the goal,
eternity is the goal.
                    "Pass, for you are pure."

<Sync # 1 (plain text):
(in respect to the enormous activity that is needed, my nervous system astonishes me with its subtlety and its marvelous resistance: long and heavy sufferings, an inappropriate *profession,*

or even an erroneous *therapeutic treatment has harmed him in what is essentially his; why last year, to the contrary, he took a firm position and, thanks to him,* I have been able to produce one of the most courageous, elevated, and provocative books that has ever been conceived in a human brain and heart. *Even if I ended my days with Recoaro, he would have been one of the most inflexible and circumspect of anyone who has ever died,* and not a man in despair. *My* **cephalalgies** *are very hard to diagnose, and in what pertains to the scientific matters that are necessary for this effect, I am better informed than any doctor . . .*)> Plain text again, this having fallen directly from N.'s letter to Peter Gast, the musician friend: Why I, I just fill my lungs with it! I finally begin to breathe *(that guy wasn't bothered about titillating the mental mullethead! a big dormitory of ideas all ready to be undone, a semitrailer filled with recyclable mental mush, and all that in the space of an ephemerid's lifetime! Could France ever tolerate impudence of that kind? To see comic beings fall away, and to cry over them, why that's Divine! Just like that! Ho! Hohohaha!)*

A Learned Man goes back into the sweaty room and wants there to be pronounced: Fatma, I knew he'd make apple pie out of this manure before he kicked the bucket! I knew he wouldn't sign off without leaving us a little bite from his bitch! He was a borderline case anyway, nothing good can ever come out these marginal characters! *Infantile, my dear Fatma!* Besides, from the standpoint of a Marxist, as Louis the Parisian Strangler has shown, the world began with *overdetermination . . . Family, Fatherland, History, etc. . . . Come on, repeat your sentence, Grandfather of the Masses! Come on, let's go, out with your Marxo-Moslem truth!*

Francisco, having decided to do *his own* paintings, because he was up to his ears in *seeing* things that for day after day had *nothing to say to him,* has had enough in seeing so much *flabby flesh.* It hurt his eyes, it turned his stomach, to see all these *huge, adipose, and pasty bodies.* <**Portrait of the Merchant in his jockey shorts! Portrait of the Sun King in his underwear! Portrait of an ass with the Queen undressed! Portrait of the Pope without his trappings!**> It made his eyes seasick! Nauseated by all this garbage! With my *Dead Letters,* I've left literature and moved on with my life! With my *Dead Letters,* I've withdrawn my reverence! *He bowed for the last time, and exited! Il a fait ses adieux les plus élégants et en est sorti!* Whence the visit at Francesco's. It had been months since I'd last been in a painter's loft. I'd had to get back to a little chaos. But that kind of chaos I'd never remembered ever having seen. I'd never seen so much scorn for order. Hard to imagine he could have cared less for order. In a corner of the studio, in the middle of this shambles, a body that has just been liquefied or that is being put back together, and over there, where the body is at the strongest point of its attempt to expulse its form, there's the fluid of the face of a deranged idiot who cries in silence, the lymph of a former face that laughs over its sterility, *an atrociously molded face: the last of our faces in the final night of our world!*

un calco atroce
l'ultimo nostro volto
nell'ultima notte del mondo!
You've been coming to visit me less frequently, Bacon said. *So must I conclude that once again you've been conspiring against me?*
I said nothing.
I had decided to write *my own books* because there wasn't anything left to eat. There never was anything for me in French literature! No, not a thing! There wasn't anybody left! Not a thing to eat, ces jours-là, in littérature francese? Not a thing! And exhausted, *exhaustion!* From reading and rereading *In Search of Lost Time* or *Nausea!* Nobody will ever know how much it pained me and whence *it all got foisted off on me, the literary police reports, the overdoings, the jerkoffs, the forces and pro-testations on the part of the ligature!* No one would ever guess how much and where all this suffering nausea originates! No one can ever suspect the violence of the devil's little point of the saffron black letters that pushed me to recover the jealous spirit of my suffered thought! *No rectifications!* All this puke waiting for the right *expression!* And no one to take up the baton! Let me tell them! No one to give me a kick in the ass! For days on end! Patience day in and day out! The extreme pain of the galley slave! The scribbler's dire solitude! True distillers of lies! Hawkers of scribblers' sour mush! The literary moonshiners! *Ah, how sad and plighted is modern litrature, how disenchanted am I!* I find this last sentence funda-mentally ugly, but I won't rectify it one bit! *To rectify!* All I've been doing for years, for centuries, is to rectify. Always rectifying and never having any time or *taste for writing. No fucking guts!* Not a nerve to write with! And if that's not enough, the distaste of writing and thinking because of this suckoff and ultramundane taste for rectifying, the sickly taste for correcting, emending, taking up, *taking care of the leftovers!* So I said to Francisco, please, no more *sewer* of literary taste! Because you know all well, you like me, you've taken the time to read my *Dead Letters*, yes, even you, my dear friend, don't ever think that one fine day I'll start rectify-ing myself and ever rectify the things you'll be reading! I can't do that anymore!

Not for anything! I don't want to work over my work anymore! There is nothing left to be emended! To rectify, *the way they take care of dishes? Never again!* And Francisco replied: *You've got a nerve, Armondo! Nerve! The Gall! Pull yourself up by your straps! Sursum Corda!* It smacked of Montaigne and was soaked in turpentine!

Aely: *In esprit there are tripes, in gust there is lust!*

Macha leaned toward the window with an absolutely wonderful contortion and she said, *so now you really believe that you're definitely rid of your ideogrammatical scruples? It's done? You think you're really there?*
I said, *yes, yes, totally, passionately, I've got to!* and in my hole I continued to rave on against the time and to fret about myself. Macha loves to speak formally with me every time she thinks she's found one of my weak points. She thinks I'm *pocked with weak points* and that all she has to do is apply pressure so that I'll push my envy buttons or so that I'll then rectify, rectify, and rectify some more. Exactly: rectify *myself! You always begin with hubcaps and night will not have fallen before you're rectifying yourself once again!* So let her say it! The way I pronounced the "yes, yes, totally," etc., wasn't very orthodox, but it surely left a strong impression on Macha. And what can be done without impressions? What can be hoped for without impressions? Given without impressions? What to think without impressions? Now Macha didn't understand that I believe that *within me there was forming an evil being who wanted to speak.*
For sure! There are days when the rectification instinct presses more than others, but in my black hole, *somewhere in London,* I sense that something definitely overcame it. Rectification was *atomized!* Modification! pensum! planum! planning! *Banished was* the time when I *worried* about literature! Presently *I am a living corpse!* It was already pretty obvious when I was still going to Peter's or Paul's café, when I was still reading books in the Goncourt style, or then again when I was happy enough to dream aloft on my two legs. *No rectification cumpulsion! No remorse! No trace of rectification!* What do I read? Water rolling off a duck's back? Impermeable? What I'm writing? Lemon dashed into an open eye? *No rectifications!* Afraid? Why sometimes a shudder, the fear of bending, but please, no more intellectual contortions, no more rectifications, no more emendations! Today, *whoever would secretly observe the way I know how to bring together the cares I bring to my cure with the conditions that favor my great tasks would not allow me to hire myself out! I've become the old Remaed of the black ashes.*

e cendra
e cadra sarta
et kama
o karuba
o kripa
okarisuma
Mirta cripa!

Summer has come back. It's banging on the door like a madman. It's invading every room of the house and nothing can stop it. I've taken my retirement. *A golden parachute!* as they say in the country whence I'm writing. *Precocious retirement! Precocious boredom!* Now I can begin to tell my story, without rectification, without having to worry about correcting papers or preparing classes. Besides, I tore up all the *syllabi* put together ever since I had begun teaching at Oxford <*Miami of Ohio!*> And, yes, that too was a good sign. No syllabus, no more syllabi for all these pretty blond American heads and for their love of syllabi. *Professor, how many texts are we going to read during the semester?* Read the syllabus! *Professor, how many papers are we required to write in your course?* Read the syllabus and rectify it if possible. *Professor, are we going to have discussion in class?* Read the syllabus. *Professor, Is There a Text in this Class?* Read. Not long afterward the entire world had somehow gotten into my syllabi. Not a single vice that wasn't syllablahlized! Not a single idea that didn't find its chosen place in my syllahbic scribblings! The last had become so precise, so *specific* that any student, if he or she wanted, could know when to eat breakfast, when to watch television, when to eat brunch, and when to go to hell. But in all that the students have nowhere to go. I still let myself be led by the *innately genital* taste that I have for integrating autobiographical elements in my writings. But that summer something had *suddenly* changed. In every event something should have forewarned me about the bad fate that would soon strike. *I should have been alerted by something.* But I wanted to hear nothing, see nothing, know nothing. I was waiting, in the little corridor of the municipal building of Providence-The-Thirty-Two-Churches, for the door of idyllic aspirations to be opened again like sesame and for the assistant clerk of immigration to come and invite me to enter the sacred conference room where every kind of denial was habitually uttered. I had *suddenly* decided to apply for naturalization in America. I ought to say that I had *brutally* taken the decision to *lose* my Algerian nationality and be rid of it *at all costs.* Immediately, illico, in order to be done with the functionaries of the consulates of the world at large, in order never to hear another word from all the little subalterns of all the Algerian embassies in the world at large, in order never again to have anything to do with myself as an Algerian-in-the-world and to be rid of the world. I was there to get rid of my Algerianity for once and for all and to be done with all the stately particles that were making me an Algerian-in-the-world. I had had enough. The bothersome fever of being an Algerian had reached a degree of such ferocity that I couldn't stand it any longer! I had to get rid of this shroud of Nessus: the distaste in being taken for anything at any border *under the pretext of my being Algerian*. For don't you see, Mr. Ambassador, that ever since you put this ill-fated nationality on sale for whoever wants it, you see, we, Algerian citizens by birth, we, the *native people* (Please note, Mr. V.I.P., that I'm putting my words between commas, as they should be, Mr. Ambassador), we are no longer seen as panhandlers! I wrote you to inform you that my passport had expired six months ago, and that six months ago I remitted thirty-five dollars, four sets of identity photos, two old passports, an official passage from my birth certificate, a copy of my bill of divorce, an electricity bill, a photocopy of my blue card, protocopy of my green card, and you still weren't satisfied! You still needed an excerpt from my father's birth certificate and a certification of nationality in order, as one of our state functionaries is wont to tell me, to have me *immatriculated!* Don't you think it's indecent to be immatriculated? *In immatriculated there is the word trick*, says Aely, *and the words mac and immaculate.* Why all this endless desire to immatry-cul-ate each other? It's been futile to explain to you that I had already supplied you with all of these documents three times since my migration to America, and it's been futile to rehearse the scenario over and over again: that in order to be Algerian for one time I couldn't mysteriously have my nationality changed. But you didn't want to hear anything of it. Since when have people been able to be *re*born out of their national ashholes? Since when have people been able to be born again in a place other than where they first saw the light of day? A person *is physically born once and only once in his or her life*, Mr. Ambassador. The folly of the day where I was born. I was born at K. *once and for all* and, alas, I can't be reborn elsewhere. Do you understand the point, Mr. Ambassador, that *I was born once and only once in the world* and, like it or not, there's nothing you can do to change that fact! But then, well, nothing could be easier than changing one's nationality! You have been very gracious to assure me that an Algerian never loses his or her nationality in the eyes of the Algerian government and state and that I really am sorry to tell you that I think it's a little odd to have to prove to you ten times a year that I am an Algerian. Thus I want to be Algerian on my own account, by my own means! Don't you see, Mr. Ambassador, I think it's easier and far more natural to be an Algerian myself than with the support of the Algerian government and state. I am therefore writing you to inform you that I am giving you my portion of Algeria, and that the portion of Algeria that is owed to me is hereafter all for you and the State. Take it! I give it to you freely and without remorse! I donate to you *the rest of my body, of my individuality, of my being, of my conscience, of my principles, of my presence, of my pertinent features, of my originality, of my distinction, of my indistinction, of my family baggage and family tree!* What I've been trying to do is to suppress this operation! I've firmly and solemnly decided to donate my Algerian nationality to Algeria, to the camels and to everyone else! I realize that you might find this formula a bit paradoxical and *somewhat* violent, but it suits me. It even enthralls me. It seems just right, because, in becoming *Algerian-American*, I can reclaim my rights as a minority citizen wherever I am, I mean, *including my own country*, Algeria, so that, as an Algerian-*Algerian*, I'll never be seen having any right and will therefore be *nothing. All-gerian-for-nothing, Algérien-rien*, that's the formula! and in two languages, yes! Hey Mister, Hasnot! The, the El, the El jeer riant! The Algaerian, the green card scum! Don't even think about it, Mr. Ambassador, but think about what I'm going to tell you confidentially: when I'm American, I'll be able to go everywhere throughout the world without having to lose hours and days in the waiting rooms of the consulates of all the nations of Europe and Navarre in order to have a visa issued in my name, all these visas that on every occasion cost an arm and a leg and all the skin off my ass. Just think of it, Mr. Ambassador! Every time I've got to go somewhere in the world, and because I'm a professional man of letters, only God knows how often I've got to drag my spats around in places outside of Algeria, every time I have to be somewhere on the globe, as I was saying, *I've got to put my best foot forward, solely because I'm Algerian.* I've got to have <Foehrr! Foehrr! It's fun, isn't it?> new photos made, show my green card, my blue card, my gray card, my immatriculation card, my *yellow star*, Mr. Ambassador <Plain Text> my identity papers, my passport, and save up enough money to assure these gentlemen of the embassy of Franconia or Germania that I'll be up to sustaining myself and sustaining my modest little tribe! I also have to display proof that I'm not returning to this *dreamed-of land* (that's how the bureaucrats of these countries believe that we lubriciously and addictively *swallow up* their country) in order to emigrate *in clandestine fashion*, but in order to do something absolutely exacting and positively useful to the international community. I must therefore put on display letters of recommendation, letters about my credit rating, letters from my creditors, letters of invitation (to a symposium, to a congress, to a mass) with rather official-looking emblems so that they'll consent to issue me the safe conduct that they would furnish *without the slightest reservation* (about his intentions or his *desires*) to any other citizen of the First World. What I find most depressing in all this business, Mr. Ambassador, is not so much the fact that I've got to pay thirty-five dollars, eighteen marks, or the required forty-two spondulicks that no one ever fails to require in all the consulates of the countries of the Fir$t World! What I find most disagreeable and most depressing is that on each occasion I have to supply a new set of photos. I can't stand having to take photos of myself! A mania for photos! With every new year this operation gets more and more disagreeable and even downright impossible. Because it requires me to see my own mug, I have to see all the *distortions and wrinkles* that the pure passing of time has inflicted on my impure face, *all without rectification!* Every time I get a new visa I've got to get a new visage. *In the word visage there is the word visa*, Elya notes. So I believe that I've gained the right not to let myself be harassed by that anymore. I've won the noble fight over the *gratuity* of my face. For sure, for me photos are the most depressing, the most painful, and the most trying of all. Between eighteen and thirty-five this was of the gravest consequence because—I don't know why or by what miracle of nature—I didn't change much until then and then especially, I mean, because I hadn't been giving a damn about my mug, with rotten luck, *je m'en foutais pal mal!* Between eighteen and thirty-five, I looked like just about anybody. Some worry about balding when I turned thirty, but *in reality* no cause for alarm. But after thirty-five, I don't know why (I think that for the moment I'd rather not know) my visage, Mr. Ambassador, suddenly and drastically began to record the violence of time. It's ridiculous to say so, Mr. Ambassador, but as of that age even the humblest Algerians begin to refuse giving the furrows in the pastures of their faces over to the State predators. As of that age, I sensed that no one ought any longer to have the right to require that a *free* man show his face. I believed that in principle a free man had won the right no longer to hide his face, but not to *put it on display*. You see, Mr. Ambassador, that I'm not talking about *hiding* my face, but of showing it only to people who are *really worthy* of seeing it. Now in our country these people, Mr. Ambassador, are dying out! At my age, Mr. Ambassador, in theory a man has won the right to be imperceptible! Have you, Mr. Ambassador, seen the photos that I sent to the consulate last week? Did you glance at the *tragic look* of these photos? I'll bet on my nationality that you didn't and I won't blame you for it either, Mr. Ambassador! C'mon, let's have a sense of humor! Lighten up! Don't be a geek! Don't be a gawk! Now there, that's our problem, Mr. Ambassador, our Algerian Problem, everybody thinks they can buy our face cheaper than anyone else, but with the little proviso that here we are *de-visaged, disfigured, photographed, immatriculated*. Now I'm too weak, too big, too grumpy, and *too distant* to continue exhibiting myself for so little. I'm not telling this to you personally, Mr. Ambassador, I'm not saying you, but I mean your parasites, I mean how your government and how the eternally "exceptional case" have made *our faces worthless on the international market. Et vous, vous vous fichez de moi.* Everybody thinks our faces are cheap! Everybody thinks Algerian faces are a dime a dozen! Everybody thinks they can *spot an Arab Algerian's* face. Now I think that's wrong. As for me, I think it's unjustified. I, well, I think they've raked our faces over, that they take our *good Algerian faces* for granted. They've reveled too much over our innate Algerian *immaturity!* Too photomized! Everywhere you set up an ambassadorial branch office <mon Dieu!> I see pullulating and prospering all these photomats that take the pictures of our slobby faces pasted in our algae-scum-colored passports! In black and white it's all the same mug of an old dried-up mummy. With or without colors it's all the same look of men wanted dead or alive! Now it's up to you. Do something so that we don't have to show our faces as if they were our assholes, do something so that we put our *best face forward* as others put their *best feet forward,* and so that I won't be forced—*compelled,* as my future American compatriots like to say—into *becoming American in order to be Algerian.* I'm exaggerating the formula a little so that you'll see, Mr. Ambassador, that I'm not taking lightly this business about visas, passports, passages, visages, immatricula-tions, and photomontages of *identity. <In immatriculation there is also "cul" and "trickle"!* adds Ylea.> That is a serious and important matter that has to be considered. Because of your coconut politics, because of the *crass incompetence* of your bureaucratic service agents and because of the advanced condition of parasitism, because of the basic paranoid personality afflicting most Algerians, because of the Algerian War and in the name of its martyrs, *a face has been foisted on us.* They've glued on us a face that looks like a mug shot, we've let our faces be taken the way whores walk down the lineup. *In immatriculation there is the word maculate and imam in power,* adds once more my favorite prophet, Aely. If it would have helped us you'd probably have tossed a bottle of sulfuric acid over our goddamned faces. In my keenest expression of gratitude, Mr. Ambassador, I beg you to accept my best and most patriotic wishes!

Here is the *delirious* letter that I had been thinking of writing to the ambassador of my country while I was waiting in the corridor of the American waiting room. At the time I didn't know they were going to take my *Dead Letters* at the foot of the letter! I still didn't know that *in our regions* they still didn't know how to allow for what amounts to human delirium and the transcendence of the gods! Dreams, Moans, Rumors, Despairs, Laughter: everything had become True, every-thing had turned into Reality. O Reality of Realities! O Sweet Creation of Reality! All is but Irreality!

Ratina Zara

Tassir Rakila!

As I was feverishly editing this letter that never (and for good reason!) arrived to its *current* recipient—a man of a very great intellectual and moral probity—the gate of temptation became straiter and straiter. I have to admit that at the time at least fifty nationalities were represented. Two little Siamese girls, *id est* Siam, played with a hula hoop, and a little Portuguese boy was gazing on them with a paradoxical envy. It was hard to tell if he wanted to play with them or if it was only the almond shape of their eyes with their polished slate color that fascinated him. Now and again he leaned over the bench on which he was seated, he stuck his face through the slats and smiled at them with an exotic look. A Hmong family was sniffing coke. A gang of Haitian *brothers* was getting ready for a little American-style voodoo act, a kind of *Vanilla Voodoo!* A Peruvian was puking a snapping turtle out of his guts. A Mexican and his lady were chewing on an old Carambas cigarillo. An Irishman was waiting for Godot. *<No rectifications! There's no time!>* I thought I saw a Sikh translating an old Tantric poem. Tunisians were debourgibuying as they usually do. A Moroccan was in a Marxist arm-wrestling match the way a Taoist locks up with a Peruvian. Taira, etc.... As I saw it, it seemed to me that an extremely precious moment of time was trickling away and that I had better things to tend to. I was thinking of what was happening at that very moment in the skies over Iraq and Kuwait, I was thinking of the Algerian War, the war in Vietnam, the Second World War, and the desire to become American *hic et nunc* appeared to me to be the most *insane* thing that a person of my age would ever want to do. During the Vietnam War I still had not passed the fateful five years required before application for American nationality. Now that it had become possible, there was being fought an even more abject war unfurling every day under our eyes stunned by bureaucrats! *<Everywhere it's the same damned thing, the same decor, the same little drama ... The universe repeats itself endlessly and stamps its feet without budging!>* I glanced at the Haitian, Hmong, Russian, Vietnamese, Mexican, Senegalese, and Turkish applicants, rubbed my eyes, and was overtaken by a great swell of nausea and forthwith got out of the waiting room.

      Now as these were the dog days of summer, and as I nonetheless want to be a teeny bit coherent in my speech, when I walked back into the street, the day had not yet fallen. A day much greater and more stifling than my thoughts could ever be. I was ready to receive the worst of all maledictions, ready to renounce all hope, ready to renounce myself, but still something seemed certain: my taste for literature, my innately genital taste *<Merzak: is that the narrator's*

nervous tick or what?>, for literary *speculation* had also reached a stifling degree of ingratitude and violence. It was as if both the sun and literature had stretched out their arms to torture me and drag me into despair. What was I doing in literature? How had I managed to get into literature without reading that this *stately lady* had absolutely refused to take into her consideration our poor human lot? *Why literature in the place, rather, of nothing?* To believe in this world or to let oneself be wafted away with it, to let it get grayer and grayer, more and more cynical, more and more mossy and morose, *no rectifications*, more and more terroristic? The thought had something in it that was more acid than vinegar, more stringent than ginger. I failed to comprehend what I had done to merit such a long life of rectification and correction. I didn't understand how I had managed to scribble so many sheets of paper to end up at the saddest of all possible genuflections. I had just reread the infamous André Gide. I had even had the gall to include on the syllabus of one of my classes the infamous novel on the *so-called Counterfeiters*. <Oui, oui, on vous croit, allez-y, continuez!> I had my students read this *fake* novel and I had invested all my energy in the struggle to make them admit (against *their* feeling and, even worse, *against my own feeling, yeah? yeah!*) that something in this novel made it worth the trouble, something really *great*. I proffered utter stupidities to convince them of something entirely fake and that I also refused to believe in. I blasphemed, I conversed with the devil and *to hell with the devil*. I was reading this book *woven with white thread, no rectifications!* just as the war was heating up in the skies over Iraq and Jordan. I was seeing absolutely crushing and terrifying images that were being sent from Somalia and my heart was still in this business, *I had the drive to continue reading!* Never had I gathered so much scorn for life. Gide! I even had the gall to reread passages of Gide that I had not opened for centuries, and as the days passed, as I advanced, backward, backward, like a crab, my dear! the nausea went up to my ears and filled my head! Nausea was becoming nauseating, more and more nauseous, so nauseous that I couldn't pass a day without a migraine. I woke in the night with my belly swollen like a cow in labor, and I passed hours on my knees, genuflecting over a toilet bowl, vomiting my guts. <C'est trop!> And as I handed myself over to this exercise of a writer sullied by his own readings, I slowly felt more and more purged of Gide, Flaubert, Proust, and the rest. I slowly felt that literature and I had gone our separate ways and that I had gotten the literary tapeworm out of my system. I moved on with my life. I was no longer a member of the Literary Sect! I was no longer sectarian! Finished! No more sectarianism! Too solitary for that! Too sick for that! Too far away! Too despairing! Too poor, for all that! Too enervated too! <Vas-y vas-y, je te fais confiance! Y'a pas un moment à perdre!>

During all this time, the time of my stupendous fever, Macha didn't flinch. Macha knew when and how not to flinch. She got up on her toes, *no, no, no rectification yet, never again!* and took pleasure in smiling at me with a slightly acid look. *You were always interested in second-rate authors, I don't mean second-rate* things, *my dear Professor of Literature, but in minor* authors. *That's why you pass life away by groaning. And if I laugh it's because, Mr. Professor, it's late and we don't have anything to eat for dinner!* Difficult in these cases at least not to rectify the shots, *plain text again,* but I didn't do anything. I too didn't flinch. To the contrary I sank deeper into my chair and replied to her, *My angel, I'll never use you again to get my story back on track. I have ambitions other than those that consist in using a character of my own invention to fill out my little ratiocinations! A true story never needs to get back on track! It picks itself up on its own!* A difficult moment, a moment of great anxiety. *Every time the best plans are thrown topsy-turvy!* At every moment I run the risk of forgetting where I'm going, not only who I am, but also what I'm doing! I know neither where I'm going, nor what I am, nor what I'm doing! And it's fine just like that! Everything seems to fall into a chaos that gives thinking the bitter taste of cold ashes! The very ashes of literature, for, on that very morning, *no rectifications,* <*Beginning over again is of no use ... what comes out botched will be just fine ... Time will take care of the rest!*>, on that morning, my dear, we were celebrating my brains and Ash Wednesday, the Ash Wednesday of literature! On that day, despite the great chaos of my thoughts, despite the burning in my soul, I have found a *placement* for the Ashes. Ash Wednesday, like the Christmas holidays, Palm Sunday or Good Friday, the holy days of Aïd-el-Kébir, the holy days of Aïd-es-Séghir, the days of Ascension and Pentecost, All Saints' Day and the day of the great Armistice, well, I just never quite knew what to do with my brains. I was dragging myself around the streets, *like a big clumsy beetle,* until day broke once again. Then I went back home, alleviated by the heavy weight of Ash Wednesday. *Another day burned to ashes just like the last! That's what it was!* But on that occasion, that summer day everywhere studded with blank spaces and full of holes in my head, on that very day, yes, *I found a useful spot for Ash Wednesday!* For me it became the day of the ashes of literature and memory. Please note, my dear, that I hadn't the slightest inkling about what schemes were being plotted against me *at that time* and what was spinning about in my head around that formula. Wasn't I writing to you from the inner depths? Wasn't I writing to you from the *end of the night?* But please note how it all *sounds just right!* The mixture of the sun, my head, my brains, memory, ashes, and literature. It rings of Victor Hugo! I can't tell how that got mixed up in my ruminations, but I immediately felt that at that moment I had a *very good place for getting my mind straightened out.* The sun that kept beating down on my head, I was drowning in a pool of ashes, the memory of the whole business was torturing me, and it was literature that refused to let me down! SSCML! Sun, Skull, Cinders, Memory, and Literature. Essay, See'em All. *Est-ce,* say, a moll? Did she, say, stop loving me? Nothing more remained between us than the ashes of our passion! Ashen Nuptials! A dead point, silence, and *still no rectification!* Not the strayest impulse to rectify anything! Literature had gone away with the sun! Literature, literature in sum, had burned away with the ashes of memory! *Don't multiply the goings away, as technical manuals recommend. And to that I respond: who cares, O gardeners of the elements of style, about your laws or your wisdom! Just let the sinuous concept of going away grab you and lead you into absolutely labyrinthian follies! A toi de choisir, ma chère!*

When I got back home, but not before I had ridden three times around Kennedy Plaza and gotten myself together in the space of a good quarter hour next to Lovecraft Tomb on Prospect Street, I discovered Macha digging through the *Critique of Judgment* and spouting her rosary, a rosary that had been taken from a little nursery rhyme and that her mother, Amalécyte, had sung to her at the head of her crib, *Amouzin, amusing, amour, amour, azur! Do you always burn with this fire, do you always have this terrifying look? Do you always have this soul, do you always have these terrifying eyes? Amouzin, amusing, amour, azur, azur, azuuuur!* I always like to get back to Macha every time I find the right moment to utter a good word, an idiomatic expression, or an idiosyncratic sound! And, for some unknown innately genital reason, *no, no, no error, no rectification yet, please, not yet,* Macha always knows how to locate these brainstorms. She immediately guesses that something happened when the right moment seems to come in the course of the day. I knuckled under in vain, in *low profile,* I composed my look in vain, I looked for Lady Luck in vain, something told me I had been visited by a butterfly! *Sartroff! Sartroff!* [Now surely that's not my true Christian name! Am I not a fugitive?] she throws a stare in my face, *What's your big brainstorm for today? So it's whatever you still are looking for to hide your old oracle! It's something that monumental? Where do you get the big idea that I might miss the right moment?* On that day, *Plain text again,* without exactly knowing why, I did not consent to her to divulge my discovery. I sank in the depths of the rocking chair and told her about my adventure in the waiting room filled with applicants. I especially recalled the Siamese sisters and the little Portuguese boy. Then, as I noted that she wasn't believing a word of what I was saying, I added that I had intended to write a long letter to the new ambassador of Algeria in order to explain to him why I had decided to become a naturalized American. After all, I was adding with vehemence, I've been paying taxes in this country for over fifteen years, so it's now or never if I'm going to make the jump, and so I plea, so I ply, I play, I grow, I growl, and I kwarrel.

Jebli Kera

Jera querulous

Kara!

Every morning the relentless face of death on my face in the mirror!
Thus it was exactly how I finished off my homily in feeling myself extremely close in spirit to Vitoldo and Antonin. I should add that my head was still giddy from the very beautiful letter that the Momo had written to Henri Parisot on Coleridge the Traitor, *Since* ema, *the so-called poematic, after blood, and that the po-ema must mean*

after:

blood,

blood following.

Let's first make poem *with blood.*
We will eat the time of blood, the eternal hell, and it was play no longer. Indeed, *voire!,* entire months had passed since I had rectified, entire months since I had seen the blue sky above my head! Months since I had de-nied, de-clicked, dis-pensed, dis-cour-aged myself, enervated! As in the *caress of skin,* the spot creates a whole fucking thing, and *there are endless locks and dams! And too, there's the ideal guy, the little delighted guy who stands at the window!* Macha had, *Plain Text,* stopped singing; I felt her close to me, very close at the moment when she just about felt like badgering me, giving me a breathalyzer test, feel out my reason, x-ray my mental anatomy, find out more about the process of my speculative thinking, in a word, on the kind of *spotting* I had done that morning. But shrewd, she never goes at things frontally. Ruseful, she always takes a tangent. *What about Gidiot?* she says. *What'd you do with Gidiot? Tu l'as jeté à la poubelle? Did you throw him out? Rumor around the university has it that some of your students think you're a faggot. Are you aware of that?* I knew she had invented this little scenario right on the spot merely to get me out of my funk. *What can you do all this time with your nose stunk up in the funk? Will you have become a stylite?* Macha the provocatrix! Macha the muse of sleepy little poems! Macha the soul milker! Macha the betrayer! Macha the abandoness! Macha the donoress!

Answer on the spot or I'll stare you down to the depths of your gray eyes! she adds because I'm fumbling for an answer. *What spotting? What placement or placements? Have you fallen back into your maniacal habits of rectification? So how many rectifications?* Nothing could ever be more difficult than tearing myself out of this funk once I got myself up to my ears in it! I stick to it like a tick, like a louse, and my Macha knows it well! And that's why she refuses to approach me. Between her and me lies a very thick wall of language and of light-years of fatigue. Macha senses well the fatigue that has burdened me ever since I refused to do any more rectifications. Macha knows quite well how much this break from literature weighs on me! She knows that this fatigue is a little machine that at all times risks blowing me up, and that's why her dialogue with the *living-dead, the zombie who I am* is so *biased.* She knows that placement can be broached only on days of a mental full moon, the days of great autoseduction. She knows that the machine can explode at any time. She has seen me prowl around in the houses of aspiring hosts in Minneapolis, she has seen me go outside to smoke cigarettes with other rootless characters when the temperature is thirty below in order not to *bother* American nonsmokers! She has seen me sound the horn of retreat in battles that I could have won simply by uttering a sigh, and she knows that all this energy that has been stored up *for no reason* might just blow up in my face. That's why Macha never attacks frontally, that's why she takes the tangent! Skating on the frozen lakes, skiing in the veinulets of my tumefied brains! On that day I kept my secret and did not reveal the nature of the setting, of the placement, or even the spot where I retreated! Furthermore, my dear, what can I say to her that's decent? SSCML? Tell her something like that, something stupid and simple? Tell her something like *See, easy, aime elle? See, easy to stop loving her? Has she ceased to love me?* I couldn't make the formula rhyme, no matter how hard I tried, in no matter what language! Something in my head told me that that had passed! It had taken place! Besides, the sun began to fall, and what could I say about my brains? Passing for sun and ashes, passing for ashes and brains, at least for me, in this very moment, *in this very spot*, but is it still a spot? But sun, ashes, brains, *memory*, and literature were a lot tougher to negotiate. For an instant I was tempted to say to her something like, *Today I saw a dog pass through the street, a poor mutt, and I thought that it was the street itself.* But I remembered that Macha had read a lot of Virginia Woolf and that she'd immediately see the trick. I also thought of revealing to her only a part of the equation by saying to her something like, *I saw the sun, it went to my head, I thought for a flash that my brains were turning into ashes*, but I quickly realized that I could add neither the *L* nor the memory. The *L* didn't work so well in the abbreviated formula, and so then I was no longer so convinced that I had been doing something about getting spotted or placed. I was thus reduced to despair, and Macha realized it well, for she then refused to ask any more questions. I heard her stirring around with her spoons, rattling the pots in the kitchen, opening and closing the oven, but asking no more questions. Thus I changed my tactics and thought that perhaps, by beginning with L I could make something come out. But the L didn't jive, it was hellish. *No rectifications, nevermore! There's neither time enough nor leisure to engage things so frivolously! No more motives, no more reasons to drag me into an adventure like that! Enough of the* Skoolies *of my crazy youth!* I really thought about dividing the formula, about transforming it into an equation with two beginnings by having Skull go with Cinders and Sun with Significant Literature, Memory going with Milieu, but it still didn't work. But not because nothing remained except for the little *pseudo*-Rimbaldian formula of the genre *the literature of memory gone as ashes go with the sun!* But what could I do with a shortened formula like that? What I needed was a complete formula, a quadrature, *the quadrature of literature, total* literature *that* I wanted to produce: *to disgorge literature! to make literature render itself! to make it render what it had stolen away! render unto it what had been stolen from it! to purify it on all accounts! to balance its aberrations, you idiot, not to purify it!*

<from Aely, the trickster, once again: *In total there is Penthotal (to a greater power)!*>

I also thought of taking a sheet of paper and a pen with a broad nib, and writing the following ideogram:

SUN		CINDERS
	MEMORY	
SKULL		LITERATURE

and giving it to Macha without adding a word. But that too had neither rhyme nor reason, it looked weird. Whatever was ashen in the sun and cerebral in literature was not in the slightest immemorial. Whatever was memorial in literature and bathed in sunlight in my skull had nothing charred about it. *Plus de rectification, plus jamais!* Right then and there I abandoned my project and was getting ready to say, *Do you realize, Macha, I think my brains have taken charge of my body, je crois que mon cerveau, caro, s'est emparé de mon corps!* But I finally rejected this formulation, too, because the sun had fallen and because the thought of it was a bit disquieting. I was disquieted! In merely *saying so,* in merely *proferring the statement,* I might be causing a catastrophe. And, as usual, Macha was the one who got us out of the mess. When she was returning from some kind of travel *along borderlines* she said to me, *Tu know, Caro mio, while you were at the INS (this is the abbreviation for the immigration services) the mailman delivered a registered letter addressed to you. I think it contains your new Algerian-born passmort! <That's how my Macha talked! Always understated! And teasing!>* And in fact, there was my passport in the big yellow envelope that I opened *illico.* There was also a little note from the vice-consul that said he hoped I would receive my new passport without delay or problem, telling me how much he had *appreciated* my study on the politics of the Moroccan peoples, reminding me that I still had to send him my father's birth certificate by return mail and greeted me, as dear brethren and as a dear compatriot, *et habeas corpus.* I fondled my passport in every way, I turned it up and around, I fingered through the pages, and checked it to see if everything was in order. I signed it, glued over the signature the little piece of cellophane that was made to keep its sheen, cast aspersions on my past life, walked over to the window where I awaited the sunset. *Good enough!*

Memory of the house of the dead # 1: The first pages are always relatively easy to spit out, my dear Macha, because they say that they can be revised later on. They say that writers can always huddle up over themselves and begin over again. **Fifth Door.** *<The dust of dead things and sterile pages, something I've never inhaled. I swear to it!>* They say they can all be erased, refurbished, etc., but in fact nothing is ever erased, everything is manipulated, period. Nothing can be erased. Nothing can be manipulated: we're all manipulated. *No rectification, not yet.* But once these infamous first pages have been delivered to you, the ensuing fear is inevitable. At any moment things can turn against you and start tormenting you. At any moment a sentence you've spat out by chance, a sentence you've taken the time to write in your *Negawit, <no rectification>,* can start swarming and want to sting you. It says to you: No one has control over his or her literary death. Nor do sentences. Sentences have no conscience. No one can underestimate what a *body of sentences (Baruch revisited?)* can do. For sentences love solitude, they love silence, and we persist in wanting to make them talk. *<In the spot where I am right now these sentences are being endowed with an ultracomic dimension! An* **underground passage,** *an old tunnel dug into the chalk during the Second World Woe!>* Sentences don't like gossip and you're making them gossip. Sentences want to be left alone, and here you're spending your time harassing them. Writers like their passages, and here we pass all our time by immatriculating them! We make garlands out of them, then we turn them into flags, and then we transform them into snakes that bite their tail. We take a sentence in order to turn it into a thought and suddenly there we are *making a stupid breviary. Amour, some* *more, in an hour, forever more, bravura encore.* At any moment a sentence can flake off the contingent moment of death and splatter into the center of a paragraph or into the throat of a writer. At any moment a sentence can be torn away from its silence and thrust into your brains. And the resonance of that very sentence is what no one can ever predict. Nothing tells of its coming, nothing. It comes unannounced. Nothing. That's why it's a sentence. Nothing. The sentence comes unannounced. The sentence that tells of nothing to come. Nothing. The most difficult of all sentences. The memorial sentence. Nothing. The sentence that has a love of ashes. The sentence that turns you into ashes. Nothing. The sentence of little nothings. The sentences of nothings at all. The sentence of all or nothing and the sentence of laughter. The enervating sentences and the enervated sentence. *No rectifications!* The sentence that reduces literature and its writers to ashes. Without sun. A sentence without sunshine that reduces literature to ashes. An immemorial sentence that renders memory impossible. A sentence without sunshine that leaves literary memory with a taste of ashes. SSCML. Please cease and desist from calling up memory. Please cease moving the moribund into memory, you're free! *Tello Tello Mannenai! Tello Tello Mannenai!* Plain Text. *Ne reminiscaris!*

<The short *sentence of my life* would probably—I was musing in my thoughts— have to be read regressively? In reading it progressively, beyond the shadow of a doubt, I was finding nothing more than *"words stripped of meaning"* … At that moment my head spun with many things that up to that point had been foreign or strange, but with a curiosity full of careful consideration, indeed, a loving curiosity. I learned to resent much more equitably our time of life and everything *"modern"* … >, *still another quotation from the great man who keeps his musician friend from letting his head spin around: for Mr. Hotshit, sleazy proof of the theory of the eternal return (A selective return, A selective one! obviously, my dear Watson)!* From the portico of the book of **Truth in Speech**: *you come as a living zombie, a role perfect in its time. You go in as a hawk and exit as phoenix.*
>*You hold the lapis stone in your right hand. By your right ear hangs the ankham flower like an earring. Your eye fascinates.*
>*You live in all truth. You are a marvel of a Mummy, extremely so>*

Yet I was able to tell Macha (with a ciphered tetragram), *Up to now I'm doing okay. Absolutely no rectification! Not the slightest tinge of rectification wafts in the air! I got up very early this morning and, as no memory persisted, I went about turning over the soil in the garden. Some rosebushes had to be pruned, so I pruned the rosebushes. The lawn had to be mowed, and so I mowed the lawn. And when everything was prim and proper, I took a closer look and went to the café.*

Nobody. Not a soul yet at the *Coffee Exchange*, so I had a moment to read the first section of the paper. I read the easiest pages of the paper while I sipped my coffee and smoked my first cigarettes of the day on the terrace. Since no one was there, there was nothing to fear. Nothing, nobody to fear. It flowed. It was okay. And suddenly, I felt it come. It was a little something that seemed entirely inoffensive. A breeze. A zephyr. A tiny jolt. Nothing but a wisp of air. A little commotion. Like a jolt in the synchrony of things. Like a little atmospheric spasm. A little breeze that lifted the pages of the first section of the morning paper without there being any desire to read them. A trembling in the air. There was time in the air. Brusquely, then, time began to shiver with the atmosphere, and I was the only being who could take pleasure in this prodigious moment. Then I would have wished that someone might pass by and ask me about the weather. I would have hoped that at least there be there an ocular witness to this little, this tiny *passage of time.* But nobody else had gotten to the *Coffee Exchange.* I was the first customer in the morning, and thus no one could share with me this minuscule passage of time. No eyes other than mine own. No conscience other than mine. No fear other than mine own. No madness other than mine. <*In the lower depths of the waters of time the apparition of the ghost behind the newspaper wasn't bad!*> I thought about calling the waiter and saying to him, *Waiter, can you, as I am, at this very moment, see time in the air?* I even thought of a lighter and less provocative formula, of the kind, *Have you seen the air of passing time?* But I suddenly realized that he wouldn't understand a thing, so I put it aside. What craziness to want to share the impression! A compulsion to share one's time! Sharing a morsel of one's heart! How idiotic to want to share one's time with imbeciles and others of the same ilk. And, finally, *the ten fingers of death to be shared!* Monsieur, you mean me, do I want to share the passage of time with you? Or as Master Vitoldo would say: Do I want to *be friendly with you?* Do I want to *fraternize with you!* He would have thought that I was taking him for a idiot and maybe that I was speaking to him about the perfume, *L'Air du Temps.* I grasped that it was silly to want to take a thought away from the air of time, that before *the air of time that passes* there is the Air of Time that stinks up the atmosphere with its thousands of olfactive megabites, and that before the Air of Time, there is fashion, and that before fashion, there is money and before money, there is the Usury of time, and before Usury, there is Luxury, and before Luxury, there is the godforbidden stench in the air of something totally fetid that makes me think I can't fail to be sick to my stomach, without my feeling nauseated, without feeling nauseated and reeking of thought. The horde of sentences had already plagued the atmosphere! But the runaround was only beginning. The runaround of life and death had scarcely begun. Memory had begun its pretty little labor of grieving. It strongly held the neck of living life in its clutches and had resolutely begun to suck its blood. *Its blood,*

blood afterward.

First of all let's write a poem, Plain Text, *again, with blood.*
We will eat the time of blood. Afterward! Plain text!

Noon-Midnight *(the emigrant's Complaint):*
Paris: *Have you noticed how we are?*
No one has seen us seated. Day and night we walk around the subway tunnel in quest of adventure. We don't have eyes for real things. They remained down below. In the Blue Country. The last time we closed our schoolbook Gagarin was making his first excursion on the way to the moon. The moon! The moon! Think of that! The moon! We still dream about it. For us it's pure havoc, a shambles of the worst kind. We've been waiting in line for hours on end!
All for nothing!
And a few drops of dew!
At Present, in Paris, between the sky and the earth
Death/Love hand in hand,
And the bittersoul of a Catoblepas!

And once again Macha came to pull me out of the muck and funk. Familiar with my lousy morning habits, *no rectifications!*, she came without ado to meet me at the *Coffee Exchange.* She shot into the great terraced room filled with its amused clients at the very moment the last sentence had just been erased, but she must have captured something from the air of the time — because after kissing me on the cheek, she immediately said, *It's strange, but don't you think there's something rather special in the air this morning?* And as I was not uttering a sound, she added, as was her wont, *Yes, I hit the nail on the head, isn't there something in the air?* And as I had been caught red-handed in a memorial metempsychosis, I was obliged to concede to her that there indeed was *something in the air* that morning. And apparently that sufficed, for she then sat down and hailed the waiter as if nothing had happened. She ordered a cappuccino and plunged into the first section of the paper. She then began to read the easiest pages of the news without, apparently, showing any signs of the effect of the air of the time. *It's strange, yes, very strange, and I'm guessing about what is about to come!*

Scholium # 1: for finally at stake is not so much the *placement* of words as, *given the circumstances*, displacing thought or maybe, in utter stupidity, of being displaced *into thought*. There's no other possibility!

The next morning I wrote a letter to the managing editor of the journal *Intersignes* to thank him for having invited me to take part in the special issue on *Destruction*, and to indicate to him that I accepted his offer to write a short article on destruction and that I had just put it in the mail. Foot courier. There followed coffee and cigarettes. And then almost an entire hour behind the great glass bay of the Lutetia where I saw people passing in every direction. A whole hour spent seeing the city as it was slipping away in the direction of nothingness. *No rectifications!* Seeing parading at least a hundred different people. Seeing passing before my eyes a good hundred people. Seeing being eyed by another hundred. Seeing still another hundred getting pushed around. Seeing a handful getting bothered. And nothing to say. *Rien à déchiffrer!* Not a single face to stare down! Not a single face that is worth my effort to stare it down! Not even a single mug worth my effort to deconstruct it! Not the least hint of a thought. Not the least hint of an idea. The ivory color of the skins appears, but *in passing*. The *purée* of all these faces, but *in passing*. The insignificance of gestures, but only in passing! The fear that follows. The fear of being shaken by the desire to rectify. The fear of beginning to remember things. A fear, too, of *doing things over again*. A fear of remembering myself. In passing. A fear of bad luck, of being taken by memory. Fear of reminiscence. Fear of the sentence. Fear of flags. Fear of the murmurings of time. Fear of the murmur of the heart. *Le souffle au coeur!* A fear of the smiles of time. A fear that time might become as porous as prose. A fear that prose has a crush on me and that I might get enamored of it. Myself of getting hooked on this sleazy prose. My immatriculating prose. My own imitating and prosing before the world. Myself falling in love with the prose of the world. I see it everywhere in her TV clothing. For don't you see, my dear, that prose has turned into TV? Right now it's the race between the short sentence, the sound bite, and the long sentence. The sentence that falls into silence and the sentence that gossips. The poetic sentence. The revolutionary sentence. The loving sentences. The democratic and love-of-man sentence. For right now, every sentence in the world is united against me to make *poetry*. I can see myself running around like a madman, but at the same time I also see a horde of delirious poetic sentences that *pass right before my eyes. No rectification, even at the risk of the greatest peril! Even where danger is most imminent! Even where everything is about to come tumbling down!* An absolute candor! An absolute *cold-bloodedness!* They run right *before me,* and I run *behind* them. And I'm in the race. We're *all in the race.* We've all sold out. We've all completely sold out, completely. Sentences, life, Brazil, Morocco, Andalusia, Chad, Iraq, Iran, and Pakistan. We've whored ourselves. Nothing left. Nothing for us. And then we sold America, Chile, Vietnam, Siam, Andalusia, and Algeria. We sold bundles of words, and when they became rare commodities, as good *souls on the margin,* we began to sell them in the name of unity. By digging into a bag of dribble. Without discrimination. *Ne discriminaris! Dawn* sold pretty well. Return. Begin again. Difference. Minority. Majority. Democracy. *Salut* sold quite well. Dismantling. Maceration. Night. Courage. *Disenchantment* was a big seller. Nihilism. Cynicism. *Ghetto* sold well for a time. I see all that a lot better, I can appreciate this *merry-go-round* from my *hole! Emigration* went like hotcakes. Everything sold well, even to the point where there was nothing left to sell. But *people* didn't have a customer. Neither did *bread.* Nor even *liberty!* Dear liberty is *intractable!* Democracy is hard to market! Democracy, what? Can't be sold? <*and if you just buy that for me you'll still be buying me!*> I was still hard at my exercise, my little morning exercise. Without rectification! I wanted to make words blossom while I waited for ideas. Make them lose their meaning. Send them packing as I was waiting to be done with my illness. While waiting to be free of solitude! A long period of convalescence. But first of all I had to *let the field of words lie fallow!* Make myself lie fallow. For six months, a year, that's it. Read nothing, see nothing, hear nothing, want nothing, desire nothing, *write nothing.* Promise nothing, plan nothing either. For six months, one year, two or three years, and, if necessary, for an entire life, <*but if, only if, I'm really up to it* myself!>, be happy to draw, trace lines, lines in every direction, long and senseless lines, and then see. If only to see what happens. To learn nothing, remember nothing, know nothing, construct nothing. Don't *touch* anything with your eyes. Don't go blind by reading! Draw with your feet, draw long lines, make lines. *Align lines.* Break tielines. If only to see what happens when I send off dead letters, *lettres mortes.* For six months to a year, write only dead letters, *lettres mortes,* celebrate the death of letters, *all in running off, when there's nothing left to tell; as for what remains, it comes from the **other,*** the ineffable, the first paradorsal!, > letters without readers, and plunk!>

For she had fiery blood
When I was young,
And trod so sweetly proud
As 'twere upon a cloud,
A woman Homer sung,
that life and letters *seem*
But a heroic dream!

@ *Rav said: Every verset that Moses has not cut into pieces, we must not do it in his place. S. answered: We can do it in his place.*

@ *Rabbi S. ben Asher said: Where you find more letters than periods, you have to interpret the letters. More periods than letters, so interpret the periods. <(and in plain text) More lines than periods, so interpret the lines!>*

I go back home by way of Didouche: *tons of stale bread, <an unnameable twist in front of the bakery in respect to rye bread!>*
There's still nobody yet in the concierge's window, and the mailbox is empty, *so much the better, so much the better, so then no rejection, no answer,* the stairs go up four by four like a stairmaster. *Jog! C'mon! Jog all the way up!*
That's where I meet the customs inspector's wife, the so-called customs inspector, trained and lettered in customs, lettered in inanities. She flags me, she's got something to say. Something that she'll only say in front of her lawyer, in front of her husband, or, lacking that, in front of a local authority, preferably a military authority: *You ought to systematically avoid running up the stairs at that pace, you might have heart problems. Even at your age you're running the risk of a heart attack!*

The sun still shines brightly. It smacks everywhere of the state and the sewer. Even the sun smells of the state. The whole world has the aroma and taste of the state. The state is everywhere. It is redolent of the state. In their melancholic drawing rooms all the writers in the building are striking against the state. I counted a good half-dozen of them. Almost one writer per floor and not the slightest hint of a thought. They look like they've all followed the same orders: writing, fiction, and prose left fallow. The state functionaries say they're on strike but it's not patriotic! Journalists of the state say that the writers of the state are on strike and that, given the current situation, it's patriotic. No idea about what a fallow field is. Unaware of the benefits of leaving things fallow. No artificial fertilizers. No sowings. No *ideas* either. *Ideas on strike!* Writers no longer want to be artificially fertilized. They no longer accept the use of fertilizer. In fact, they don't even accept prose anymore. My favorite prophet, Aely, tells me that *in prose there's rose.* Therefore they've stopped writing. They prefer to let nature *go on its own.* Give their brains a chance to get their health back in order. Let prose *rise up!* Against the state. No more intellectual manure! No brain fertilizers for the state! <*What a shingle for a bookstore!*> That's what I was thinking about that morning at the Coffee Exchange. It came back to astound me. But I still refused to rectify. That's the point of it, period. I didn't rectify. I didn't slip back. I didn't budge an inch. No concessions made. Volleys of memories from the city and the dead, and I refused to flinch. I held firm. I was hard as marble. Memories come back by the shovelful, and I didn't slip back. Even when the Algerian customs inspector's wife added, *all the same the young really have it! They run up stairs like billy goats on a mountainside and they don't miss a heartbeat! Darn! You're a god with all your goodwill and misericord!*

There's not a beat missed, Madame, because there isn't any heart. I don't have the heart to enrich the state. No heart to *escribble* inanities. No heart to write an apologia. No taste for writing panegyric. No heart to think. No heart to budge. No heart to be. No heart. *Now do you want to commit treason? What about the people? What are you going to do with Algeria?*
What destiny? What revolution? What democracy?

Algeria, *demolition.*

Lella, *Plain text,* vanished into the elevator. *And what about us? Have you thought about us? Us, the older generation! We who've scrounged around for your welfare of degenerate attitude of African latitude!*
Aely's blue notebook: *"In misericord there's cord and misery"!*
Retreats, marriages, celebrations on November 4, the cult of the dead, Monuments to the dead, Islam, Fraternity, *fraternization,* and nerds! *What are you doing for fraternity? What are you doing with taxes? Who'll pay for your retirement when you're an invalid, ready for the nursing home?*

A parade of invalids. In Algiers, in Paris, in Marseilles, and in Montreal. The same parade every day. *Invalids of all nations, all you have to do is climb out of your wheelchairs! Unite!* The construction of the great mosque under three crescents—Araby, Islam, Algeria—is moving ahead at full speed. AIA. A mausoleum stands where there used to be a grove of nut trees. Next to the mausoleum there's a marabout! Patriae, Fratriae, Idolatry! Where there once stood an office building there's now the construction site of the new Paris Opera. The frogs aren't stupid! I also counted a dozen professors in the building. *Shovelfuls of Professors!* Professors, well, they're a little behind the times. They don't have an inkling about the virtue of leaving things fallow. Production, copulation, reproduction. The panic of passing a whole day in abstinence. Publish or *pas riche!* Worse than Americans! After getting rid of scruples and other quirks they publish a monograph and other little works! They think they've got something to say about how writers name things! Zola and the proper names for smut and filth! Proust and his narrataire-à-terre! Flaubert and his words for nostrils and noseholes! All they do is dream about *immatriculating* their writers! Poses, costumes, all university malarkey! Nomination and denunciation! The whole university is in its Sunday best! Its breath stinks! Fetid! They hate fallow earth, they hate peasants and pastures. University, yes, that's Productivity. "At the University Productivity Is Our Most Important Product!" Geee! University and the national charter of invalidation! University and the national charter of idiocy! University and the immatriculation of writers! *Poet, gimme ya green cahd'n kissmyass!*

<You big baby!>

Let's let Macha have the last word, she knows how to put it elegantly: *I knew your grandfather! He would be ashamed! Shame on you! Simply put, it's shameful! Not just shame, but all the same it's shame! Who do you think you are! That's the last straw! Honesty! Probity! Three whole volumes on usury!*

God will make up for this on your children's account!

When you're older, when you reach the golden years, you'll see ...

When you're in a crunch, you'll see that it's not easy! Now just think, Madame, I've got two handsome children (both male!), born of a Frenchwoman from Orleans! What madness! Treason! Blasphemy! From that moment on I understood that he had committed treason, and that he had to be exterminated.

Plain text: <Not from that moment on,
we never beg the question of testing our mettle or krypton of being,
we liquidate, we destroy, we murder,
I remain with the marble veins ...
even the little bottleneck pain is bombarded
no choice, no judgment,

no taste,
no appreciation,
  tasting
  swallowing,
  sipping,
  etc.
no tongue, no idiom
no bullshit!>

Sync # 2: The inner flash of passages falls faint when the electric lights come on, and he took refuge in their name. But the name of passages became a sieve that let through only the bitter essence of Past Time. (This strange power of distilling the present as the most intimate essence of Past Time is what, for true voyagers, gives the name its stirring and mysterious power.)

Fortunately for me, nothing came in the mail from Providence. *Plain Text.* Now that I've put a good twenty-odd miles between me and Kouba-the-Two-Mosques, the mail has stopped. It has dried up. *Jean-Jacques* has no more cause for alarm. *He's not waiting for any letters anymore.* He's begun to lie fallow. A fallow folly. Now that the Atlantic lies between Kouba and me, it's all *dead letters.* No more *Kztl!* between Algeria and me. Letters no more. Prose no more. The prose of the world is all dried up. It's gone tchoufa. No more Kultchure! No more peelings to pick up, that's for sure! But *n'aies pas peur!* as Macha says, *be not afraid, Joc* [That's not his real name, *clearly!*]
if you swoon in your name of Joachim
be not afraid
for names are no more than wisps of smoke. Adventures, happy voyages, Joachim, your name was too good for me after all,
Phoenix,
phoenix abolished in ashes
or *Fenimore*   <*Fais no more! Be done with things!*>
destined to respond to this name Mrad **X**
is worth being written Rmaed (Ashes)

     and Μουραδ

in haggardese (Arab)
gray hair
gray flannel slacks
and even gray eyes on certain days following the armistice
and to dodge the question, to avoid being called in question
In pasture, I threw to the Sphinx
Mourad's common name
  they wish to infer that
  on the day of his birth
  the world was all dried up
and now, one by one, every letter of my name has begun
to blur
and here comes *Ramadan!*
in sum
not enough to talk about
not enough for much rubadub
not enough to yoke the masses!
Is this a decisive step in the direction of peace?
You who venture in the whereabouts
you who come from the littoral of cities
watch out!
danger!
for every edifice only holds onto a single hair
and what does it finally mean? So what is it all about?

مراد

Somewhere a DAEDALUS at the northern climes will not return:

LAST TIME SEEN THE YUSUF ROAD (ALGIERS) AROUND

THE GREAT SONATRACH BUILDING. NO NEWS SINCE

MUST INFORM THE MINISTER OF THE INTERIOR. MAY

BE IN POSSESSION OF A BOGUS REAL PASSPORT.

NEW NAMES MRAD. OR RMAD. OR MOURAD. TRAVELS

ALONE. POSSIBLE DESTINATIONS: SWITZERLAND, BELGIUM,

CANADA, OR U.S.A. STOPOVER IN PARIS, MARSEILLES, OR LYONS.

POSSIBLE CONTACT: NICOLE TACHE IN MALLEMORT.

PROVENCE.

The general consulate: *one of these days he'll take refuge, he'll get calm with passing time*, age, experience, wisdom, money, children, marriage, responsibilities, tasks, teaching, knowledge, sexuality, cholesterol, Freudianism, *fatigue, they all wind up getting tired, they all finally get the point about what life is all about, they wise up, they get back in line, they sow their oats! No sweat, I'll pin your Shitsky down!*

Whoever used to say (*Aerd*, the cacochymous bard): you're instructed to leave my language the way you found it and my cabin that you have not built and my body whose power of labor you covet and my dreams whose wealth you envy and my speech whose meaning you deform and my brains whose sap you tap and my skin whose softness you desire and my name whose meaning you can't decipher and my thought whose birth you fear and my thought whose meanders you traffick and my death whose birthday you celebrate,
for he alone knows the infamous crimes of Oedipus,
denn es gibt keine Form in der Natur (le Maur?).

> *He has no longer been seen alive, but that proves nothing, he might still be hidden in the Casbah as in the good old days of the war of regional liberation. Maybe he also left the matrimonial territory in search of other adventures. Maybe he took sanctuary in the cellar of 78 rue Ahmed Ghermoul so that he could dedicate himself to his labors of "écritchure"! Maybe, finally, he was turned into a scorpion or into a vulture after having swallowed too strong a mixture of mescaline and Kateb Yacine. Another possibility: he ODed on Burroughs cut with a Pound Punch! The question has to be explored. Contact Franz K., 2 Denkenstrasse, Prague. Or Rûmi, Stratosphere!*

and may the wind blow black and with pestilence on the day of the debacles,
and may the wind blow black and with pestilence on the day of your nuptials,
and may the wind blow black and with pestilence on the day of your reconciliatory rituals,
Read Boehme <*Jacob!*> on that day if you've *got the leisure*, because, as for me, the scenario is stifling.
Coryphée: "Don't get riled up like that, c'mon, buddy, ya know, there're many less-depressing things to consider in life! Look at the sky! Look how clear and limpid it is! Look at the sea! Look how clear and limpid it is! And behold your brothers and sisters! Look how they dance! Look how they celebrate the glory of the year's end in joy! Look how happy and handsome they are! Look at the earth! Look how it's in bloom! Look how it exudes sweet perfumes! Look how it is pregnant with the seeds of summer! Look how it is greening everywhere! Look how it offers itself to our craziest desires! Look at the mountain! Look how it invites us to rise up! Look how it exalts the loftiest thoughts! Everywhere nature seems to be celebrating the saturnalia of philosophy! Everywhere the earth gives and is felicity! and everywhere, it bubbles and trembles with joy!"

Sure, sure, but nothing will ever shatter the dark night of our distaste,

nothing will ever put to an end the obscure night of our treason and our denials. Stop!

A misdemeanor of composition! Death and composition! The devil with composition! Sex and resurrection! I had paid an honorable fine, I had sworn that I would never rectify my shots, I had promised myself to live a silent and frugal life, but there I was slobbering and "getting over" things before "moving on" with my life. I hear only groans, and currently I am living in *a kind of pain that never pierces, an empty dark, sinister, muffled, drowsed pain that lacks passion, that has no natural expression . . . I see but I can't feel to what degree [the elements of nature] are beautiful. The élan that inspired me is dying, for what can this spectacle do to free my heart from this suffocating weight of things? It would even be vain to contemplate this dim green light that lingers at sunset; I am forbidden all hope of finding near to outer forms the passion and life whose origins are in ourselves!*

and at this moment you dare to ask me, "What are you doing?

What do you want to do with your bag of bones?"

They disfigured me forever. Now all I can do is go away

HEIMATLOS

But *alas too late for Taenia!*

You will, I hope, excuse me!

For they've thrown sulfur on my linens

and I burn

I burn everywhere,

"if he's unhappy, he only has to return to where he came from" (said by Madame Perez)

The Hydra has returned

(about 1960)

and there's no other island for his majesty Bigshot!

No other countries for bibi!

Where do you think you'll find refuge?

Who do you think will care for you?

Who do you think will worry about you?

When I return from a little *Italic voyage* like that Macha always watches out. She walks around the house and starts to put together everything that recalls history, everything that recalls Algeria, everything that recalls Algiers <especially rue Didouche Mourad>, everything that recalls *outer reality*. She starts to behave with me as if I had gotten drunk on the milk of amnesia: remember *Tabarin?* And do you <*she displays a photo of the narrator on the hump of a camel*> remember that? And that

<she puts a piece of amber under the narrator's nose> tells you something? And that? <she tosses on the bed a copy of *Portrait of the Artist as a Young Francophone!*> And that? And that? *That's enough!*

Addendum or how Macha turns into a *Strader* (i.e., a Mack truck with a *front cab*): *You write the way you read, or do you read the way you write?* <You better make up your mind, and pronto! Time is passing, and the *cockroaches* are waiting! Time slips away, and the literary police are waiting for you!> I'm spending a whole afternoon examining a prospectus for China. $3500 round trip, a trifle! But I'm falling back on a *trip* to Ghardaïa-the-Ochre! After that, a ballad in the park of the *Lake of the Isles with Macha.* She still doesn't know that you can't pet the Canadian geese, *that the black-and-white Canadian geese just don't like that!* yet more thoughts on the depression around the book! She cuts through my mind the way a comet flies through the heavens: You have been born to get us out of the dumps of the human imagination! <I am thinking: an antidump mode of thinking!> night has almost fallen, <I am thinking: *three days and three nights have gone by since I've caressed Macha's inner thighs on the mattress in the attic! Am I getting senile or what? Is that why she craves to* caress *the Canadian geese?*> The kids have been throwing us topsy-turvy! Not a minute of peace! Not a moment when we can be alone! I'm reduced to caressing her thighs as she reads Kant. *Under a desk in the Louis Philippe style:* a primarily synthetic apperception of thighs! A transcendental deduction of breasts! A monogram of her face! The schematism of little greyhounds! You're acting out a *scenario,* you're already succeeding and repenting for it: if you don't watch out, you'll put another little brat in the world! Right now you're restricted to fornicating in the attic! <*The satyr in the attic!*> *Remove everything but your panties, ma chère, I know my way around there!* A malingering finger suffices to spread the little shroud of pink cloth that protects the perineum! The most sensitive spot in the universe! *Delicatessen!* A little cup of slightly acidic honey at the base of the thighs! A choice morsel! It makes me horny! I try to graze, I begin to lick her softly, but Macha's already tickled crazy, she can't stand it, she thinks I'm a pig, *I'm for naught, that makes my dick go limp, why don't you bite my neck, I love to feel your dick rubbing my ass, don't you like it like that? If it's no, then buy a lollipop! It'd also get you over your sempiternal desire to have a blow job! What a maniac!* <*How to measure the gap that exists between diurnal man and nocturnal woman*> It's hard for her to turn the page of a hot potboiler, *Plain Text,* all the while she holds my fat head in her hands under the legs of Louis Philippe! This time my little ruse works! <A compliant hand: her dirty mania for stoppering my ears with the palms of her hands when I drop the periscope and take the submarine under

the waves! The survival of a deeper archaic instinct? An atavism? When the homunculus is in rut, better not close his ears shut! Better let his gills breathe! In case a predator wants to whisper it in his ears!> From my point of view in the conning tower *everything's rosy right now!* When he sees her a few months later with her *cockpit forward* and her rosy cheeks aloft and aloof, the *Henry <Now what's he still got to do with you?>* doesn't mince his words, *there's still another that's fallen on rusty nails without warning!* Macha is as red as a tomato, *no rectification! Right now, let's assume!*

Algeria, *demolition*
<later, later! For now, the Archonte story!>

Memories of the house of the dead # 2: When, *Plain text,* writers want to account for the condition of their thoughts, they invoke the country of their origin, they pull a white page out of the drawer of their desk and write a calligraphy of the name of their country, then the name of their town, then their date of birth, then the <virtual> date of their death. For writers above all want to be born of the ashes of their mental disorder, they want to tell the story of their afterlife, they first of all want to turn everything into ashes, they want to kill, they want to die, to die over and over again. It's incredible what they won't do to nourish the belly of potential literature! *The automaton!* Thus there exist piles of mucus of desire. And lots of ashes in the end! And who are the writers who don't have a taste of ashes in their mouth? And what is literature without this descent into the ashholes of hell? Sure, they all begin with the mucus of literary memory. The same mucus sticks to their fingers. *Il leur colle aux doigts!* No way to get rid of this mucus. They begin with a very healthy, very praiseworthy *drive to write,* and no sooner than they begin to write the literary mucus rises to the surface, right from the time they begin scribbling an abominably sweet and acrid *narrative impulsion* rises up in their throat. A quadrature! A swell of literary ashes! A ligature of literary deceit! They all want to break the ligature of sterile literati! Ligatures up to their ears! They never stop fooling the world with their ligatures! You'll write me a hundred literary sentences without a single ligature! A hundred sentences without a trope or figure! A hundred sentences without the foolery of figures! Utter your sentence, Gramps. I beg you to francophonify to your heart's content!

An excerpt from Aely's Black Notebook. "In the French tromperie *there is the word* trope! *In figure there's a fig! In literature there is [to a higher power] the words litter and atchure! Too many literary aches, hatchers, spoiled and stillborn litters! Too much litrachure litters human mores! etc."*

Everywhere literature litters the empty streets of the Ramadan. Geoff <the narrator's guardian angel> slowly works through the meanders of *Dead Letters*. From time to time he is heard laughing in his corner, muttering, *I can't believe it! Good Grief, this is Madness! Hey, Ben! How do you explain that they took this stuff seriously? Were you out of your mind when you wrote this book? I couldn't dream of a bigger hoax than this! This is pure madness!* And even in plain English!

An excerpt from Aely's Blue Notebook: "**Of the Spiritual Automaton**: <the four pillars of literary writing ever since the beginning of time:
— NARRATIVE IMPULSION
— A DRIVE TO WRITE
— RHETORICAL EX-PULSION
— THEORETICAL REPULSION

       A narrative impulsion without a drive to write is **lifeless.** *A drive to write without a narrative impulsion is* inert and will be defined as **deranged.** *This double (im)pulsion with rhetorical ex-pulsion is* **estranged.** *The conjunction of this*

      IM>
             } *PULSION*
      EX>

without theoretical repulsion is simply **blind.** *I shall define the* **spiritual automaton** *as the synergetic functioning of these four vectors. As it is very rare and very difficult for a writer to bring together the 'points' of these four* automata *without going crazy, we shall conclude (1) that authentic writers are rather endangered species; (2) that real writers have to have the most robust mental and physical constitution; (3) that 'real' literature can be reduced neither to the taste that writers have for narrative, nor to the taste they might display for theoretical speculation, nor, finally, to the taste of well-wrought sentences. Thus, in our opinion, literature need not be concerned either with narrative, literary prose, or even the reader. Thus there remains a great* inherent *wisdom in real literature, <i.e., whatever is not the ligature of mental flunkies, i.e., not shackled by the ligatures of rhetoric, i.e., not spoiled by the magma of Theory*">.

Algeria, *immobility.*
When we were at the Mandarin, *sure, sure, everything's all mixed up, Macha, everything's mixed up in my head, but don't blame me! Blame Aely! Blame it on this devil, this literary theorist!* I understood that we had been free for a long time but without hav-

ing to go through a trial by fire in order to be aware of the fact. It was up to who-ever would be best able to endure! Literature as a trial by fire! Writers, a call to cigarettes! Literature considered as opium smoke! <*What a spiritual rapture! What inner worlds! Was this then the panacea,* the nepenthe pharmakon *for all human suf-fering?*> The point basically assured us that K. had been an inveterate hash smoker! Hadn't he already stunk up the Algerian atmosphere of literature for more than half a century with his shooting star? Didn't he already put us in a state of perpet-ual trance with his stale tobacco of Fondouk? I smoke, I stink, therefore I think! *Fumare et petunare ergo sum!* We were stinking in order to see if we were worthy of literature! Literature as an art of stinking! Congenital anti-Cartesianism? Inveter-ate smokers! Hashachins! Hashassination! Assassin poets! Literature and stench! Lit-erature as a physical test of intellectual suffocation! Literature and smoke, litera-ture up in smoke.

I *am not* at home in the city of asphalt.
Forever I've been equipped with the sacraments of the dead:
Newspapers, tobacco, whiskey,
Scornful, ultimately *discontented*, a flâneur![2]

gone back home, I think I stink I sink in
the house of stale and old tobacco,
I consult the oracle at Bastos,
I call for the gods with a Gauloise,
I scoff at the sphinge with its Virgin tobacco,
with all the windows closed,
the Hubris incarnate!
Next Friday, if it pleases God, I propose to get drunk!
Who says it better?
Summing it all up: O. narrative impulsion: O. theoretical repulsion: 2! In other words, the machine is entirely off-track! The ordeal of the seance of the Mandarin threw me into an absolutely extraordinary state of dereliction. Rhetorical *ex-pulsion:* not at all! And so, *how can anyone dedicate themselves to the labors of writing in the middle of so much noise?* How do we get out of all this stench with a head chock-full of Midrashic aphorisms? How can we belch a thought with my head heaving for tobacco? I look with scorn on Aely. I look with scorn on Elya. I cast scorn on Jabès (may his soul

---

[2]By poor M. B., *The Domestic Sermons of Mourad Bensmaier.*

rest in peace after all). I cast scorn upon myself and feel myself sinking into the green armchair.

Elya: In the learned name of Jabès, there is *Yabess* who, in savage language, means dry, arid, *sec!*

Caro, Macha said, without leaving the room where she prays for the return of the coming year, *Carissimo, do you know that the energy you unleash in forcing yourself to reread the **Artificial Paradise** is enough to kill a bull! Can't you get out of this perspective, even for a second? Why don't you go ride a bike around the block a few times before getting back to work? Don't you think literature can get along without you for an hour or two? For the love of God, just an hour or two! You'll calm down, you'll be okay, I'm sure of it!*

Treatise *Sota* 34 b: "Ah'imane constructed Anath, Cherchaï built Alach, and Talmaï built Talbuch."

Myself? I tinker and rummage around the attic. I construct a *mobile cognitive map* of my spiritual wares, I force myself to *destabilize* my mind, I take pleasure in getting out of my mind the *condition* in which it is placed, *Undo Typing*, in undoing its static mentality, *Edit Again*, rip it away from its stability, *Repaginate Now*, I am laboring with this *task* like someone sent from the bomb squad. A bomb de-fuser, I rip it away from its bombast, *Short menus, Preferences, Commands!*
Courts menus, préférences, commandements!
And always no rectifications!

Judges 14:4: "He looked for an occasion to slander the Philistines."

Algeria, *a lie,*
between the *pshat* and the *drash,*
a lying low, a kind of fallowing: read the same work fifteen times, twenty times, a hundred times, at the foot of the letter, "the folded wing of the mind."
After the fiftieth time, something is happening in the *filigree of the words, in the filigree of the sentences, at the end of the thousand and first time the meeting with the mummy takes place,* a meeting with the mind,
a meeting with *death itself,*
but it's agonizing. Now what can be done? Quit thinking or striving to think?
First of all make some stench, take a drag on a fresh Gauloise, get high with *every kind of tobacco,* turn my head into a pile of cut tobacco, shove a lead pipe up my skull, no rectifications! *Nope!*

Again, I'm in the café. *Do you remember the whirling dervishes that I had a chance to see in Istanbul? You're whirling, you're whirling, you're whirling about yourself and you're the only one not to see that you're whirling around a void! The only one who can't see you're twirling around! C'mon, buddy, relax! You're not the man who makes the world turn around! It turns on its own! If we had to count on you, the great fall would have taken place long ago!*

Sync # 3 (in plain and full text):
I am a Mummy of Truth.
I have presided over the rites of winter (Minneapolis, Minnesota)
and over the rites of summer (Algiers, Amen).
I am a Mummy of Truth.
I arrive at the hour as the interpreter, to defend my heart,
in this room of Truth . . .
Just in voice, I arrive as the interpreter in my hour, to defend
my heart from my mother, under the smile of the god . . .
Just in voice, I conjure up the Bennou,
the phoenix of my spirit. I discover the passage. I enter into knowledge in the sanctuary of the serene life. Light radiates from the burning intellect.

Algeria, *melancholia,*
it doesn't stop, and it's hard to take, *no rectifications!,* with one and only one conso-
lation: no dogs in the streets, no cats in the streets, it's too early for the animal clan, too early too for the sebsi smokers and the domino players, too early too for the bearer of shadows, too early too for the *men* of this city, but that's because all the bistros of this city are closed, it's because all the whorehouses of the city are closed,
and as it's the month of Ramadan all the *bars* of the city of A* are closed,
she, still delightful, *You're always talking about leaving, about letting things go, leaving it once and for all, getting out, and you haven't budged an inch. That's not very Catholic, wouldn't you think?*
As it is the month of Ramadan, that I take on the ordeal by fire is out of the question. We'll stay put calm and collected in a corner of the *Brasserie des Facs* or the *Tabarin,* waiting for the three shots of cannon fire that will announce the coming of *Dhôr.*[3]

---

[3]*Dhôr,* twilight.

There is a Marxopath (Nono), a future homeopath (Siphi), a patented politologist (Omar), a great Popoteur (Ameyar), an Image-feeler (Merzak, called the *Great Maker of Images* or even the *Polypalper of images!*), two paperscribblers (Abdou and Doudou), a Papou (?), and a scriptopath (yours truly).

The streets are empty, the stores are empty, the sidewalks are empty, the souls are empty, the future is blocked, *l'avenir est bouché!* and the inhabitants of the city, aphasiac flâneurs, resemble the *passengers of an immobile ship.*

Ameyar (as I breathe through my nose): You see, what really bugs me the most about this goddamned Ramadan is not so much the fasting, my dear brother, but that I can't smoke! When I can't smoke the taste of a dead cat sticks in my throat! I can't even strike up a conversation with a whore because my breath stinks so much! It bothers the hell out of me! When I don't get my daily dose of nicotine I can't even get a hard-on! The remedy for this, Zella, Zella, my wife, damn it, my zealous wife, is to put golden tobacco in my evening bowl of soup! So then she'll do anything, even sprinkle a full pack of Afras, the abomination of Algerian tobacco, in the banana soup! You get the smell of the recipe? Can you imagine the stench of my breath the next morning? <he sticks his fat iguana tongue out at me> After that people say that I'm writing my editorials *as if I were on drugs!* From one tobacco to the next! You've got to give up your erection! I can't sacrifice the erotic life of my wife for the Ramadanic imperatives! My wife has inalienable rights! Islam can't do a fucking thing about it! And then, in every way, in spades or in a royal flush,[4] I'm neither a Musule nor a Moscule!

<Come on!... Come on ... Let's get back to our chronicle!... I'm losing you once and for all ... but you know I've still got my headaches! But that's no reason (Plain Text again):>
After closing the door to the future with an iron hammer, they left in the direction of the port. They all had their eyes closed.

Nono: What are you eating?

Merzak: A jujube. What about you?

A stick of chewing gum.

American?

No, French. That's all I could find.

What's going on in that country?

Old-time writers, you know, are dear souls!

Language isn't just the portal on the left!

Language is not within everyone's reach!

---

[4]*De toutes et en une trois cartes! That is, in every event?*

In the daytime, we stutter,
In the nighttime, we speak like prophets!
Sure, we had time enough to drink and to see it coming,
        See what?
The trains that pass near the port,
The ships that unload their cargo on the docks,
A blond girl with chestnut eyes,
And behind her, a whole army of kids who whistle at her
And who was laughing?
The cop (he was going to take his retirement the next day)!
He let it happen?
Yes, completely.
Here confusion always reigns.
Who do you think you are, God or what?
No, I am not thinking.
Then why the hell are you bothering us?

The investigating officer: I see that you have consumed an incredible amount of energy to reach such meager results. That's alarming! I imagine you stay up day and night so that you won't fail to seize the moment when it is revealed to you. What a disaster! This typically petty Algerian game will be the death of you! Let's have a drink! C'mon, let's blab for a bit! Let's chatter! When will it finally sink in that you're never going to *break off*, my children! Mr. Death is the most democratic creature in the world! He'll respect everyone!
—For what reason do we have to listen to you, O bird of evil!
—I am returning to you from the end of all things human! I'm human no more!
—(idiotic laughter) Hee! Heehee! Haha! Thaoura Zira'yia!
—Today's youth doesn't respect anything or anyone! May Alla have pity on them!
A chorus of today's youth:
—Yes! We've been wronged so much we're hanging from a rope! (Sardonic laughter!)
Eh! Mamyia! Thaoura Zira'yia!
—You're playing with your life as if it were a game of dominoes or dice!
—A roll of dice will never abolish your song-and-dance! (Laughter!)

Sleepless nights
Opium of sleep
The moon shines over a smoldering sickness

He is pale
His laughter is dry
His lips are swollen
His head is round (uncharacteristically)
He stands motionless
While we observe
The *weasel* of time slithers away on the horizon! ·
O *former Masters!*
Please tell us what you are doing!
Tell us *what* to do! What can we hope for!
We hang by the words on your inspired lips!
We're all ears
And we can't stop waiting with bated breath!

All my writing projects are presently arranged in manila folders,
they wait only for the end of Ramadan,
they will be the first to leave.
I made a meticulous classification in preparation for departure: except for pictures,
everything else was left *in quarto* folders <*isn't it madly teasing?*> in every color: yellow, orange, red, blue, pale green. I had never imagined that the world was filled
with so much ink and paper, I had never had the slightest inkling, even in my wildest
fantasies, that in my dreams I had blackened so many white pages! *no rectifications!* I
found a whole box of old lithographic exercises: all marks of calligraphic wit, pic-
tograms of the soul, a young and impetuous (and slightly naive) soul, *drowsiness*,
stupor, and with *spattering sperm.*
The mother believes that it makes Ramadan because no one can eat, drink, nor
smoke during the Ramadanic month: *Since you've got exams to do, once in awhile you
can make an exception or two, for example on the day of the* written *exams, I'll make you
a little bowl of soup and a Techekchouka for lunch!*
She doesn't know that I am taking advantage of the occasion to practice what I preach
about the *sickness of leaving things fallow, out to pasture.*
*Do you really think that you'll soon be leaving for France? I added: your brother's sweater!
Up there you'll be needing it more than he does! I sewed your initials on the inside of the
cuffs of your shirts and inside your socks!*
Right then she offers the narrator a cigarette and stuffs another between her lips: it
will not be seen that Lellac's children, the three children of a Moslem mother and
revolutionary, who accepted to go and play at being the virgin in paradise while

her offspring will go off and roast in hell! *Maybe all these stories of hell and paradise are idiocies, but I think I'd better take out a life insurance policy right now! If you're going to go to hell, my son, I have to follow you! Smoke, smoke a cigarette, my son, smoke a cigarette — the kind of cigarette they give to criminals before a firing squad — with your mother!* <Texto!>

They're ramadaning, he's *fallowing:* taken for a good Moslem because he's fasting, he takes advantage of Ramadan to put his diabolical plan to work. No need for the toilets in the *Brasserie des Facs* or the *Tabarin* to jump into the ordeal by fire, to drink in catimini, to *think* in catimini, to *stink up* in catimini, to *groan* in catimini, to *fornicate* in catimini,

no need of *alibis* for writing (Plain Text),

no need of Earthly Nourishments: overnourishment, population explosions, both crass and mass, fascism, revolt, Camus: *overnourished, overpopulated, desert, the absurd, phtysique!*

his written exams are *excellent*, the best he ever wrote: flying, free, paradisiac!

Aren't you ever afraid of always mashing up your ideas over and over again? If I were in your shoes I'd really be afraid! But I do know that I don't think I'd ever want to be your wife!

The directress of the group of young Communists is decidedly delicious: Marxism, History, Revolution, idealism, Materialism, Dialectics, *Telos*, social criticism, Free Love, *a boat en route to Vietnam! from door to door doses of propaganda, future, liberty, equality, fraternization, whole garbage cans overflowing with bread on the eve of Ramadan.* What she doesn't know is that I never had the slightest intention of marrying her: *marrying* the directress of the study group! She's pretty, ripe, really attractive! And smart! That balls me up!

In the Office of the Secretary General of the Single Party (SGSP): Ameyar <he is on a mission: has to do a report on the next congress of the SP> first of all, spell out the contradiction in this country of dopes: *they make them fast all day, they beat around with their singlemost thought: stuff their bellies with food! Along their way back home they buy a loaf of bread at every single bakery they go by! A loaf for Samia! Another for Rashid! and another for my grandmother: she really likes having a crust or two! And then there's still the Shôr!*[5] *There is this invention by the devil to make us more miserable than ever! A loaf for the baby in case Nana doesn't find any powdered milk at the pharmacy! My dear brother, that's also needed! Do you see the contradiction? You're empathizing the crud? At this moment compatriots have patriotism at the gut level, therefore they're stocking up!*

---

[5] *Shôr*, dawn and the little meal that is taken during the month of Ramadan before sunrise.

Note well that they're nothing more than pretexts! While waiting, the bakers have their shingle over the street, they fatten up, they construct villas on the hills over Algiers that look like cardboard boxes while the country is in ruins! A vicious circle! It perpetually turns on death! The country is one that wants to turn to death! Bread, death, and frenzy! It's a safe bet that if we were to succeed in changing the national diet we would be free of the yoke of underdevelopment!

Siphi <*quoting Aragon by heart*>: <One of the most sordid of all French sayings is *It's a safe bet that* ... It makes the eyes jump out of the head of whoever utters it! Don't roll your eyes so romantically! How long do we have to be nailed to and spin around on our chairs in this back room? Wouldn't it be better to take in a movie at the movie house with a .38 at our throats?

Ammeyar: First, there's a shortage of .38's and second, yesterday the theater burned down to the ground! Another one of the assassins' plots! We'll take advantage of this audience to ask the SGSP if the Single Party can help us rebuild it! This country needs culture! A strong dose of culture or the country's in the shit! An overdose of culture will not be cause for harm!

Coryphée: *While they fast the grass is growing!*

Siphi: *If we had as many filmmakers as there are members of the Single Party this country would be the flower of the Maghreb!*

Algeria *(in the middle of the night)*
the writer returns from afar:
the directress: *you realize now, the country is also turning! It's turning and you're turning with it! All the turning dervishes! They're all idiots! They're draouchas,*[6] *as they say in our country! They're all thinking dervishes! Thinking idiots!*

baba batra 12 b: "Ever since the Temple was destroyed, prophecy was taken away from the prophets and given over to simpletons and children."

And currently? Currently, since there isn't even any cinematheque, he's getting ready to leave without informing the directress,
he thinks from over there he will write them a little letter to show them how and why to say something clear and rigorous, to say something completely inexact but rigorous accompanied by a picture of his face *withered* by travel, *I have traveled, I have not found, I am still traveling, with best wishes,* and a picture of his

---

[6]*Draouchas,* from *derouèche,* in spoken Arabic, which means an idiot or a simpleton.

shriveled body, *he'll also tell them how much he appreciated their friendship and admired their courage*: in short, what is hardest to say, *Plain Text*, without stooping to ridicule,

a required passage by way of Nice, *on the surrounding heights*, to visit a pusillanimous musician and the fishmongering wife and to track back through for a last time the *ascent* of the *Nietzsche Road* between Eze-by-the-Sea and Eze-Center, to go and shake the mayor's paw, have a drink at the *Méditerrannée*,

see for a last time the fireworks in the hills over Nice, take a quick turn around the Museum of the Saracens, *non-sense!*

In truth, I still ought to see Kouba again, but I really better get all my damned papers together: that's still a significant part of my job. If I'm going *to make it* it's urgent that I refresh my memory a little. I whistle between my teeth in imagining how the inspectress of culture will blow her stack when she sees how much I borrow from non-Francophone literature. I'm jubilant when I think of the rage that will shake her sternum when she finally believes she's *discerned* my method. *Inviolably problematic conditions have to be made*: she gets back what she always loved to repeat to everyone around her!

Nothing, however, could be healthier, and *nothing could be better for one's health* than this little climb up the hills around Eze-by-the-Sea: to reread for the last time the historical marker, to transcribe its contents in the little notebook of pretexts and if money allows, go in the direction of Saint Moritz, go to the old bakery where Nietzsche ate the burned crust of his bitter life, see the deer in the park, look everywhere for Nietzsche, smell the perfume of Lou-A.S.'s hair, <Lou Automat-Spirit>, take the train for Venice and disappear in the veiny streets of the empty city, *no rectifications*, unless accompanied by a *deer-referee!*

Blue Notebook: *"In Venice, there is Venison, Vein, venery, and vision for whoever has ears to see and eyes to hear"* (Aely). In Nice, there's "nice," yet, because the summer's nice in Nice when the sky is blue and when one is madly in love.

Journal: Reread Emmanuel Levinas's *L'Aù-delà du Verset*.

and *after death*, take the train back to Paris,

and carry along only one book. *Make your choice!* you can't really travel—and I mean really travel—with a *huge pile of books*, too many books weigh you down, they beat you down, they mortify, they mollify—especially *theoretical books*, especially the books that are *supposed to be theoretical*. First of all it weighs you down and at any moment can change the flow of your ideas. At any moment they can make you keel over, at

any moment they can take you hostage, tempt you, slow you down, intimidate you. *An indigestion of books! The great dark night of books!* Plain Text, *it is imperative* to alleviate the weight of books with a single book, to be rid of all other books with a single book, to *lend oneself* to one book alone in each mental season. For, *after all, it's nonetheless better if we read only three pages of a four-hundred-page book a thousand times more in depth than the ordinary reader who reads everything, but never once a single page in depth. Better to read twelve lines of a book with the greatest possible intensity, thus to penetrate them in their entirety, as they say, than read a whole book like an ordinary reader who finally knows the book with as much awareness as the airline passenger knows about the countryside he is flying over,*
<how light is the baggage we carry throughout eternity!
how long is the passage we follow from day to day!>

It was only in the train from Marseilles to Nice that my sentences were going to start flowing again, *sentences at high speed/slow and dull course of ideas,*
pain,
the extreme pain of thinking
a flow unleashed: thought/disorder of sentences
ideas in slow motion, in constant struggle with the sentence,
but don't give way too quickly,
don't let up too quickly,
don't give yourself to the sentence too quickly,
better to have fear, to face the void, than the wanton abandon of the sentence!
give oneself the time and make the time last,
make the sentence endure, make it endure pain,
make it suffer under the time of thought,
Five-minute stopover,
Five minutes of slow motion,
Marseilles, La Ciotat, Toulon-La Seyne, Hyères, Bormes-Les-Mimosas, Calvaire-sur-Mer, Saint Tropez, Cannes, Antibes, Nice, Nice, ten-minute stopover, *passengers going to Monaco, Vintimilia, Bordighera, San Remo, Imperia, and Genoa on Track 4, crossing the railroad tracks is strictly forbidden, travelers please use the underground tunnels, Local Train for Monaco, Track 1.*
At Penn Station <Newark> it's the same thing: there are those who come along in passage with us, those who are only passing through, and those who are there because they aren't going anywhere else, those who are here will remain here and never leave,
Pass on, let's go, pass, you're pure!

Algiers, *pillage*
as it happens every evening, an hour of reading with Macha,
from the window of the sunroom we can see branches that *madly shake in the wind.*
Macha is seated in the green armchair, she has put on her shawl studded with gold
and silver, a trace of autumn-colored lipstick adorns her lips.
Klimt because of the golden hue, *Venice* because of the wind and the sails, *Rossetti*
because of the grays, the confetti, *the thinker!*
Our weeeekly hour of reading!
"Probably, the interpreter answers, <*I am reading out loud and in a clear voice*> these
are industrial wars. The people have neither commerce nor industry, they are not
obliged to wage war; but a class of business people <*I underline 'business people' with
a strong tone of voice*> is compelled to lead a politics of conquest. The number of our
wars inevitably increases with our gross national product. As soon as one of our
industries fails to get its products sold, wars are needed to open new windows of
opportunity. Thus we have a war of coal, a war of copper, a war of cotton *[and currently a war of crude oil!]*. In the Third Zealand <*Loti would have said Iraq or Kuwait,
today*>, we have killed two-thirds of the population in order to make the rest of them
buy our umbrellas and suspenders."
     I read this passage from the *Island of Penguins* to Macha, and she
answered spontaneously, *that's the way it is in the Coral Islands, and even recently in Pan-
ama and even lately in Cuba,* with the Bay of Pigs and at this very moment in Iraq!
I said: because we couldn't wage war, we began to loot our own country! They've
starved two-thirds of the population in order to cause the others to emigrate and
to sprinkle the country with slogans! The virulence of the looting is in direct pro-
portion to our incapacity to produce anything of value! Usurers love Algeria because
it loves to fall into debt! Twenty billion fat francs in a single generation of degen-
eration! Who can top that? Sooner or later that's what the Master saw in his cav-
ern: *every day, once we stop to think about it, that's just about everything that we experience, that we are governed by a hypocritical, mendacious, and crude government that is,
above all else, the most abominably stupid government that could ever be imagined,* he
replied to us, *and we think we can't do a thing about it. That's what is really frightening,
that we can't do a thing about it, that we are happily reduced to the incapacity of seeing,
but of only seeing, how from one day to the next this government is becoming nastier and
increasingly intolerable! As a matter of fact, this nation has stooped to the lowest level, the
Master said, and soon it will have renounced both its raison d'être and its spirit. And everywhere we hear this disgusting malarkey about democracy!*
It's dismal, absolutely dismal, and it's far from over!

Scholium # 2: \<I copy into my black notebook\>: "The difference between Bolshevism and liberalism is superficial, while *they share in common a profound perversion:* probably the tentacles of the same monster."

1. Wars are unleashed in order *to create debt.*

2. War is the supreme, *even the most atrocious* form of sabotage.

3. "A nation that refuses to go into debt enrages *usurers*" *(Ezra Pound, "Labour and Usury").*[7]

Algiers, *misery.*

The city in which I amble about before departing looks like a city that has just been sacked, it *resembles* nothing, it is falling down toward the sea as if an earthquake had just devastated the area, it is deracinated, it is sliding down to the sea as if it were falling to its demise. The sea will soon devour it, it bears a formidable weight, a formidable *gravity* currently weighs upon the many sustaining walls the French, Egyptian, and Italian engineers erected so that the Aurassi hotel would not carry off a third of the city in its crazed course toward nothingness. The surrounding walls of the city are closed, local authorities fear that the citizens will flee. The cafés in the center of town are deserted, everyone has emigrated in the direction of the northern edge of the city, in the *heights* over Algiers, at El-Biar, the Telemny, Hydra, whence the extent of the devastation can be best seen, whence the disaster can be seen coming, whence people will be in the first rows of seats to see the city get swallowed up by the sea, whence the city can be seen slowly falling to rack and ruin: *an attempt to save it, nonsense.*

Plain Text: What goes away from this city will be what has passed through it: the wind!
The house saddens the dreamer: he leaves it.
You know, we're all transients, people in passing;
but who will follow us? No one who is worth being named.[8]

August 1965, Algiers: the Hotel Aletti *where I await the deluge:* the bearded man with his *so what, so what, big deal, we'll do better the next time,* they don't lose anything in order to attend to these *infidels!*

---

[7] For more disgusting details see "An Open Letter to Jean Baudrillard with Seven Scholia," *Intersignes* 4 (1992).
[8] By poor M. B., *The Domestic Sermons of Mourad Bensmaier.*

July 1981, London: Trafalgar Square *where I await the coming of Death*,
September 1973, Paris: Place du Trocadéro *where I await the coming of disaster*,
August 1991, Providence, Rhode Island: Kennedy Plaza *where I await the coming of nothing*,
September 1964, Oran: Place de Martyrs *where I await Nora*: with her brown and hazel eyes, swirling hair, flowerbeds in bloom, and on the ground one of Nador's old oriental rugs: *what happiness, what happiness, what joy! what pleasure! what liberation, an eternity!* <**but we stiffened up, full of defiance, to wander again, with panting breath, lost and ravished, among the craters!**>
Macha: Are you still thinking of her when your nose is stuck to the window pane? C'mon, how long are you going to go on suffering?
—*I can't tell. Five or six years. Maybe more. But I'll get over it.*
—*Fantasies, yes, they're fine, buddy, she tells him; fantasies like yours don't cost a dime.*
To avoid the emptiness and the wandering, I mark down: <Philiphor, sewn with child> in Vitoldo's "Bakakai" or Arnolfini's *<Scenes from the Life of a Faun>*: formidable apologists for modern times. Worth being cited as examples, in an era when everyone makes a show of Le Pen and makes a point of the errant myth (in other words, of the ultra-idiot!)
(here it's almost impossible to bear the temptation to rectify).

But once we got perfectly settled down in the train things really began, to be dis-*figured*
in the way one is disfigured,
to write in order to be unrecognizable,
to write in order to be rid of one's name, of one's face, and of one's memory,
a memory without name,
une légère modification, a slight change in the air of the time,
cleansing, a matter of cleansing by means of emptiness,
to subtract by tens, hundreds,
thousands, ten thousands, twenty thousands, one hundred thousand words a minute,
and then see
the crazed flow of images, the crazed flow of sentences, the crazed flow of words,
before,
  impossible to think.

Macha: *Why do you disfigure me with that stare? You look so ferocious when you look at me that way! Is something wrong? Pourquoi me dévisager ainsi?*
She laughs,

Plain Text, in the cooler there's a carton of fresh milk, hard-boiled eggs, and Italian bread. The foreign passengers are drinking, *the speed of the sentences is frightening*, without really being thirsty, *Plain Text*, they are eating without really being hungry, the young woman in front of them tears her baby away from her breast. She says, *it's a crying shame, it hurts me to cry about it*,
the young man who is at her side: you ought to wean it as soon as we get back to Paris. He's too big to *get his big bowl of soup at his mother's breast*.

The embryo of the story:
it can take at any moment, it can turn sour, it can spin off-track, if it takes, it's horrible, but if it doesn't take, it's horrible too,
Total surveillance over the rhythm that takes or doesn't take,
At any moment, everything can turn to vinegar,
A shard of literature or a literary fetus,
An embryo of a human being: at any moment it can become a *subject* of his Majesty Mr. Death!
The young woman: Did you remember to call Lisette before you left? The young man acquiesces: oh, yeah, it would've been a catastrophe not to leave her a message before leaving; you know, her birthday is *sacred!* We'll have to send her a little card from Nice, *early tomorrow morning*.
The young man: For your birthday last year she *didn't even* telephone, *so there*. The young woman: Yes, but *Mother*, that's not the same thing, don't you understand! She can do things that *we* could *never* fathom ourselves doing. The young man: This ritual of birthdays is really becoming a serious *pain in the ass!* Marie, can't we get things done once and for all? To lay down the law *once and for all* that no one will celebrate anyone's birthday! *Enfin cela mettrait de l'ordre dans les choses! That would be really nice!*
Meanwhile: Circumstances make it impossible for me to concentrate, I can't read under these conditions, and above all else, it's not even a question of *thinking about* thinking. All this claptrap derails my train of thought! This bellyaching rips the sum of humanity off my face! *I begin to stutter!*

Gigantomachia of sentences *at high speed* in the *Marseilles-Nice Express*, the Phocean. I've got to do everything in my power, and while there's still time, so that it doesn't *take*,
grumble,
*what became of **Dead Letters** with their trillions of soldiers*

their trillions of dead bodies
when I had neither a man
nor a dime nor a language
but the music of the spheres whistling in my teeth,
700 trillion kilos
and a ballpoint pen
but avoid *that it takes* at all cost, even in an
<?>*embryonic*<?> *form!*

I *fell:* the damp ground, barer than an earthworm, more *elementary* than a bacterium, a real larva, an embryo, a mollusk, my teeth turned to pablum, the skin of my belly, the skin of my neck, the skin of my ass, the skin of my face, the skin of my hands, the skin of my soul, all these skins *completely shrivel away* under the press of my thoughts! *no rectifications!*, and I have no power to *rectify* everything that falls and slips away, I would give a child the shivers, I could be a geek in a circus, I could be put on exhibit in a hospital. *A real freak show!*

Macha: *You know who you remind me of?*
Myself: . . .
Macha: *Well, you make me think of a doddering old man! No, it's not funny, you're a frightful sight! Is it because you're far from your beloved country that you've gotten your-self in this state? Admit it! We can turn around and go back to Kouba. Morning and evening prayers! Daytime and nighttime prayers! Muezzin and loudspeakers! I know a lady who'd be ravished if she saw you coming back home!*
—The Mater or the Matrie? (Plain English Text)
—Any difference?
—'f course not!
What do you ask, then?
—Dunno
—You Jerk!
Should I give any indications of time? of place?
Can I tell what day and what hour?
And the ties? relations? linkages? coherence? Can I flash back in time? And go back exactly where? How far can I go back in time?
Ah! How Algiers weighs on me! Ouch! Ouch! How Algiers makes me despair! Algiers! Algiers! My love! Algiers, my bête noire!

Journal Bis (in plain text): The only sentence I could salvage from the disaster named Gide during the season of migration to the North:

"… and every one, according to the imbroglio that his head is thus preparing, is lost, if I may say, *he writes,* in their own particular labyrinth."

At first, I kinda laicized the Idea! Despite the Germanicism, despite the philistinism, despite the Gidism, all ambient! I thought for a moment that I was going to be reconciled with my former teacher, but no sooner than I had turned the incriminated pagette, I recovered my old Christian idealist, as soon as I had turned the page, I recovered my very old, very sleazy, and very boring and very glitzy moralist! "Conserve the *forthright purpose <?>* of not cutting the Ariadne's thread no matter how *enchanting the labyrinth <?>,* the attraction of the unknown <?>, getting your courage back into shape

… This thread will be what ties you to <!> your past. Follow it back. Get back to yourself. Move on with yourself. For nothing comes from nothing, and it's your past, that's what you're laboring on right now <?>, that's what you can build on!" (the Schmidtian *viruses <?>* are mine own, Malcolm Mrad!)

Bullshit, pal! Ill-digested philosophy! >< Gide's stomach was too delicate to really *make* philosophy! *Get back to Him! Get back to Yourself! Gather yourself! Get yourself together! Back up! Listen to him! Don't listen! Ceins-toi, Virginia!* Only the capital letters were missing! My stress! I put emphasis on the periods and strand the *ifs!* I put accents on here and there and get out of the muck! I mean, paludal swamp of *Gidea!* And from there, it's *gidiocy!*

Further on he insists: "Therefore don't linger in the labyrinth, nor in the arms of Ariadne … Move on, pass further on, beyond!"

It is I who am stressing! Why would I pass *beyond* Ariadne? And why wouldn't I want to lay over *in her arms?* Haven't the Sirens been singing for centuries that she was the most ravishing of all women? So then why would I *pass my hand in there?* What the hell d'ya care if I pass my hand there where I'm thinking of Ariadne? Fuck! Fuck off! And if I didn't already like the *outrages* done to passages?! And if I had a predilection for *outrageous passages?!* And what if I really wanted to *pass* my hands on Ariadne's *beyonds?* And as if Ariadne's exaggerations, beyond all presumptions, that attracted me in the first place? Lemme be rid of Gide and his *passoutrages,* his outrageous passings beyond all what who in hell gives a damn! How did I get there? What are the *conditions* for such a "lapse" of tension? What priest is he hiding in a Rhetoree like that! Better to *rip* the past off the past! And the present off the present! And the future off the future! O Sovarardhi! To be rid of writing on Gide!

As soon as there is a get-together, as soon as three or more people occupy a room, I begin to see better how things happen when somebody dies, I understand better the *mechanism* of death, in seeing it thus reduced, in seeing it multiplied by one, then by two, then three, then shit, that gives a better inkling about how we can die without even realizing it, dying without *even shrieking! no rectose!*

But the best thought comes from without, it can only come from without, in the street, in the candy shop, at the bakery, in all the little stores where there's *contact*, a surface of contact, between the inside and the outside, you're inside and, at the same time, you feel yourself grabbed by the mental blaze of the Outside, you're still motionless, but pregnant with the steps you're going to make,

feverish, in labor with the ambulation that will carry you off, with the anger that will *put you beside yourself!*

But for the moment, in my opinion you've been sitting too long in this room without curtains, blinded by the sun, crushed by the heat, your skin turning to jelly, your body becoming a bag of skin, a big bag of skin that conceals your mood factory, a bag of very supple skin that protects as well as possible from the old blood-suckers (bags of blood), that hides you and shelters you from the gusts that swell you up with pure air, *no rectifications!* a bag of skin that retains odors, dams up the mucus, conceals the shit factory, *slut*, the mud factory, behind the skin, under the skin, mentally flip the skin over to hear the whir of the factory.

I still can't always see the *50 trucks of mental* on the horizon.

See the *workers*, talk a little with the *workers* in the factory, hear a little of what they have to say, see a little of what they're doing in this nerve factory, *a dismemberment of the worker's soul, what are you going to do? Dismember our souls? What are you going to do? Begin to cry? Appeler les flics? Sue me? Me traîner en justice? Poison me? Put a cover on my nerves? Put me in a straitjacket? Straitjacket me in literature? Immatriculate me in francophony?*

The choir of the outraged: That is exactly what we would like to do!

There's no pity, no compassion, no misericord,

don't forget the inhibitive restraint of [   ],

Censure! Censorship! A fear of fatwality!

Everything can be dismembered, everything can be destroyed,

but that won't change things one bit,

it won't do a thing, it serves no purpose,

so what remains to be destroyed has to be destroyed,
we must humbly and methodically destroy what remains to be destroyed and

                     Begin *in the middle of things, in the middle of time, then slowly unfold*
according to the folds,
while myself, I was waiting in his return for a better understanding of ideas, a clarifi-
cation of the secret about how ideas are manufactured, but not really a factory where
there was an inn or *a simple studio;* I was waiting for a *revelation*, and so the image
of the factory didn't hold up. Maybe the studio, the studio of creation was better, an
art gallery, a gallery of artisanal ideas, a gallery of ideas as they are being formed, a
studio for the deduction of ideas, a gallery for the pottery of ideas molded, glazed,
fired, and baked; a studio for the insemination of ideas, a gallery for the birth of ideas,
of the dismemberment of ideas, of the deconstruction of ideas, of the coffering of
ideas, the qualification of ideas, the production of ideas, for the repair and maintenance of ideas *under the skin:* when she came back into the room my taste for ideas was
gone. Her entry threw all the ideas *topsy-turvy*, it was *disconcerting* for ideas, nothing
remained but brown chestnut and hazel-colored eyes of the ever-silent young woman,
the sinuous body of the ever-silent young woman, more than the immense mental
buzz shattering my temples and and very strong lateral thrust that plunged into my
back and up to the nape of my neck, in the direction of the *continental drift,*
the young man still doesn't know the rules of the comedy, the comedy of a day, the comedy
of love, comedy, comedy, gelato al limone! Gelato al limone! Truly, a head full of molasses!
No reports were outstanding, nor discourse, nor analysis, nor dialogue, but only a
simple breathing of souls about to leave, a long respiring of souls in decomposition, a soul pitted against a soul, a soul that breathes the soul of another soul, a
soul enraptured, a soul enrapted, and against this soul another soul that is being
enraptured, and against this soul a soul that is being rubbed *like a wave on a beach of*
fine grains of sand, and against this always, ever-wavy soul, a reef that licks it, a wave
against a reef that hooks onto it, another wave against a reef that is shoveling into
it, while another wave still catches it and another still that lets it go, that lets it go
to get it back and to disappear, and then reappear, *just in time,* just in time to heave
over itself and gather itself, to beat down and embrace itself, just in time to gather
itself and to dissolve, and just in time still and still again to stretch out and swoon,
just in time to *ravish itself* and to begin to ravish, to ravish as a wave that dies and is
reborn of its ashes, like another wave that cries while it holds its breath and that is
reborn like a phoenix that breathes and is reborn of its ashes while a woman heaves,

no rectifications! no remorse! (Plain <English> Text) / When she, and though some said she played / I said that she had danced heart's truth, / Drew a knife to strike him dead, / I could but leave him to his fate, / For no matter what is said / They had all that had their hate / *I said, I had strength enough to say it, that she had danced the truth of her heart! For despite whatever they say, we took the rap for our hatred! A full tin cup! A whopping pile! Ah! Mach! Machallah!*

(The Coryphée: *C'est lui qui est mort? Ou c'est elle qui est morte?* Voice-over: Is it he who died? Or is it she who is dead?
The Choir: *L'amour, c'est comme une dent de lion!*) Voice-over: Love is like a dandelion!

N* is about to leave for Switzerland with her husband and children, they won't come back for a year to two, *the nanny says.* Boy, that poor lady really looked like she was in the dumps! It was at that very moment that she appeared to recover her love of life, right when *he* decided to leave Algiers! I suspect he sniffed something out, you know Ada, he's like a dog, he doesn't think, he sniffs, he smells people, he gets their odor in his nostrils, but you know, because he's too proud, he's too lazy, and these things just aren't done among the Kda! The Kda aren't haywire! Let's get packing and be on our way!

The odor of thought: *l'odeur de la pensée*, thought with its odors and predators, the predators of the thought of idiots and others: let me *smell* what you are thinking, and I'll tell you if you interest me! Let me *smell* your neck, your hair, your armpits, your ass, your sex! *I find your odor very interesting! Tell me what you smell of, and I'll tell you who you are!* I *smell* that something isn't quite right! I *smell* that something isn't going the way it should! Ada *smelled of* something! And because she smelled like a dog, I lost N*! He packed up his wife and his baggage and beat it! Algeria stank too much for him! Algiers stank too much for Ada! A *suffocating* stench of a woman in heat! An unbearable odor of sweat and sex! A mortal odor of wet hair and perspiration! The loving sweat of human shit in heat! <in order not to be *eaten*, in order to avoid circulating the *smell of her thoughts*, N* spent whole days thinking that Ada was only a *man*, N* spent her nights deluding herself: *I'm a bitch! I'm a bitch! I have to* smell *that I am a bitch!* Ada sniffed her up and down and jumped back with horror: *You're only a bitch! I married a bitch! A bitch of a woman! Hell, I can't fuck a bitch! A bitch! They snubbed me with a bitch! She dirties everything wherever she goes! Along your way everything gets polluted! She pisses on everything she passes! A real bitch! A real bitch that stinks like a woman in heat! But how I long for her! How she*

fascinates me! How I want her! O Allah all powerful, how can I become a dog? Can I be a dog who doesn't know he's a dog? Look how I smell things so well! Look how good my snout is!> Retrieve N* in the midst of the mountains by Lausanne or Geneva? Should I go and crawl to Geneva? Go back down the Yellow Pass again dressed in a plaid shirt with lederhosen and hiking boots? *Grüss Gott* and biscuits for lunch? See Geneva and die? Or else veal sausages vaudoises with steamed potatoes in the Buffet de Gare at Château d'Oex? Waves of hope, waves of fear, waves of despair! Hour after hour of waiting! Waves of boredom! The narrator *feels* he is at the end of the line. All these sleepless nights, all these long evenings without end, all these hikes in the mountains without any horizon in the distance, all these lies, all these aunts, cousins, mothers, all this democracy, all these rats in the streets, all this sterility, all this cowardice, all these women under veils, all these blind alleys, all this pretentiousness, all this muddle and mess, all these stupid political measures, all this confusion, all these economic *errors*, all this tumbling down into the sea, all this furor, all this black bile, all this rage for chaos, all this impossible revolution, all this beer, all these cafés, all these bistros, all this Muslim wine, all this Muslim beer, all these Islamic liquors, all these orgies, all these rapes, all these Islamo-Marxist compromises, all these sustaining walls, all these menaces, all this bestiality, all this garbage, all this *night*, all this stupidity, all these marks of idiocy, all these stupid arrangements, all these cultural *embezzlements*, all these thefts of culture, all these people buying into stupidity, all these cultural mummies, all these thefts of language, all these rules of good conduct.

I discover again the jealous spirit that thinks it knows better than I what I am and that is stupid enough to believe that there resides a character or spirit in this city of the damned, in other words

        what?
        Ramoudi
        Rah iräneck
        Ouelham
        Fi känek

I am the old Rmad
        the Cinderella of the farce!

So much rancor toward thinking, so much hatred of the mind, of ideas, so much hatred of intelligence, all this anger against freedom, all these hyenas, these ten-cent Islams, all these *renunciations*, all these cheap compromises, all these scapegoats, all these emigrants shoved under the rug, *<unwanted! You're unwelcome here!*

(Plain English) *Go back where you came from, Mister!>* all these bugaboos of incon-sistency, all this religiosity, all this allahlick sex, all these ayatollahick mausoleums, all these ayatollaïc mosques, all these atavistic mullahs, all these languors, all these hungry bellies, this entire surface of Algeria *in heat.*

Aely (little black book): *Nobody knows the power of a forked tongue!*

Reflection Machine: You have to have been juvenile to *let yourself go like that,* to *write like that* and at that cost: whenever you want to write down your thoughts *you swerve out of control,* you've got too much hate boiling over, too much fear *when a little cold blood would do you well,*
too much accumulated resentment when you need to *look at things coldly,* with a head that is cold and clear as steel, cold as ice, when you need a will of *steel.*
You want to give your version of the bile that eats away the youth of a country that's crumbling, the youth of a country that is howling, when everything *is swerv-ing out of control* because of so much ignorance accumulated over aeons. It's too late, there is too much accumulated idiocy, too much boredom heaped up; it's too late, there's too much stockpiled imbecility. Too much hate where the country would be better served by cold blood; *the ravens of thought always crow too late,* the ravens always predict the coming of evil, the evil of the coming year, *Nevermore,* the evil of the expiring year,
before:
cold-bloodedness

cold-bloodedness *above all else.*
Let's first of all write a *poem* with *cold blood.*
Afterward we shall drink the time of blood!
You have to have been juvenile to let yourself fall into degrada-tion like that: *What will become of you? What will you protect of yourself?* There's the *slogan of modern times,* the slogan of times that are *born again* modern. We have to protect, safeguard modernity in our underwear. Dress modernity in lace panties: with the lady who says, but what will become of us without things *modern?* What will happen to us if we aren't modern? No, no, please don't let the modern go! It would be ruinous! Without the modern, my dear friend, we'd be lost, finished, it'd be the apocalypse, disaster, no, no, let's not let flag our desire for modernity, moder-nity and revolution, modernity and desire, the modern is not the past, the modern is the future now: she's enthralled and tipsy? Yes, that's modernity! It's death up in

ashes! The pretty lady is high on modernity, modernity gets her high, she's drunk with modernity, modern from head to toe, modernity comes out of her nostrils, she *smells* modernity in her skirts, she feels that *that's what's* modern, *it has to be* modern to the flesh and bone, she feels modernity in her everywhere, and everywhere she is modern in *front* and modern *behind (that's why she wears a miniskirt and leather boots for the season)* and she couldn't give a damn if *American* feminists — among others — don't agree with her, *first of all, my dear friend, because they're afraid of me!* They aren't in complete agreement with her because they can't see what is modern in modernity, they don't see the modernity of the modern and the modern of modernity in the same way that they can't see the *Italianness* of Italy or the *Frenchness* of France. Revolution will be *modern* or it will not be.
Is all that serious?
Is it politically correct?
*Everything they say is a dirty **mentor** that has always been on my heels!*
I despise the intuition that allows people to know everything the very second you say something, when they don't even give themselves half a second to think about it
(pure duration, the pure endure).

Scholium # 3: *"There is a modern sense of tragedy: it's a kind of great turning shutter that cannot be opened or closed by hand."*

You have to have been juvenile to have *cried such bitter tears,* to have cried for so long, to the end of the night; you must have been young to have cried *in solitude* and have been so fearful, young to *have loved* and have harbored so much fear, young to have *so patiently watched over* everything in such fear, young to have *militated* and been so afraid, young to have *continued to live with so much fear eating up your insides.*

Algiers, *falling down,*
impossible to ride a bike in the city: the streets are too hilly. It's a city for peregrine falcons and buzzards! *Now what are you going to do now that she's gone?* says the nanny: Can you finally leave Algiers, leave this city behind me *as if it were a buried and dissimulated fable covered over with a triple key?*
Why triple?
And why a key?
Because in the entire history of this city *some kind of stupid preconception about its mystery,* a mystery of Keys, of Chiefs, of Clans, of General Secretaries, of high-ranking officials in the Single Party, of Prefects, of Monotheism, of marvelous marabouts,

of allahlaïc Mullahs who *enslave this people, that up to now has never been able to bring itself to the point where it might start thinking,* even if for one measly moment in thirty years. That's what **depresses** me, what depresses its fifty meter readers of natural mental gas, where will the antidepressant come from? Where will a counterthought surge up? Where will there be born the cries that will shriek against this disaster? Who will wring the neck of the simple sickness of my thoughts? Who will restore to my thoughts the sepulture that they once deserted? When did they leave the howled befouled harikaried bowels of their birth? When will they stop sucking the blood throbbing in my skull? When will they stop discharging the honey of their diffuse faith in my flunky brains? *Sorry is the country that needs a martyr!*

Aram Assouli
Mana ani
Martori!

I have just closed the door on my fifty years of slavery and I still can't drive a car: an *irremediable* descent and fall, a descent to the end, to the very end of time, a cohort of human magma and the debris of the thoughts on Yusuf Road, a dribble of human magma and of *debris already thought* on Yusuf Road, an unfurling of humanity sacrificed and of *aborted* ideas on the Rue du Telemny, of body heat and *asphyxiated* hopes on the Rue Mohammed V, *a dispersion* of human intelligence and desire on the Rue Ben'Mhidi, of disfigured martyrs and displaced rage on the Place des Martyrs, youth ruined and forgotten *everywhere.*

I climb the stairs that lead directly to the Chemin Pouyanne, I can stick my tongue out, there's nothing to put on its taste buds, nothing to make it salivate, nothing to *edify* it, a useless muscle and, furthermore, *it's pasty:* entire nights spent taking drags on lousy cigarettes, entire nights spent swallowing lies, entire nights spent speculating and expeculating, entire nights spent stinking up, entire nights in *stumbling and stuttering about,* entire nights spent in useless labor, *entire nights in laboring like a dumb ass! It's impossible to browse around:* too many Moorish cafés, too many zombies in the cafés, too many domino players, too many pinball players, too many veils, too many women in veils, too many veils carrying women off in their folds, too many ghosts, too many mysteries under the burnous, too many whispers, too much laziness under the whiskers of bearded men, too much *indolence,* too much frustration, too much anguish, too much mental chaos in the atmosphere, too much theology, too many unattained desires, too many inchoate desires, too many inconceivable ideas, too *many men,* too many pretendants, too many *oukalas,* too many leagues, too many cliques, clans, clerks, too much oblivion, everywhere, *no rectifica-*

tion, no, not yet, for the people are lacking, they are still lacking, while you, you are enamored of your own poetry.

But that, says the occult, that, that's what you must keep ineffable:

<For I, yes I, I love poetry, and poetry alone> you will never dare to say it, Oh yes! for there is the obscenity of the matter: it is because the petty-bourgeois idiom, the erotic slap in the face of Madame Obscene Petty-Bourgeois is one that has forever been in love with poetry.> Every day I see you removing yourself a little more, there's almost nothing left of you in your writings, there's nothing left of your youth and of your hope in your writing, nothing left of your body, your thinking, nothing left of your story of boudjadi, nothing of your battles with modern history. Because she is serious the young woman who admonishes the narrator—and how she admonishes him with love!—wants to let him know something about his fate, and what, voice-on, nothing left of your youth and your hopes, how she speaks so justly, how she utters the bare truth, how she hits the nail on the head when she says that nothing, nothing more of my writings and my hopes, nothing remains of all my crap, nothing remains of my rage, there is nothing left of my worries, nothing more of my moodiness, nothing left of my passions, nothing left of my insomnias, not an iota of my fears, until the time when night falls once again, until the moment when the dark night returns, not a trace of my blind readings, not a trace of my blind wanderings, not a trace of my blindest memory, not a trace of my tracks left blindly behind me, not a trace of my blind larceny, of my fears, of my falls, not a trace of my oblivion, not a trace of the blood of the blindman within me, nothing remains but the black night, not a trace of my little scrawls, nothing more than the black line of my broken fall. But (in plain English), okay guys, that's enough! That's good enough!

Memories of the house of the dead # 3: The only spot, Plain Text, where I might ever want to set my feet again before leaving this city, the only place where I might stand the rigor of finding myself enclosed once again in the city of A*, he says, Ammeyar reported, and that is the Museum of Modern Art of Algiers, the soi-disant Musée du Hamma, just above the Jardin d'Essai, yes, it's in a passageway through the city of A* and there, there is still a place where I might die with my conscience at peace, the only remaining human place of the city, the only place where I still might go again to breathe a little fresh air of freedom, the only spot where I might once again get myself together! because it's probably the only spot where a little fresh air remains in Algiers, the only spot where a little fresh wit exists in Algiers is in the Musée du Hamma, the only building that has yet to be profaned in Algiers, the only shack that high-grade individuals will not yet have spotted and degraded no rectifications! and, in turn the only place that will not have been *looted*, the only place that will have remained sheltered from their will to plunder, the only place that will have been shielded from their *gaze*, the only place that still protects—*without them having the slightest inkling of it*—objects that their greedy hands have not sullied, the only place they have neglected to rummage, because of the *crass stupidity* that identifies them as warring businessmen, men for whom art doesn't have a cent of *value*, for whom art is useful only as *decoration*, for whom art is what you hang on the walls of the living room and the dining room in the officers' quarters, is the Musée du Hamma, the only place that has yet to have any *attraction* because, he said, *Ammeyar reported*, just before leaving the city, the evening before my final departure from the city of A*, the only place that I have ardently dreamed of seeing again, the only ramshackle building that *came to mind*, the only place where I could find a last *refuge*, a last breath and wisp of love for this crazy city, a last smell of the air of this city of senseless carnage, a last image of this city of wild desire, *no rectification*, when I needed a penultimate lungful of fresh air, I went to the Musée du Hamma where I found, in this shack that every inhabitant had *forgotten*, in this shack that no one had been condescending enough to *visit* since the country gained its independence, in this shack that the *minister of culture* had himself consigned to oblivion, in this shack that the human beast they call the *public* had *neglected*, in this shack *that the painters themselves* had abandoned, the place that the *soi-disant* art lovers had *scorned*, for, he said, *Ammeyar reported*, it was in this *deserted lodging by way of the small fry of the city* that I could imbibe a bowl of fresh air for which I'd been thirsting, air that I needed in order to tear myself away from the country of wild love, in this dilapidated shack where I could withstand the extreme pain that was breaking my heart, where I could drench for a moment the fire that was burning my brains to ashes, *because of this country of incredible beauty, because of this city of senseless violence, because of these inhabitants of maddening genius*. It was only among the colonnades eaten away by the salty air of the sea and the prickles and spines of the rosebushes, *no rectifications*, that I was finally able to fill my lungs with clean air in this asphyxiating country, on the terrace of this enchanted piazza, yes, *in this passageway of the city of A** that I could once more smell the *air of thought*, that I could once again imbibe the air of this freedom of thought. I paid my 350 dinars and quickly found myself again in the immense disorder of bodies that the stone had taken in the hardness of its folds, Bourdelle perhaps, Maillol maybe, yes, Maillol maybe, and its aphrodisiac goddesses, maybe, *no rectification*, Carpeaux, to be sure, Degas, yes, but nothing could be less sure at the moment, especially for Degas, Maillol, and Rodin, perhaps, because it was in this little shack lost in its bougainvillea and its wild roses where I gathered myself together on the very evening of my definitive departure from the city of A*. It was on the second floor of this shack that I wanted to see again the Marquets and the Delacroix, just two, three, or four of them, not many canvases in sum, just a few *works* by Delacroix and Marquet, maybe, very few works that seemed to be *lost* in the midst of other lost, less illustrious, not as *remarkable*, less **notable** *works*, but such marvelous *witnesses*, all so *vigilant* and *enervating* and even so *lost* in a world, a city that was slipping and falling down into the sea! The guard's children kept me company during my walk through the museum. I even played ball with them in the Marquet and Delacroix room, among the Renoirs <yes, maybe Renoir, maybe even a Renoir after all!> and the Géricaults, a Renoir, maybe, *a real piece of larceny!* and a Géricault, *the disaster!* a tiny little Géricault, you might have said a *Géricault for children!* a Géricault for *decolonized citizens!* and then a little cohort of tiny, nameless paintings, a theory of little specks of *anonymous* colors, after the two or three Delacroix, *after* the tiny Renoir, *after* the tiny Géricault (in plain English!), *it's a pity!* Entering the Grande Salle I finally glimpsed one, then two Khaddas; one, then two Issiakhems that were brandishing and clattering their swords in the great *silence* of the Musée du Hamma, one or two Khaddas and an Issiakhem that were dueling in the great *void* of the Musée du Hamma. Do you get the point? In the midst of the Delacroix, the Marquets, and maybe the Dinets, one or two Khaddas in the darkest room of the museum, one or two Khaddas that attested to the dilapidated condition of this nation's culture, one or two Issiakhems, in the room where the windows were tightly sealed, that attested to the artistic void of this nation, a Khadda and an Issiakhem that pointed directly to the cultural disaster of this nation, *no rectifications!* Not a single Baya, do you understand? *Not a single Baya!* Can you fathom that? Two or three Delacroix, two or three Marquets and not a single Baya, a tiny Renoir, one or two Marquets and not a single Baya, a Delacroix or two, a Marquet or two, a Fromentin or two, a Dinet or two, *but not a single Racim! and not at all in the last room* of the museum. What else? A *tiny* Jean-Désiré Bascoules, maybe, and a Maurice Bouviolle, a *tiny* Maurice Bouviolle, a *Villa Abd-el-Tif* by Maurice Bouviolle maybe, and then, maybe a *tiny* Paul Jouve and a *tiny* Charles Brouty, Paul Jouve's *The Tiger* perhaps, and Charles Brouty's *Algiers Yacht Club*, perhaps, maybe too, but we can't know for sure! Yes, nothing could be less sure! For how can one distinguish an Etienne Chevalier from a Serge Choubine *at such a distance*, for *in extremis*, despite the fragility of my eyes and my health, *I could still tell* what *belonged* to an Etienne Dinet or to a Eugène Fromentin in this museum. I could easily *recognize* a Racim in the midst of the shambles. Yes, I could have drawn a Racim from the lottery and put my bets on it, but how could I *distinguish* a *Caravan at Sunset* by a

Eugène Deshayes from a *Caravan of Nomads at El'Kantara* by an Antoine Gadan? How could I tell what it was that made *Rocky Landscape, Southern Algeria* by a Constant Louche and *Bou-Saâda at Nightfall* by a Maxime Noire? There was maybe also a *tiny* Marius Petit and a small, *minor* work of Charles Brouty, but it was hanging in the most lugubrious room of the museum of the garden of the essay (what else was new?). I can't recall anymore, my memory is fuzzy, because it was already getting late, and, the guardian said, Ammeyar reported, *there aren't enough art lovers in this country to allow us to illuminate all the rooms of the museum throughout the blessed day. My son, it's a luxury that cannot be afforded, a luxury that in current times only the generals can afford with impunity. But the generals haven't the slightest interest in Art. Pass on, go on, let's move on, you're young at heart!*

For the thousandth time I reread page 57 of the only book that I brought along with me in my cave: I found strength enough to reread page 57 a thousandth time, maybe the two thousandth time, maybe the three thousandth time: *not a single word was out of place*, not *one word didn't belong there! That's what frightens me!* You might say a mountain, a mountain that reigns in the firmament, the only mountain, *nothing in excess:* I was seeking the *secret of production*, I was seeking the error, *the tiny error*, but I couldn't find it anywhere, I was looking for the crack, the fissure, that was everywhere, but I couldn't find it. I looked for the *smudge*, but nothing, it was all for naught, a self-contained page, followed by another self-contained page, a page that *refused analysis*, followed by still another, even more perfect page, a crystalline page preceded by yet another, even more crystalline page, so I looked for *fatigue*, the memory gap, the nervous tick, the *style*, the little *thing that made it tick*, but I found nothing. *It contains its little formula within itself*, like a madwoman who scoffs at reason and meaning, like a goat that grazes the mad grass of reason, *no rectifications!* It seems to purr, it seems to scold with a maddening self-assurance. The little sentence exhibits an extraordinary pride and at the same time nothing is out of place, nothing that might cause it to keel over or to *vibrate*. It makes a *quarter of a turn*, you might say that it was controlled by a demon, and I'm in despair, I'm at my wit's end, but I tremble with joy, for I know, I know with a crushing certitude, that no one will ever succeed in *unveiling* its secret, that no one will ever succeed in stripping it of its secret.

In the attic I happen upon an old typewriter. It's a QWERTYUIOP, an old *English* Olivetti that lost its blue-white-red ribbon and that hasn't been used since the earliest days of writing, since the time when writing still retained a *sense of itself <nonsense>*, since the time when writers still had their *dignity <nonsense>*, since the time when the writers of this country *<what country?>* still had *good taste <nonsense>*. It works like a dream *<that's a good sign!>* and it *still seems to work, so I lift it up on an old Directory style table*, slip a fresh piece of virgin paper into it and begin to type invisible letters! The first invisible writing of modern times! From now on I shall write the way *sculptors sculpt! Hereafter I shall write* with a hammer! From now on I shall write *with claws!* From now on I shall write *with a rake and an eraser!* Plain Text, *It's decided! Understood! Concluded!*

Siphi *<hysterical, ecstatic, Estherhàzyish>*, hunkered down, raised his hand, scratched his nose, polished his canine teeth, ran his hand through his hair and said: *No ifs, ands, or buts about it, it's understood and concluded that thirty-six buns make eighteen sets of butts!*

T W O

(*1992-the present*, Minneapolis, *fall 1992*, Providence [Swan Cemetery], *June 1988*, Paris [Père-Lachaise Cemetery], *April 1963*, Oran; *summer 1989*, London, Algiers, *at all times*)

So then? So then the officer went in through the door by the garden, *the back door*, and he said: Mr. Mrad, *since that is the way you spell your Christian name*, I must regretfully inform you that we have just received confirmation of the truth of the threats that weigh upon you since the publication of your *Dead Letters!* Our ambassador in T* has been apprised by a reliable source that the entire affair was not one of the KGB's practical jokes <*a hoax by the KGB, he said with precision*> in order to bother <*annoy, he said with precision*> Madame the Prime Minister, but this is something extremely serious that unfortunately has nothing to do with the Russians! The latter have other irons in the fire and at this point do not have any interest in infiltrating our country or any other nation in Western Europe. Some special agents have *put out a contract on you, they want to bump you off*, please excuse the expression Mr. Mrad, those are the words of our ambassador! As of now you're going to be shot down, eliminated wherever you are and no matter what you are doing! *Set an example* (in Plain English). Our informants are formal: they want to make an *example* of you, make things such that by way of the example they make of you no other writers of Arabic or Muslim origin will have the pleasure in going in the direction that, according to your detractors, you have taken in your acts of writing, and, of course, through the *publication* of your book! For them you're only an agent who has sold out to the American and British secret services, and they would be well served by you if you tried to discredit, before the very eyes of the Arabo-Muslim world, the authenticity of their revolution. The most paranoid elements see a manipulation by the *Zionists!* Therefore, as we are wont to say in our jargon, I kindly beg you to understand that there is not the slightest insinuation of irony in what I am going to tell you. We therefore are telling you (in Plain English), *They want to rush directly after Salman and knock him off!* In other words, they really want to gun you down quickly and right now! Perhaps you have had wind of the fact that the sale of your novel is forbidden in practically every major city in the free world! In the United States the Customs Service has not allowed any copies to cross the border into American territories! Even today an exceptional meeting of the House of Representatives and the Senate has been called to decide what measures must be taken with respect to the authorization or interdiction of the importation and sale of your book in nationalized American territories. The theme is the same in Paris, Rome, Madrid, et cetera. As a consequence you surely understand, Mr. Mrad, that as you are a permanent resident of our nation my duties include protecting you and fending off every attempt that would be made to slander or hurt your person! <*Is this finally the beginning of a story that will be surreptitiously inserted here?*> You clearly understand that it will not be possible for us to let you go about your daily affairs as you had in the past! As long as the threats were merely a rumor, it appeared necessary — but no less sufficient — for us to invite you to vacate your studio at 22 Parkside and please hereafter move into this area of the city! But currently we know that your life is in real danger, and that to protect you some draconian measures must be taken. In any event, in your case London has become a very dangerous city. You will therefore have to leave London at your earliest possible convenience! We had first thought of finding you a place in a little town in the French provinces, Mallemort or Puyricard, for example, and for this purpose we even contacted the French minister of the interior and the DST. But the operation promised to be rather *onerous and impractical* for reasons that it would be too long and futile to show you in detail! For no less *abstruse* reasons (*recondite reasons*, the inspector stated), which I will not reveal to you, we have also considered sending you to Warsaw, but the most recent elections have made this project no less impractical! After a good deal of research it has been decided that for the moment, *for the time being*, the officer stated, the surest thing to do, *the safest thing to do*, is to send you to the United States. Not to

New York or Chicago, you realize, for there both your enthusiasts and your detractors have been swarming and seething over you of late, but to *Minneapolis!* Contacts have been made, arrangements completed, so all that we now need is for you to sign the agreement! Let's end this on an optimistic note: in our eyes you are an immigrant like many others, you're perhaps a little noisier, perhaps a little more visionary, <*Ahem! Humm!*> but that doesn't matter (in Plain English) *it makes no difference to us*, because from our point of view you have broken no laws, you have harmed no one, you have not been involved in politics, the incriminated book in question *is after all nothing more than fiction (Good Lord!)*, and we rarely wave the death penalty in front of writers who stray from good taste, or writers who *transgress*, as critics say, the norms. (In Plain English) *We wouldn't have given a damn about this fact if your life weren't endangered.* I might add that since Oscar Wilde's condemnation for *pederasty, we have seen worse in the meantime!* I don't believe that we have ever condemned a single writer? What do you have to say about this?

I think it was incredibly stupid to send Oscar to jail, *Officer! What a stupid idea, a real mess!* (In plain English) *I am coming to the conclusion that privacy, the small individual lives of men, is preferable to all this inflated macroscopic activity. But too late. Can't be helped. What can't be cured must be endured!*

I would have been happy to state the above and then, *yes, yes, surely, no doubt, evidently*, or as Bartleby might have said if he were to add his two cents, *I would have preferred not to*, I would have tried to save time, I would have asked for a little time to reflect a little on the matter, to mull it over with Macha, with my children, my lawyer, God, the pope, the secretary general of the party, who knows? <*It's really stupid, really stupid! Cover your tracks!*> I said (in Plain English), *you know, officer*, as the great French poet, Stéphane Mallarmé, a poet who was a great admirer of Anglo-Saxon literature, an excellent translator of Poe and the author of a very eccentric little English dictionary, as Mallarmé used to say (in Plain French), *qui écrit se retranche!* I believe, Mr. Officer, that in all this there are no changes expected, whether in Provence, Warsaw, or Minneapolis, *quelle différence*, what's the diff? *What difference does it make?* I'll simply move and take things up again, pick up where I left off, take the baton from Mallarmé, *but in a Muslim context*, I'll pick up from where Antonin the Mômo left off, *but in a Muslim context*, I'll take the baton from Baudelaire, but in the territory of the Muslim king: but don't you see, Monsieur l'Officier, *maybe it is none of your business and I do apologize for that*, maybe that's not your cup of tea and I beg your forgiveness, but quite curiously, you see, quite curiously, *it's funny, isn't it, very funny in a way.* Last night when I was rereading this curious little book by another one of the damned of the earth, why yes, the book of an Iranian writer, *Buried Alive* by Sadeg Hedayet. *Do you see what I'm getting at, officer? Can you see? Buried Alive!* Enterré vivant! *This guy died in Paris over thirty years ago,* this guy wrote like a madman in Paris where he lived in exile, this guy had to be exiled from his country where everyone took him for a madman, a basket case, a paranoid, a writer in outer space, this guy was interested only in suicide and poetry, and before he died, before *giving himself over* to death, he nonetheless found the strength to write this *little poisoned book* that correctly takes as its title *Enterré vivant,* the prophetic title of *Buried Alive.* He wrote this book in a basement or in a maid's quarters in Paris, and he declared death on himself by bequeathing to us these *Flowers of Evil.* He declared death on himself by leaving this writing of a victim of suicide to the conscience of his contemporaries all the while knowing that this book would be *read,* all the while knowing that one day the poison he had distilled in his brains of a mystical opium eater, knowing that the magma he had secreted in his studio of the death of modern letters, knowing that the slobberings he had puked up in his drugstore for the death of modern letters, knowing that the plasma he belched up in the mental mucus of his dereliction, that the blood he spat on the white sheets of his mental rage would not, for all that, one day find a *reader,* all the while knowing that this sap of maniacal pain of ambrosia and of the acid taint of death would not, for all that, one day haunt his blood brothers, Hedayet donated his cold blood to the death of Iranian literature. Three times he gave his blood so that the literature of his country might live. *He suffered so that we would not suffer, he died so that we would live! Let life and the good works of this suffering* be done! What would be more astonishing now if the same fanatical mafiosi want to *bury me alive?* Don't you find it a bit astonishing that the death threat hung around my neck *does not originate in the government or the citizens of my country,* that would have been *logical,* but from a country that ought to have nothing to do with me or could give a damn about what I do or don't do! After all, it's my *native country* that I have taken up in the torment of my writings, these are the *customs of my native country* that I have taken to task, *the attitudes of the people of my country* that I have submitted to an X-ray vision by unleashing the madness of literature, by unleashing this whole primal horde of sentences in dire distress. But as you can well observe, Monsieur l'Officier, the *ban* did not originate in *that country.* It is not in that country that judgment was pronounced. *Is it because in my country literature is still respected and admired? Is it because in my country liberty is still cherished? Is it because in my country people still know how to read? <Merzak: does he still believe in Santa Claus or what?>* but from the country of this great suicide of literature! Sadeg Hedayet *was* buried alive, but don't you see, Monsieur l'Officier, in burying him too quickly, much too quickly, as if in a rush to die, *à la hâte, these guys—they didn't have the wisdom of Solomon—rushed him out!* They buried *life! Death clutches the living,* no expression will have ever been so ironically revolutionary: by *taking his own life,* by burying himself *alive,* Hedayet became the *vigil* of what is alive in us, in being buried alive in opium, Hedayet became the implacably *living* testimony of every force that struggles against death. By burying himself *alive,* Hedayet ended up making incarnate the vigilance of life, the vigilant life that casts shame on all forces that hate life, the vigilant life that casts shame on all forces that harbor contempt for living life. By burying himself *alive,* Hedayet allows us to look at life directly, from the deepest pit of the tomb where this world scoffs at death, where death snickers at the dereliction of his world. Hedayet the vigilambulist, don't you see, Monsieur l'Officier, Hedayet the *vigilambulist in a world of somnambulists, Hedayet* awake and alive in a deadened, brutalized world, Hedayet *conscious* in a world astonished, *stunned,* a world stoned, *beaten down,* drugged, abused, Hedayet *preoccupied* in an idle world, Hedayet *despairing* in a world of *desperation!*

(In plain English) *So it is my turn to say, I really don't give a damn!* The first-class burial that you are preparing for me is in *the order of things!* What you are doing, what we are doing, what I am going to do *in complicity with you* is to *bury* Sadeg Hedayet a second time! In sending me off to Minneapolis, by inviting me to *go and bury myself alive* in Minneapolis, you're not burying me alive, you're burying Sadeg Hedayet, Sadeg Hedayet's *vision* and, why don't we admit the fact, Monsieur l'Officier, Sadeg Hedayet's *sacrifice!* By protecting me the way you do, you're not protecting me, *you don't protect writers from their destiny,* it is not *liberty* that you're defending. By *defending me the way you do, you are protecting* nothing, you're protecting nobody, you're defending your *bosses,* you're defending your clients, your *clientele,* against the fear that is eating away at your stomach, you're defending yourself from the acid that eats into your ideals, you're protecting yourself from the poison that contaminates your institutions. In a word, you're giving yourself an *alibi* for a dying democracy and you're making a show of your complicity with the most ignominious of all *conspiracies!* By *defending me* you're revealing your leanings *toward a defunct democracy!* You, as Europeans, you've taken the Marquis de Sade out of the confines of censored books in your libraries in order to bury him in paperback! *Sursum Corda! May Sadeg be spared! We can't let Hedayet be buried a second time through the intermediary of a second person! Through the intermediary of Dead Letters! Lettres Mortes Modernes! L.M.M.! Hell-même m'aime!*

As for me, throughout all this time, what can I tell you? I made my little speech and I said, *yes, yes, evidently,* to be rid of the officer of Scotland Yard-KGB-CIA-DST-SM. Clearly *you've got to bury me alive, yes, you have to, for sure,* but that's not what will be of service to democracy, that's not what will get democracy out of its delirium, that's not what will get your democracy out of its indecency. *As for me, throughout all this time, what can I tell you? I was thinking of taking a little step in the direction of politics <Foerh! Foerh!> An error worthy of praise. But what a handsome piece of stupidity! For it's too late, it's finally too late for the ineffable fate that is so desired ... Fall back in place, screw your head in place, we've fooled around enough, enough dreams, enough life, get on with it!* But the officer once again: *One more time, Mr. Mrad, if you don't mind, it is obvious* that *under the given circumstances,* it is *out of the question* that your wife and children be allowed to follow you to the United States! There are too many risks involved! Your *spouse* would do well to remain in London for a period of time. One person is easy to spot, but four! Can you imagine what that means! With four people stowed away in the United States, why that's tantamount to suicide! *With all due respect,* if you allow me to say so, Monsieur Mourad, it seems to us that for lack of another solution your wife might prefer to return to France! *She obviously wants to return to where she belongs!* She thinks it would be better for the children if they were to live near their grandmother, who, as you know, has taken up definitive residence in Eze-sur-Mer! (In plain English) *Obviously you have your say in these matters,* but, as Mômo the rootless, Antonin, the man tied, bound, and ligatured, *from now on*

my occupation is to uproot *hell so that,*
hell having revolted against me,
pounded upon me,
driven me to despair,
felt itself alive,
wanted to discuss,
believed I had been forgotten,
combined mixtures, different things,
sought to be rid of me
          by crushing me
          by replacing me,
it's the battle,
I can't forget it,
I can't be the victim,

I can't fall into illusions,
                    fly,
                        go awry,
don't lose footing
don't abandon the feeling of my imperviousness
                        of my reducibility
                        of my exclusivity
                        of my originality
                        of my solitude,
of my absolute unicity based on a single word,
                        demeanor,
Atena Tanit
Rut sustenit
Ramar!

But no *demeanor* can be hoped for on the part of the officer who couldn't care less about one of Antonin le Mômo's little puppets, and who would give a damn about my *mourning*, for the officer didn't see that I was *trembling, because it seemed to me, really, that Hedayet never had to die. I could never believe that one day this voice might expire. I was afflicted by these painful words, but at the same time I was amused. Hedayet had been correct, he had predicted that one day his own people would force a writer to bury himself alive!*

As time passes, the officer continued, life will not be so risky for them in Paris, in Nice, or Aix-en-Provence as it might in London! (In plain English) *Again it is mainly a matter of security, a matter of safety!* Obviously we will take care of the *move!* There is no need for you to be alarmed about the *practical and financial aspects* of the affair! *We will back you up and don't you worry, Sir!* In the present circumstances, Mr. Mrad, you are a rich man, indeed a very rich man! A recent conversation we had with your editor assures us on this point: perhaps your book won't be *read*, but it will sell *like hotcakes!* <Rubbish! Fiction and damnation!> Curiosity, *Mr. Mrad*, the sick curiosity of the *greater public*, the ignorance and the fanaticism of the *human beast* are sufficient! Watch out, *Mr. Mrad*, watch out for the *human beast!* They all want to know what a book that brings fame and fortune to a simple writer *looks like*, but *at the same time* they also want to condemn it! Nothing could be more stimulating! *A real kick! A real one, my dear friend!* With all due respect, Monsieur Mrad, they are truly interested neither in you nor in your book, but merely in the *fate* of your book! What piques their curiosity, you see, what stirs up the interest of the *human beast*, is understanding how a book can destroy the goodwill of its writer! For paper and words! Mere words! *Flatus vocis!* You see, what intrigues them is that a book can kill a person! To grasp that would be like selling their soul! They can't restrain themselves! They have no *manners*, my friend, not even one iota! I hope I should never forget that fact! The interviews you agreed to have with the BBC, with France-Culture and Radio-France-International had *surely* better be canceled! If *we* are informed, then so are *they*. In respect to your round-table discussions with Pivot, Patrick Poivre, Apostrophe or *whatever-you-might-call-it*, and with Bill Moyers, and so on, *you will clearly have to decline all engagements!* Getting yourself on the air with people like that is out of the question! There is no way your security can be guaranteed in open spaces like that! You would be a sitting duck! You will be able to visit your wife and children in a place that can be specified when the proper time comes! We will keep you informed when our offices have determined exactly where and when you can meet them again!

In the jungle of the cities, (in plain English) *no rectifications, we live among our accumulation of things behind doors festooned with locks and chains, and find* it *all too easy to fear the unforeseen, the all-destroying coming of the Ogre — Charles Manson, the Ayatollah Khomeini, the Blob from Outer Space! Nobody has read my book yet and yet I am buried alive! Amazing to see how politicians have gotten so good at inventing fictions that they tell us are the truth! It then is incumbent upon us to start telling the (real) truth, the truth of fiction, und so weiter, my friend!*

In the attic I found an old card from North Africa, a glove that must have belonged to a giant, and an object that looks like a Neanderthal's heavy club *<it's called a bat, Mister, a bat!>*. Downstairs, they might say somebody is surveying the five square meters of the kitchen, I catch my breath: *maybe Macha and the kids have returned?* Cut!

Reread page 73 with infinite patience: it is enchanting: its simplicity disarms me, it seems so simply *simple*, it seems so stupid that its *evangelical simplicity* is what makes it so radiantly beautiful and crushing: it has surely refused to make any concessions to anything or anyone! *Ens Simplissimus!* And I'm bewildered to think of the soul at peace of the person who wrote it! An extreme fatigue after a long agony, but an abundance of light, a fear of the northern lights, but much sobriety, disquiet over the underground, but patience above all, yes, a great deal of patience and pain withheld, a lot of that, but now, in passing, in the city as in the country no one bothers to worry. Absolutely no one, not even the priests, the censors, the educators, the politicians, the ayatollahs, the capitalists, and the communists, would even raise an eyebrow, to *squint their eyes, at least squint and assume a scandalous look, <preposterous, mon cher! Infamous! Blasphemous!>* but presently, a flat, total calm and silence reigns over the real brutes, the *so-called* **modern readers,** true cynics recalled **modern readers,** who are proud of themselves. Do you hear them? *Get lost! Go to hell! What drivel! This is pure crap! What crawled up this guy's ass! A louse! A cretin and a vandal! He's a provocateur! Let him go peddle his wares! He ought to have his teeth knocked down his throat! Good for him! Justice! Sacrifice! Burn, baby, burn! Reclusion! A crematory oven! Poison! The Galleys! Hell! And the runaround starts up again!*

no, no, nothing, truly nothing,
no more bloodstains, never more?
no, no bloodstains, no, nothing,
it's because they aren't looking closely, no,
if there is something that someone finds out of order,
yes, it's true, it's known.

In fact, I have been reading the first seven lines of page 73, and I can't get into it any further because further, I think, I know for sure, is pure adventure. Further ahead is the unknown, for me what follows is already the coming of death and always the black rain of anxiety. To go further ahead means condemning me to an even greater solitude, to go further means condemning me to have nothing more to say, further on, nothing, and fear above all else, fear *in addition* and the dire confusion, further, there remains only *whatever inspires a fear of dying.* Further on, there are the consumers and a very great fear of bothering the neighbors, further on, there are the means of production and capitulations of every kind, further on, there are the dormitories that look like Tokyo and men in factory uniforms. *They eat standing up without paying any attention to people around them, they eat standing up with faces that look afraid, they eat standing up with the hands of assassins, they eat standing up with the eyes of opium junkies, they eat standing up the very flesh of their own mental disorder,* so what is needed is first of all that they start fasting on their own, that they begin by fasting in order not to bother the living-dead, the zombies, *no rectifications!,* so that they won't have too much to think about, in order not to disturb them during their siestas, in order not to shake them out of their torpor.

What must be avoided at all cost is *recapitulating*, the bitter taste of *recapitulation*, *in recapitulate there is capitulate*, the bitter taste of memory and repentance, so that what is needed is silence, silence before all else, silence, and then silence that follows and is forever fallow,

after which the disorder of ideas,

silence, after which impossible thoughts,

silence, after which long nights of insomnia,

silence, after which the pain of thinking,

silence, preceding the *impossibility of thinking!*

silence, after which the agitation of thinking!

silence, before thoughts get buried!

And presently,

May they be fearful! May they give up their thoughts!

I don't give a damn!

In the attic: The world is turned topsy-turvy. Every time I go up to the attic I can hear steps *in the foyer* of the house, steps and voices, a woman's soft voice and voices of children who are playing, and apparently, the sounds pass up through the chimney: *Am I losing a screw or what?*

Right now he just put the machine on *sleep*, something that he taught electronic equipment, right now, he has left himself fallow, he has put himself into a fallow mode, his *placement!* his *innocence!!* his *stupidity!! his arrogant stupidity and his stammering agony!!!* and nobody cares about what he does, nobody cares about what he thinks. *Does he think?* <In his case *what does think mean, anyway?*> Right now, no one bothers about what might be passing through his head, no one is around to think of asking him what's going on in his mind, *nobody is around to offer a penny for his thoughts!*

He says to the young woman: (In plain English!) *Who cares if I stop writing? Who cares if I stop thinking? Who would ever give a damn?*

He says to the very young woman who faced him on the terrace of the café, a café *that looked directly upon a Passage*, if I were to stop writing, who would ever care? Who would give it a moment's pause? If all the people that are in this café suddenly decided to stop thinking, who would ever care? If the six hundred people who were registered in this Sofitel for the International Congress on Francophone Literature suddenly decided to stop thinking, who would even stop for a second to think about it? (In plain English) *He says <what do they care though the whole land squeals*

like a rabbit clenched in a weasel's jaws?> What is the heavy pensum of the thoughts of all these people gathered here? What is the weight of our thinking, what is there to ponder about all this francophony, *anyway?* And the young woman replies, Don't be dramatic my friend, you're exaggerating, you're very *pompous!* Things in life are much more simple! And turning toward her brother, a man who seemed to be the spitting image of her brother: look how our friend is *so full of himself!* Don't you find that quite *extraordinary?* Don't you think he takes himself a little *too* seriously? She uttered *too* with a tremolo in her voice, while the narrator said, without really believing at all in what he was saying: *You only believe in things halfheartedly, maybe that's why you say what you are saying in such a patronizingly cocksure way! The last time someone told me what you had just said to me I was scarcely twenty years old, and the woman who was speaking to me was a whore! Only whores accuse people who believe that things are* fully *as they are, Madame, but you're not a whore. So how can we solve this mystery? How can we make heads or tails of this coincidence? How can we piece it all together? Do you believe in coincidences alone? Is it only a coincidence? And above all, what do you know of what makes* **too?**

Right then the brother said, what if we were to *chatter* a little about something else? Why don't we change the subject? Why not the weather? If we simply decided what we'll do on this radiant afternoon? Wouldn't that be better? So much seriousness! Too many weighty things to think about! I much prefer chatter. I'd much rather close the door on all the cares and worries of the world! The world is not equipped to sustain us anymore! It has sustained us for thousands of years and now it's finished! It's given and endured much too much! *Nature wants us to return what she gave us! She wants her money back and we have no money left! Elle voudrait que nous lui donnions quelque chose en retour!* All we have to give back to her is our debris! It amounts to saying that we have nothing left to give back in the bargain! We have wasted everything, *absolutely everything!* The young woman: *Come, come, this is stupid! Men sitting in cafés are always idiotic! Let's go over to the Trocadero and see the skaters, they're great to watch in the summertime! They do great things!*

They leave the café without a thought as to the consequence of what has just been said, without a trace. The only *trace* they left behind are those crumbs they scattered around the heavy iron table where they were sitting, which begin to attract pigeons, *no rectifications!* They walk toward the nearest subway station and the three of them have a total age of ninety. The young woman is about as old as a rosebush and she's the youngest of the three. She laughs, she speaks, she walks. You might say she's dancing. You might say she's singing. Her eyes are chestnut and hazel colored, and are very deep. You might get lost in them. She raises her bare arms to the sky and says to the narrator, *how is it that you can continue working and make do for all these years without having earned a red cent and so far from all your friends? and so far from your country? and, too, so far from yourself? also so far from your cares?* The question is easy for her. For me it's catastrophic. The question marks begin to multiply.

To say that I'm just making things go? That I'm not making things go? That things have never been going? That I've never stopped working? How can she say all these things in the same breath? Give in to depression, give in to stupidity again and again? Is that what she expects from me? I say, one never loses real friends *when one is really far away.* She replies, *Out of sight, out of mind.* I say: that's incredibly stupid. Out of sight, *in* mind, when one is *really far* away. But first of all one has to be *really* far away! She replies: You feel that you count among those who have *really* gone far away! Now isn't that a bit presumptuous? How can anyone ever know if they have *really gone off or away?* How can you tell if it is not some kind of transcendental illusion? You believe you've left everything: *I've left everything, I've left everything,* you shriek at the top of your lungs, but in effect you have left nothing at all because you have taken everything along: car, pictures, little dog, Rosebud, Mommie, fetishes, bric-a-brac, a pile of jasmine flowers from grandmother's garden, a pressure cooker, *Halhal,* allali, Ah! La la! falbalas, tralali, tralala, wild lavender, fantasia, medical records, notebooks, pens, erasures, cameras, academic theses, dental prostheses, credit cards, just like these people who *break their habits* and *venture off* in these gigantic caravans where they have *reconstructed everything,* even the granny's portrait, they've even brought along rubbers and a camp stove in Yellowstone Park, rubbers and a camp stove in Yellowstone Park, *did you see them the way I saw them or do you want me to draw you a picture?* She laughs, why the doubting lady is laughing! The others leave with their books and letters from all their paramours in order not to forget the slightest thing! Have they really cut the ropes from their moorings? Or rather have they brought along the essentials that count only *for themselves?* Have they really taken flight, or have they just gotten lost along the way? <Siphi: *I kinda like this one, kid!*> Screeches of tires on the cobblestones of the Avenue Wagram, spits and chugs of the number 63 bus, the brassy show of the sky over our heads. The road back is lost forever!

The time I spend in the attic increases. I have carved out a comfortable little *working space* in front of the window that faces the *Porte des Lilas,* from which I can see Zooey and Franny Ziegler having fun scraping the bottom of the stream. *Their objective?* to save all the larvae of the frogs and *minnows* from the world's disaster. *Another min-now! Another one! Yeah! Don't let him go!* Up here I can hear the pitter-patter of Macha's feet and the kids crying in the distance. Everything passes by my eyes as nothing ever had before, *no rectifications!* As in the song: *Dad's upstairs. He's doing his affairs. Mom's down below. She makes things go.* At my feet all the teeming stuff of life! The *minnows of life, my friend! On the horizon, a fat black octopus has just spurt his electric ink on the blind white horizon above!*

I remember, I remember well: the mineral solitude of the blind,
The mineral solitude of the blind
fermi al sole sulle soglie,
on the thresholds, immobile in the sunlight
la furia incandescente delle voci
the incandescent fury of voices
dentro un mondo di tenebra: cosi oggi,
at the heart of a world of shadows: so in this day,
solo nella città grande
alone in this great city
io mi abandonno al muro di una chiesa,
I abandon myself at the wall of a . . . mosque!

He remembered N* in '67 or '68, when she wore a taffeta dress: with her chestnut hair thrown behind, flowing over her shoulders *like the mane of an Arabian horse.* He recalled her face, when she had the look of a madonna, *no rectifications*, the face of a Gioconda who was coming back from a dance on the night of the fourteenth of July, and the provocative and smiling gaze she cast upon him just before she vanished behind the door of the harem. Yes, he said to himself, this woman must understand that she will be responsible for the fate of my life from this point forward. I must find a way of letting her know that she has captured my soul, that my soul has been taken hostage in her prison of azur and golden hair, and that if she does not act, I may soon be lost forever, I might never recover my bearings, I might never find my way back to myself. I followed him *blindly* in the winding streets of Paris. You shall be my guide, she said, you'll be my argonaut, with you I'll go everywhere. I'll go into the cafés, I'll jump into the dives, I will enter into the *Passages*, I'll go through the oldest sections of the city. I will go into the slums, the two of us will march ahead through the night, forward, until no place remains that has not been trodden under our feet. I shall be your queen, you'll be my king, I will not be afraid, you will harbor no fear, I'll have no more nightmarish memories, you'll have memories no more, I shall be without a past, you'll be my future, you'll be without a future, I'll be your past: <I thought her formula was astonishingly beautiful, even if I couldn't quite understand it, even I couldn't even detect its cruelty>. She added with violins and harps: I shall be the present of your past, you will be the present of my present, just you and me, we'll be one, together, the present of our future. I am at this very moment the present of your past just as you are the present of my present, just you and me. And further, what more could one ever hope for? What more could one ever ask of writing? What could one ask of the bitter bile flowing in my veins? *I climb up, I drag my demons behind me up over the cliffs of Algiers. Life and letters amount to nothing more than an old heroic dream! Night casts its dark and blinding shroud over the houses of the city!*

Hot to trot and rip one off!

I am *the period style* of Macha in a cold-blooded bath, <*an entire period of time, surely! and full of folds!*> I'm all bound up with Machin-Macha, she winds through my mind at every moment, a mind that has become a sinister period style. I should have gone in reverse and committed suicide back then in order not to let all this carnage get unleashed another time. *Too much talk in the sleazy dives, too much mush in the maché of paper books, too much sacrifice for the sake of my belly button.*
But that doesn't stop the doctor from finding me in good health. *You'll die beyond the age of the Bible, Monsieur Mrad. You'll reach a hundred, and the air in Minneapolis will do wonders for you, believe me! Get outside, breathe that air! Go skiing, go skating, it'll relax you and keep you in tip-top shape.*
On the dead-end street next to where I live are the Zieglers. Their house is right next to ours, our yards touch each other and we can dip our tootsies in the same *pond*. As Mrs. Ziegler says, wet your feet, wade a bit in the cold water, it's good for your heart, and in *an approximative French and stuttering diction*, dip your feet in zee cold water and you vill zee dee *rézeultss*, Monsieur?
Monsieur Mrad, Professeur de théologie. *Theology? Oh! Why, yes! That's splendid, it truly is!* <yeah, sure, but for how long?>
In front there are the Lendstroms. He's a psychologist, she's a lawyer, *no psychology! only tanning.* Since I moved onto the dead-end street they haven't yet even said hello to me! They probably think that with the way I look I won't be around here for long. *Why bother, dear? These foreigners! They come and go like mosquitoes!*
At the entry of the dead end, *the so-called secluded area of our dreams*, Yackoff, the

refugee surgeon. His specialty: genital prostheses and sex-change apparatus. He is bent on showing me the films he smuggled out of the Soviet Union in the stuffing of an armchair in the period style of Alexander the First. *Professor*, I am sure the films will quite impress you, I don't know if theologians are much interested in this kind of thing, but I can assure you that it's a phenomenon that probes moral and philosophical problems of great importance! As I often say to Vava <*his significant other!*> *you know, really*, surgeons are philosophers in their own way, they constantly confront problems no less complex than those put forth by professional philosophers. Valentina <*Yackoff's better half!*> nods in approval, but doesn't utter a word, because she is repainting for the hundredth time the *pond*, but this time I spot her applying the paint in an unlikely way, she's bent over her canvas in an inhabitual pose, I sense that she is really strung out, *technically*. Yackoff continues, I can transplant any given organ of one sex onto the body of another sex, without any major *technical* obstacle. I can transform the sex of a man into the sex of a woman, and vice versa. But *morally*, Professor, *morally, well, that's another kettle of fish!* As soon as morality enters the picture the problem gets much more complicated, because we're no longer dealing with a purely technical problem but an essentially moral problem, and that's why we need the help of people like you, Professor, because for you, technique is what is lacking, and for us philosophy is what is lacking. We're speechless in the face of these questions. A young biological male comes to see you and says to you, Doctor, I want to become a woman. You've got a charming young lad of twenty before your eyes and his problem, Professor, is about a sex change, he's *physically* a man and *psychologically* a woman. Now what would you do, since you have in your hands the power of performing this miracle? What are you going to do, Professor? What are you going to do when you face a problem like that, Professor? Are you going to treat this problem like any other organ transplant?

Just let Mister Professor be, leave him alone, Yackoff. Don't you see that you're a royal pain in the neck with your sleazy stories of organ transplants? You know, that's not what you want to tell your neighbor who has just moved into the house next to you, is it, Monsieur?

Rmad Bensmaïa, <*ashes, ashes, in hagarene idiom*> Madame, Rmad as ashes in Arabic and Bensmaïa as the son of heaven or son of my heaven.

Isn't Monsewer Bensmaïer a bore with all of his stupid stories?

Bensmaïa, Madame, Bensmaïa, A, I, A, at the end, Aye-Eye-Aye at the end!

Oh yes, Bensmaya, I see, you must originally be of German descent?

Algerian, <algorithmic>, not German, *Algerian*, <seismic>: Ich bin nicht ein Deutsch, Ich bin ein Algerianer!

But Mr. Benslama, what in heaven's name is an Algerian doing in Minneapolis at the end of our century?

Bens*maïa*, Madame, B.E.N.S.M.A.I.A <*B as in boy, E noir, N as in nuque, S as in soot, M as in Malte-Laurids-Bridge, A rouge, I jaune, A, as in aphony!*>

Ah! *worry not!* Someday I'll wind up pronouncing your name correctly, Mister Theologian, you'll see, but I should tell you that I can never remember proper names, I always twist them around at the beginning, but once I get it, I remember it for good, <she points with the index finger of her right hand to the upper right lobe of her brain> I never forget it, for you see, you're the first Nigerian that I've ever met in my life!, <a pause>, you belong to the community of colonizers, don't you?

Now don't you see, Vava, you're the one who bores the Professor with all your stuff about your bad memory and proper names. You realize, *Professor*, Vava sometimes even forgets my name! Do you realize that! She forgets not only her husband's name but her daughters' names too, Syria and Taniochka, she has them pulling their hair out! One time it's Sarah, another time it's Samia, and another, it's Sillia. Nobody knows what to make of it! She mixes them all up! But in other areas she has an elephant's memory, I can assure you!

Yackoff! Yackoff! You're not going to tell the Professor your story about the playing cards again! Tell him anything you want about me, but please, not that one! That one, dear, that one is worn out! Let's let our new neighbor the Professor tell us how he plopped down in Minnesota!

And what tells you that the Professor wants to tell us what brought him to our neck of the woods? Wouldn't this be a rather indiscreet question, *Herr Professor?*

Now you're beginning to speak to our friend in German, Yackoff! Dear me, we're not in Germany anymore! You know, he's never gotten over leaving Munich. Whatever German he remembers is stiff and dead as a doornail! *Es ist eine Überraschung! You ought to be ashamed of yourself!*

I wasn't intending to speak with *Monsieur le Professor* in German, my dear. I simply said *Herr Professor* inadvertently, only because I spent the afternoon reading Professor Minkowski's monograph on pancreas transplants, a remarkable study from all points of view, that happens, my dear, to have been written in German! Thus a matter of *reflex* and not of a *lapsus* or a *slip of the memory!* Apropos of memory slips, Professor, have you ever read the study Dr. Freud wrote on this phenomenon? It's brilliantly intelligent and subtle, but I have the sneaking suspicion that Dr. Freud was well aware of the workings of the nervous system but did not take adequate account of the biological aspect of the matter! Our brain, Monsieur, our brain is a very complicated machine! And he treats it as if it were *a simple digital calculator!* What's your opinion about this matter, *Herr Doktor?* Can you tell us what your feelings are about this theory? Do theologians have an opinion about this phenomenon? What do theologians think about the nervous system?

disorder,

rupture, rupture of ligatures,

rupture of linkages,

Ah! if only all ligatures were ruptured!

Valentina then replies: Whenever Yackoff happens upon people with whom he can discuss things that are his passion, he grabs them with his tentacles! So I advise you, *dear Monsieur Radar,* not to answer this question! Mister Professor! If you answer you're finished! He'll never leave you in peace! If you answer you'll see! In any event you've had your warning!

Every passing day persuades me more and more that the house I inhabit functions according to the principles of *spiritual communicating vessels:* when I go up to work in the attic I let the spirits that are busy in me stay down on the first floor or in the *basement.* In order not to stir them up, I spend more and more time up in the attic! I only leave the attic to go and eat something in the kitchen and when I go to bed, in the wee hours of the morning.

Only when he goes to bed at dawn does he twist and turn with fury in his head, for a long while. He too, like so many others, had a horrible nightmare, but although there was nothing really horrible in it, in the morning nevertheless his eyes were streaming with tears, he stuffed his head into his pillow and he breathed heavily through the fabric **in order to make the weight of things, the great stone of dawn, vanish from his heart,** *what must have been especially horrifying was what he knew all along, but he still threw himself into the trap, again and again, because there was a trap in the dream, the dream unraveled the same way every time, in front of the butcher <the Censor?>, a middle-aged woman <Macha? The Ligature?>, a neuter creature, who boasts to some people present of being able to charm him, yes,* **Mrad,** *and the proof, the young man, it's he, will jump against his will onto the tracks of the trolley that rolls toward him, he laughs, a little perturbed, incredulous, but keeping calm, and accepts the coins amounting to twenty fillérs that have a strange form — square, not round — with rounded corners <his* **Dead Letters?**>, *in order to buy his ticket, but no, no, responds the woman a little insolently,* **that was the point of the trap!** Having stated this remark, which she pronounced as if it were a magic formula, she opens the living-room door onto a man who looks like Abraham Lincoln

and the Ayatollah Khomeini and says, smiling, *Mrad, I would like to introduce you to Mister Péter Esterhàzy, the son of Thomas Bernhard and Anna Kiss. He has been burning to meet you for a long time! Cut!*
In the dormitory of thought, inches away from the success of breaking all ties once and for all, two inches away from the success of making a definitive rupture of all ligatures! you have to write this little novel for us, you've been taught how to wrap up a good story, so what the hell! What's keeping you back? *Quick, write your novel!* All we're asking you to do for now is to *provide local color*, give us a smattering of a few *barbaric nuptials*, a little infibulation preceded by an excision preceded by a little circumcision, or else a whopping marriage in the seraglio! They'll love it! Put your obsessions aside for a few months while you're in Minneapolis, *but my head is aching, it's burning!* Many writers would *dream* of being in your shoes! Six months of literary reclusion! Six months set aside to ride their hobbyhorses! Six months, a year, all for a single preoccupation, for a single goal: writing, creation, don't you get it, Monsieur Mared!
Aely: *In Mared there is maldreamady!*

Scholium # 4: "*To do* in French means to shit. Example:
Ne forçons par notre talent
[Let's not push our talents]:
Nous ne FAIRONS rien avec grâce
[Graciously we will get nothing done].

Progress, yes, in writing, but at a snail's pace.
Algiers, *disaster*
after which, deracination, exile, boredom: the utter bore of these words, the bore of these meetings, these cults, the bore of this culture, the boring friendships: *Amitiés Françaises!* Algerian friendships! Franco-Algerian friendships! Togolese friendships! Netherlandish friendships! Business friendships! Paternalistic friendships! Ugandish friendships! Swiss friendships! Literary friendships *and assholification:* assholify myself, after which I Algerify myself, Arabize myself the way they sheer sheep, transform myself into the Plural Maghreb, after which, I pluralize myself in getting assholified, pluralized in being Minneapolized, francophone and Maghrebian literature, as if I were getting anabolized, Maghrebian literature as if it were a cure-all, francophone literature as if it were a cataplasm, Francophony as cacophony, Francophony as sheer boredom, Francophonia just like America, Francophonia as

syndicated labor union with unlimited responsibility. *In Francophony there is Franco!*
We'll francophonize them, we'll francophony them! Then we'll see what happens! Hey! Get
a load of that francophone! Francophonissimo! I'm at your service, Generalissimo!

What we are seeking, don't you see, my dear friend, what we would like you to do
is to have you *Algerianize yourself, effortlessly, in your best demeanor,* in every one of
your thoughts. What we want is *pure Algerianity!* We need good family-style Francophony! After all, the greater portion of your *public,* your *lectorate,* your highness
and most serene Master, is majoritorily and apostrophically French! *<rather more!>*
and so what we therefore need is some good old-fashioned francophoney of French
origin! eF.! eF.! eF.! *<Elle fait fi! de Fous! Fhe's defying fou!>*
If I really weren't in such a bind, if I didn't have to make ends meet, I'll tell you
right away, I'd be done with it all, I'd erase everything, nothing would be left, but
not *that <he clicks his tooth with the thumbnail of his right hand>,* not a bit for francophone literature and its admirers! If I didn't have to grub, if I didn't have to pan-
handle, *no rectifications!,* I'd erase everything! Especially my *Dead Letters!* The only
really nasty book I've ever written! I get the point . . . the *dark and bitter depths,* sure,
everything, yes, I'd suppress everything. *<Too late, Pal!>*

Immense worry over assholifying: assholify to the max so that Sadeg won't ever
again point his finger at me, *bury him once and for all,* get rid of him, get rid of his
ghost *by means of an intercessor:* francophone authors are rare and highly valued.
Mummification: The Mollahsons are taking advantage of my state of
reclusion, they are taking advantage of my weak and sick condition
to infantilize me,
to juvenilize me,
by making me forget
who I am
and WHAT I have done
and that it is I who have
@ the preponderant
2. the prosperant
3. the secret language!
Carouta Krata
Inume soerna!
surrounded on all sides . . .

Suicide and assholification,
I've got to bury Sadeg Hedayet and get assholified,
bury him as I get assholified in Minneapolis,
burials of Maghrebian literature by its bachelors, even
burials of Algerian literature by its Molasseshons,
burials of Maghrebian literature by its own writers, even,
burials of literature by Francophony and francophone of every kind in new cultural
spaces: first-class space, young space, expressive space, French space, the space of
dreams, minority space, gay-lesbo space, protected space, money space, Muslim space,
space à la mode de Caen, Maghrebian space, Beur space, Khorote space, pleasure-
dome space! Quebecois space of Francophony, postmerden space with added boredom, space of freedom, anxious space plus death, verbose space, adipose space, space
of contrition, space of volition, space of suspicion, space of racism! Deafness *in the
midst of so much din! After all that health matters little, illness doesn't mean a thing, and
life even less!*

Scholium # 5: *"The more we concentrate the greater the amount of ground we lose."*

The cultural attaché: *You're telling me that a writer doesn't have to have any gray matter upstairs and still be awarded a fellowship from the Ministry of Culture?* He looks
furious, he's ready to take the maquisard by his neck: *Is that what you're insinuating?
You're telling me that they can leave chicken scratches over all this expensive paper without having a single worthy idea? They can drown us under their tons of mental compost
without knowing what in God's name they are doing? It's loathsome! I am going to consult
with the Dalai Lama and other competent authorities, I'm going to cut appropriations for
fellowships, annul subsidies, forbid all travel outside French territories, reduce budgetary
allocations for national education, curtail visiting positions for foreign intellectuals, sus-
pend all imports of foreign books, launch a movement against all professors, forbid all basic
research.* The deputy attaché: *But Monsieur le Cultural Attaché, it has already been effec-
tuated, in his great magnanimity, the president had already* granted *these privileges … at
a certain time, dreams were especially violent and painful, here he could awaken again
but, on the one hand, in falling back to sleep he continued as usual in any given place or
another, but later he was only dreaming that he was awakening, he knew that it was the
time to be prudent. The trolley arrives, while he suddenly remembers that he is going in
the right direction, but that he would be crazy not to climb aboard because this impossible
woman, etc.… and that's when the woman with the chestnut and hazel-colored eyes said,
Monsieur Mrad, I have the pleasure of introducing you to Monsieur Péter Esterházy, etc.*

Before his departure for Minneapolis, the state nuncios and police officers had advised him to get a domesticated animal, a dog or a cat, to keep him company, to take his mind off his business. He wouldn't be alone, he wouldn't be bored, he'd overcome his solitude, get over his identity crisis, recycle his psychological and mental pigshit. You'd have something to talk to, you wouldn't be alone, you'd have an ego distraction, some *diversion, humanity, distraction,* even your neighbors would be hoodwinked: a man who loves dogs can't be all that bad, he must be truly *human,* the animal is an outer sign of wealth and human sensitivity, extreme impassibility of orders, the extreme passibility of memory. Think like a shitting pig, *that's what is typical of our state functionaries of literature! Think in heaps of mental pigshit! Everything that looks like pigshit gives them flights of fancy! Crap or pigshit, provided it smells like a dirty cop! Provided it sounds like a real lie! Their way of understanding poetry! Their own way of understanding the hardships of poetry! No rectifications! Right where the Moor cries in his ears you really burrowed down, you old mole! They say you've got to burrow poetry! How do you burrow poetry with cavities! How do you chomp into a line of poetry with teeth literature has rotted away! With their mouth full of pigshit they feel right at home! <Here we feel right at home!> For that, with the pigship of lies they think they've hollowed things out! They've burrowed and hollowed out their minds the way they hollow out a tomb in a pig's ass!*
<Lemma: "The great pains of the inner sanctum are the abominable sphincter of being squEEZEd all around,
the black picture of beings
Now the fight has to begin. It won't start without opium!">

Rather rapid regrets for literature: There's always enough mental pigshit to bury a living writer, enough literary crap to neutralize a bothersome writer, enough functionaries of state criticism to make literature go to rot, enough ideological muck in which any writer who tries to think will drown, enough Francophony to bury literature for good, enough Algeria to destroy all thinking!
Progress in literature, full speed ahead!
Urgency of literature, pretty slow!

Every week he took the *Minneapolis-Rapid City* train to carve out a space in which he could give himself over to accelerated work on mental writing. He reserved an armchair in front of a formica folding table. As soon as the train started moving, he released himself to his passion: one word per every passing telephone pole, one sentence per every passing silo, one paragraph per every passing station, one chapter every city of more than 20,000 inhabitants, a novel every city of more than 200,000 inhabitants, *all the way to Cincinnati!*

This time, dear Aunt Adelaide, he wouldn't waste his time writing children's stories, especially fables, or little parables with little pearls of wisdom, short pieces, well-intended anecdotes, *no rectification*, little, well-turned things, now that men having proved that they decidedly lacked all sense of humor, men having decidedly become much too serious for his taste. *Yes, people weren't Little Red Riding Hoods that he manipulated in his imagination, little figures who were happy to live under his wolf's gaze!*

I worked like a dog, I labored *like a slave*, I kept banging my head against the wall *like a prisoner on death row*, despite all of Madame Yackoff's harping. *You shouldn't be smoking so much, Monsieur Rmaed, you're going to ruin your health (in plain English) you are going to kill yourself, is that what you want?* Work is piling up like pigshit, work is heaping up in the abode of the recluse, work is spreading all over the home of the hanged, *with all my fear I could never invite anybody inside.* I've blocked a door with piles of paper, going out of the house isn't a solution, breathing the air outside isn't a solution either. I've cordoned off the front door with yellow police tape, the garage door is still open, and so is the door to the backyard, the one I called the *Porte des Lilas*, because of the lilac hedge that grows by the little stream and because of one of the lesser ways into Paris, I can now cordon off the garage door in order to resist the temptation to drive my car, in order finally to be done with modern means of transport and in order not to be obligated to talk to Hans, my other neighbor. Every time he sees me tinkering inside the garage, he intones, *Monsieur Moerad*, the health of your lawn will suffer if you don't *mow* the grass at least twice a week, the grass gets stiff and hard to cut. Look, don't you see that it's already burning off, look, there's dandelions all over the place, *it looks like a field that's been left fallow*, but letting things go to pasture isn't good for lawns, lawns aren't meant to be fallow. Fallowing, Monsieur Ramed, means the death of the lawn, leaving things fallow, my friend, *that's for peasants! for farmers!* The people who lived there before you, a young fireman and his very pretty wife, had a contract with Chemlawn, a green lawn business. You pay them two hundred and fifty dollars a year and they'll take care of everything, they'll treat your lawn chemically, and all your worries will be over, everyone in our dead end has a contract with them, don't you see the difference between your lawn and ours? Look at the color! Yours looks like *an alfalfa field that's just been cut.* If you wait any longer, it'll dry out completely and you won't be able to do anything about it. You have to understand that with the Lendstroms, the Zieglers, with James and Molly we make up a good little community and that good lawns make good neighbors. If you want me to drop a line to Chemlawn and ask them to send a person over to look at what you've got and discuss how you can improve it, you'll see, you won't be unhappy with the results. It's miraculous what the experts from Chemlawn can do with your lawn. In no time they can transform sterile ground into a *green space* <*aha, so there, fascist green space, emigration from popular fascism, ecological fascism, political platforms against all fallowing*>, if you don't keep up your lawn, you'll be canned, Mister Theologian, if you don't get things green, you're the one who'll be mowed! The same green, the same green grass, grass will be green or it will not be, or *out you go! no theologians on this block!* No writers set out to pasture on our turf, *this is a quiet and secluded area and we love it! Our kids love it, too!* Do you understand, Monsieur Rmaed, we're really happy in our secluded space, and besides that's why we decided to move into a dead end, here it's called Golden Valley for that very reason, because of the happiness, because of the peacefulness, because of the calm that reigns over this little international community, because of the *hard-earned, honest* money we make, and because of the *quality of life*, thanks to our neighborhood and to Chemlawn. There are Russian immigrants who love America, Polish immigrants who love America, Uruguayan immigrants who love America, <*and American Indian aborigines who abhor America! What America did they make for us! Look at this America! Stop all Americanization! They've turned us into aborigines! Help us, oh please, Althusser!*> I also emigrated, Monsieur Rmaed, that's why as a good friend I'm telling this to you, because all that really counts is my loving and dear wife, Marie, and James and Molly, my dear neighbors, who are *true Americans,* James the retired general and his wife, Molly, the retired school teacher, and Marie, our educator who holds a degree, Marie, my wife who holds an advanced degree as a wife. I'm joking and I'm not joking, Monsieur Rmaed, my wife holds a diploma as a model wife. She did three years of matrimonial studies, she even has a Ph.D. in matrimonial studies,

So you get the idea all the same, three years of *puericulture,*
three full years spent in the culture of puerility, and centuries of cultural puerility, getting assholified, puerility and culture at will, *tenured and perpetual cultural reclusion, assholification forever! Puericulture and francophone literature in total disorder! They've ratified me like a rat!*

(in Plain French) Maintenant, c'est assez, soyons un peu sérieux!
We were saying:
No more screwing around
with laws,
with the catechism,
with Islam *in general,*
with midnight mysticism,
with the Torah,
with the faith,
with the world *in general,*
with man *in general,*
with woman *in general,*
with theory *in general,*
with history *in general,*
with Algeria,
with Arabic,
with the Koran,
with language,
with Marxism,
and with death *in general,*
with time,
with nature,
with literature,
with life *in general,*
and in a general manner of speaking
everything that, my General, is general!

California Court, Golden Valley: The dead end turned into a camp cut off from the world, the dead end turned into a concentration camp for white, adult, socialized persons (the *general* WASP!), quick, I have to board up the garage door immediately, burn all my travel notebooks, destroy the outline for my future piece on Destruction, throw away my *intimate journals,* get all this stuff together, tie up a bundle of my *love letters!* and, *so that I won't raise any suspicions,* so I won't let the cat out of the bag, *no rectifications!* so that there won't be cast over me even *a shadow of a doubt* with the slightest outburst, with the announcement of rain, with the storm clouds on the horizon, with snow flurries, I've got to put it all into the fireplace and turn it into ashes, *and my neighbors will only see signs of fire!*, ashes of francophone literature, ashes of Maghrebian literature written in exile, ashes of every exodus, ashes of the love of letters, ashes of every love that goes stale and rancid in my love letters, *but keep only my reflections on the spiritual Automaton,* keep only the blue notebook on spiritual automata, and then sign a contract with Chemlawn so that the neighbors will leave me alone, put on a good show for the neighbors, green up my lawn the size of a postage stamp and rigorously set my brains to pasture, and hereafter write only on kraft paper, write only on yellow sulfite paper, write only on fallow paper, write only on paper time, going on *papering things over, stumbling over,* putting Magrhebian literature out to pasture, putting Maghrebian literature to fast stutter stumble stammer, and then, franc*aphone* literature, but please, no cat, no dog, no parakeet, no fish, no domesticated animals, especially no rectifications: who domesticates whom? do humans domesticate animals, or do animals domesticate humans? An open question. Today I finally see the intellectual blackhead that blinded me for so many years: man domesticates the animal in order to get rid of *something* <add = X> that horrifies him! The wild animal that sleeps within! The smooth-skinned dragon that he conceals beneath his eyes of a domesticated animal! The little pig that dreams beside the window! *Man assholifying the animal in order to domesticate himself!* It's the same old story! The same compulsion to domesticate! The homilies of the void! *Erasure of all historical allusions!* Erase everything! Slay everything! Contempt for everyone! Abjure everything! The writer who francophonizes with literature has become a domestic animal, he has finally been domesticated! *Homo homini domesticus! L'homme est un domestique pour l'homme!*

Notae in Programma while they are ramadaning, I'm fallowing; while they're stuttering *I'm stammering! Stamphering! A lifelong enemy of all forms of psychology, of all sociology, of all cosmology, of all bestiology, I really don't understand a thing and would not be who I am if I began to understand what they're about; but I'll continue suppressing everything I need to show off my competence, on this point a competence or an incompetence.*
   Surely animals are always getting me dirty and they bother me with their abject ways that can only be gratified when they piss on my muddy turf!

<*La fin de la vie, c'est un bouquet* (in plain French)> presently the *soi-disant* narrator is talking with Yackoff and tells him how much he admires the paintings of his compatriot Marc Chagall: *Oh, yes! Chagall! surely, Chagall forever!* Chagall gave me the idea for the little story I am writing for my younger son, it's called *For Algeria, for the Mules, and for the Others,* and I've based it on the title of Chagall's painting: *For Russia, for Mules, and for Others,* do you know it? *Like Chagall, I want to surprise this*

world in the unmoving eye of the bull! Here Algeria would see its life flickering within!
A reducing glass of pain, a heavy destiny of rain without the voices of the wine harvests!
—You're talking about gold and blue, friend! I was unaware that you have this talent, my honorable neighbor of Abyssinia!
—*Just a quote, Alas, just a little quote, my dear Yackoff!* a little eccentric deduction off the top of my head! What many people haven't noticed, Yackoff, is that this painting was finished *before* the great revolution of October 1917, and I just read an idiotic article by someone who *saw* in this painting a *critique* of the Soviet Revolution, *a pictorial tract* <O mule! O mule!> against *totalitarian rule!* a plea to return to the old Russia of the czars, but that's a pure anachronism! How could Chagall have made a critique of the revolution before it ever took place! Sure, he was clearly a visionary, but how does he go from there to the mule! *from there to the mule!* dear Yackoff?! Chagall was *for* the revolution! Damn it, look at his reds! The pure tone of Chagall's *magical reds!* The pure tone of Chagall's *magical blues!* Chagall was betrayed by the Revolution, Yackoff! *It's the other way around! Just the opposite, dear Yackoff!* This painting was done in 1911 and is now on display in the Museum of Modern Art of Paris at Beaubourg! If you ever go to Paris I advise you to go and see it, neighbor Yackoff! It's a real masterpiece, comrade friend Yackoff! It has lots to say to someone in transplants and transplantations! *Didactic, dialectic, tic, tic, and toc! A peasant with a pointed hat gesticulates and pushes forward a little mule loaded with smooth goatskins filled with wine: Don't you see?* Mules are everywhere! Even the greatest writers can't get along without them! They much prefer the company of mules to humans. That's a calming thought! Nothing could be better to keep you company! A very calming thought! Why not? *The mule had the most delicate of all possible souls, he even found a footing to show how delicate it was!*
Yackoff: Spassiba! Vava, did you hear that? Did you hear what the Professor is saying? My friend, you're speaking with *enthusiasm* about the revolution! With a lot of enthusiasm! You seem to know what a revolution is all about! That's very interesting! Did you ever know it from the inside? Did you ever rub up against one, or are you satisfied merely by *imagining* the revolution?
<Elya: *In enthusiasm there is in sum mi-ass. Les révolutions sont criblées de (plain English) half-assed jackasses!*>

A measured defection of the sentence, the homunculus is made with the irony of the sentence, little by little the homunculus is made through the treason of the master's sentence, he knows well he has to go out and find the criminal sentence that wanders at large, but the wimp looks pitiful in front of the sentence that laughs in his face. The longer the sentence extends, the more the wimp feels hurt, because the sentence offends him, then folds into two, then into four, twelve, forty-three pieces, the sentence *crumples* him up, the sentence without a figure, the sentence without a body reduces him to nothing. The more the sentence unfolds, the more the wimp hunches up, the more the sentence gets rowdy, the more the wimp gets hoarse, *like a muscle without a bone! Clearly there can't be a real crime without the evidence of a piece of bone!* Now there, maybe that's the master's secret: he has created a sentence without blood, a simple sentence that *kills* all pretension! A criminal sentence! *The last supreme anguish, the supreme fatigue, the supreme loss, the supreme void, that's me!* Nothing of that order in the dormitory of Algerian literature, a very long corridor of boredom protects it from candidates, many candidates, and very few elected writers! A great dormitory, a great soporitory, a great yawnitory! Sodom and Gomorrah revisited! *Francophony, you're getting more!*

The '80s, the quatre vingt, *in bold text!*
Algiers, *springtime activities:*
they have caught another Algerian writer in misdemeanor of writing, on our territory, you see dear emissary of liberties, in our country writing is a misdemeanor, we amputate the hands of burglars and petty thieves and it clearly follows that the tongue will be cut out and the writing hand—left or right—will be cut off, according to public opinion, of those who transgress this taboo! That's our way of showing that we are the last human beings who really take literature seriously! Do you understand? It makes writers responsible for their actions! Before they start scribbling they'd better reflect twice on what they're doing!

Haul up the verb, you construction workers! Now let's be frank and honest about these matters, earnest Madame Johnson had stated, *Let us be honest about it!* good Martha Johnson repeated to everyone who wanted to hear. This house is the *healthiest* of the neighborhood, it is erected on solid ground, its foundation has been built with reinforced *concrete.* When my poor Lewis undertook building this house, it was on the most *concrete* foundation that he wanted to have this house constructed, a house that I never would have sold if my poor mother had not just recently passed away, she died barely a week ago and now everything seems so empty to me. She gave her soul to God just a week ago, and since then I feel completely alone in the world, but you will see how happy you will be in Mr. Radmer's house. You will see how much the house will make you happy, and you will be happy because it is a house that was built by a man who was happy to build it for the wife and children he loved. You will be happy because this house was conceived by a man who really knew what happiness is all about, besides, that's why he always used to say to Marie, your future neighbor, *I am building my dream house*, he used to say, *my house of happiness, a house that has been conceived for people who know what happiness is all about <les gens qui savent ce que c'est que le bonheur>*. That was his formula, yes, that's it, a little slogan that doesn't sound like much, but that's worth its weight in gold, and then all this happiness slipped through our fingers, all this happiness has vanished <she means *tout ce bonheur s'est évanoui!*> we used to be right here, right on this sunny porch, we were smiling at the first lilacs of spring when he complained of a little pain, right there, right by his heart, and then he went to lie down on the sofa, and when I came back with a glass of iced tea, he had already left us. Life is so precious, God only knows how precious life is, he left us without even being able to say good-bye, <he left us without a good-bye kiss!> he left without our telling him how grateful we were to him for having dedicated so much of his life to making us happy, yes, without saying a thing, just like that, as if nothing had ever passed! But now I'm getting distracted again, said Martha Johnson, here I am, letting myself tell you stories that you probably don't even care about, Mister Redmer, you probably have enough worries of your own and here a driveling old lady is heaping her problems on you. I was saying then that this house was a solid perfection, it was solid and honest, a house built on concrete, a house the way they don't make them anymore, but you should know, Mister Bensmaïer, you ought to know, and I'll be very honest with you, that some parts of the house are *unfinished*, there are two or three little things that my dear Lewis didn't have time to complete. Take, for example, the stairs at the entry, did you see something odd when you went in? Well, the stairs at the entry aren't *finished*. My dear Lewis poured the two squares of cement at the base of the front door entry, but he didn't have the time to build the *deck* that was going to hide them from view, so as you have probably seen, you can't go into this house without passing by two big slabs of concrete that look unsightly, the first thing that you see when you want to enter this beautiful house are the two big slabs of poured concrete that are a little bit of an eyesore. You know, it wouldn't be as bad if we were living in California or in Florida, but in Minneapolis, in a city where it snows more than half of the year, in a state where at a moment's notice rain can turn into sleet, when, big slabs like these, they are a crime, concrete slabs as smooth and slippery as those might bring you into court for liability, anybody can come by and break his back, which means that anybody could sue you, <*anybody could sue you*> Mister Armada! I should have closed my eyes, I could have pretended not to see anything, as if I saw nothing, heard nothing, knew nothing, but in memory of my poor Lewis, for his memory and in memory of him, that is something I could never bear to do! I could never do a thing like that, I would never have done it if I knew he were still living, he would never have left anything as ugly as them in full view. I know that he would have *willingly* finished the work on his own, I know that he would have happily finished whatever he had begun, in honesty, for the love of doing right, for this love to see things get done the way they should, so I am persuaded that you too, Mister Rmada, you're also among those people who like to see things done right, I am convinced, I immediately saw that you were among the kind of people who like things to get finished, I saw it in your face, I saw it in your eyes, I saw it *written* on your forehead, in the distance between your eyes, a distance that has a *largesse*, of view, yes, of view about it, and at the same time a very great intellectual acuity and a very exacting sense of good craftsmanship.

Already, well before the debacle, to write: for me it seemed plausible, I thought it right to be encloistered under lock and key in a basement, a subterranean tunnel, a tower, an old apartment in the city of A* *<no more, no less, Adèle, Juré>* get a padlock and be assured that the hinges are tight and sealed. The mania of enclosure *<Saha! Saha! so that's the way it was!>* lasted entire years, I felt wrapped and caulked like *Beuys* in a woolen and felt cage in order to get the clandestine merchandise out, *trabendo, trabendiquement.* The hardest part was not so much finding *what to say* as finding the *form* that would allow the sulfur jaundice of our black thoughts to be *inhaled, no rectification!*

List of <formal> difficulties: (1) *proper* names: what name can be given to the enervating red color of the flower of the Bougainvilleas of Blida in springtime? A *rogue* red such as Francisco suggests (the other, the sacrilegious poet of the *Nioques de Printemps* and other *spongiatures*), or *blidique* red, *<bleeding Red>*? What name can be given to the odors that waft from the toilets of Tabarin? *Arabic Foehn* or *Fun odiférant?* etc.) (*prudently, I began by naming things all over again, giving them the renown they merited*) (*I will return to this: for this is surely a machine that has to be assembled and taken apart*); (2) learn not to be afraid of words that resonate in a kind of oblique way: Mahcound, Gabriel, Hamid, Humid, Aurora, Gégène <something ungentle, something annoying that a certain part of the world's population feels when they face *Generals*>, Angoulevant, Avunculaire, *Kadjeglegjen*, etc., and give to these energumen words a new and fitting definition; (3) determine exactly who are the recipients of our cataracts <Greek, *Kataraktês*, "fall">: the People? (What People?) O un Amy? A mistress *<add: former>* the President? the Party? *<add: unique!>* Mommy? God? *Tel Quel?* Paul Valéry? Lukács? Father Engels? The Abbot Oration or Marx? Et cetera.

I therefore decided from now on to write only under the injunction of a *Stimmung* (acute toothache, fear, anguish, sickness, H, rage, black holes, abulia, priapism, etc.) in order not to lose the connecting theme of *(appropriate articles)*: idea, fear, anguish, sexual desire, conviction, affect, pruritus, pain, hope, priapism, <and especially priapism>, etc. I soon began to write *without rectifying* and, for once, things started to *take form* without my having to experience the least the slight hic hesitations fear cup cough, that time I could go without delay *hic* to the end of the alley, *hic;* (4) determine what, in the current conjuncture <*with what delight we pronounce this substantive!*> was most apt to give an idea of the situation in which we had gotten all bound up *(semicolon);* (5) put into a second category of importance the typographic, graphic, mirific aspects of the quadrature of the book: I had repeated it to myself more than a thousand times, Macha never tired of reminding me about it: *You're not made to tell stories, what you need, is ... (but she stopped there):* it was understood, yes, that was enough! Short pieces of writing with networks of lines cut by knives illness native lands mousetraps ravines labyrinths corridors lairs knots where my body might finally find a toga fitting its nerves and stand up remain seated lie down make a half turn stay put okay for 5 *(re-semicolon);* (6) and even if the text doesn't get finished, *I have 8 armies, 9 energumens, 1 ton of opium, 1 ton of cocaine, 1 ton of heroin, goods, cold alcohol, hot cereal, manioc, sesame <add: open>, mushrooms, chestnuts! Why do you, you leaning towers of jelly, want the answer to be a characterization and that a point cannot be, that it might first of all have been an object? I might cause myself harm, and that's it!* <*O just, subtle, and powerful opium! ... you hold the keys to Paradise ... >;* (7) then, space (but don't make a mountain out of a molehill of space): it can be cut, pruned, recomposed, *cut and pasted*, skipped over, sliced, put forward, selected, played with a pinball machine, be censured, be precious, gallant, elliptical, anacoluthonithic, metaphorific, metonymythic, *after all* (things [seem] to be done always the way they had been); (8) accord oneself a reader (preferably a woman reader) ideal, a <type> (a <typesse>: kind: Arno Schmidt's she-wolf: <Käte> for example, and after which: *ket! Ket! Kztl!*), *a fauness that would have suffered the same sickness, the same fears,* the same nervous system, it would suffice that he or she returns: as story, vector, end, parousia, anemia, *erotion, jubeluption, adherage, loukoumade, mucilage, collusion mouth-sex, tongue-brain!* (9) get into the rhythm of the *Spiritual Automaton!* Let it purr! Let it spread jaundice to everyone who holds poetry in contempt! *(But all the same go to the point of claiming that the Sheik Rimbaud is French!* What nerve! What lack of perspicacity! What bad taste! Ah! Gide, for example, *he's French, and how!)*, <<Go back over everything in me that is *French*>>

ADIAphoria: to become the bearer, the exclusive (?) importer of rancor and spite that have really taken their place in the *immediate present!* Smoke rings of Virginia tobacco that tickle my nose while I scribble my lines! *Great aspirations* of wisps of smoke! Great expectations sent to the winds! An *assassinating* mood this morning! Gray crosshatchings everywhere in the sky that look like clouds of ashes, *no rectifications!*

(another difficulty) The choice of verbs: how can an action be expressed that consists in smoking while the hangman pulls the noose down over your neck? How? *Write as if you were giving your reader a pain in the neck!*
Think of (an open list), (10) the *frame* of the action: a farm, a dormitory, a cheap apartment building, a classroom, an editing room, a subway corridor, an express train, a bed-and-breakfast, a California campus (an abundance of choices finished, *A choppy sea, the Wind from the East is at gale force!*); (11) the *narrative structure:* striated, crosshatched, kissyfaced <pretty sharp, eh!>, beveled, refined, hybrid, lacunary, partitive, programmed, scurrilous <now and again>, utriculary; (12) the *montage?* Montaignian! From one pickup really to the next! From one *tertre* to the next (so the critic can *thumb his nose* at Proust and at Antonin the Mômo on my nose!).

Pass Go, Baltic and Mediterranean and go directly to the next Rome, pummel the verb, send signals of every kind to an unknown recipient, a recipient who doesn't want to *decline* an identity: copies, doubles, rubbings, maps, decalc*omanias*, moltings, mutations, mutisms, mimeticism (the Snake sheds its hard, *compact* skin and slithers back into the crannies between the Rocks), fake passport, bogus *identity photograph*, a forged signature.

At noon I'm back home. It was a furnace outside. I turned on the radio, plugged in the refrigerator, and I waited. A whole day passed in limbo. I couldn't get a handle on what was going on (or by): the smell of wilted flowers in the little blue vase, the smell of the lilacs, the smell of my thoughts, the smell of books, the smell of mothballs that wafted from the mirrored closet in the hallway. The mountain of winter garments that had to be recycled. A heap of anguish had to be sorted through. Ready to leave:
—Your body is now naked. You can look at yourself in the mirror. Are you the one I am seeing?
— ...
—I see that your body has a history, that your body *is* a history, everything is a history, my dear friend, our common history, that belongs to us, you and me, Macha! Just you and me! On your belly the scar of your case of shingles, the sacred fire (in

that way the souls of the damned console themselves for dying little by little); I have *two* scars on *my* belly: a cesarean for Hams, a tubal ligation for Djams! O, you're goddamned loathsome! And then, present, in order not to be outdone, your *infamous* **Dead Letters!** That's the last straw! I warned you! I begged you to leave these satanic sheets in the drawer! But *Monsieur* wanted to show his contemporaries what he was so capable of doing! *I can't stand you!*

—There is nothing *satanic* about my *Dead Letters!* There wasn't an iota of satanism in the letters in general! Satan is the body and soul and spirit and sex of people who don't know how to read! Satan is brought back to life every time a nation starts to act like a censor! Satan is reborn of his ashes every time a nation wants the body of a writer *dead or alive!* No matter what writer! I *am* this writer! In the name of the God of God of God I am this writer! I'm just anybody!

—Not anymore! It's because of your vanity! Your overblown vanity as a writer and the pride you take in being a *subaltern!*

—Former teachers and generals are the ones who created subalterns, the noncoms, the underlings, the flunky servants, the corporals, the courtesans! It's high time that a subaltern stopped writing like a courtesan! What, ex-colonial *Vanity! Arrogance* of a subaltern! Arabic *pride!* It all stinks, Macha! Neocolonialism will have to pass! Obscurantism will have to be eradicated! *<I realize that enlightened readers can go ahead without detailed explanation, but there still exists an undocile kind of censor who, armed for the duration of his whole life with a single book, understands nothing of its contents, and in front of whom the most important developments are not at all superfluous!>*[9]

(Think of the moist warmth of their bodies entwined, they're *burning* to make love. *Ahem! Ahem! Hey kids!*)

This time I find myself in the disorder most productive for poetic creation, but what would Macha think of all this chaos? *What would she think of my infinite solitude?* What would she think of all this ravioli I'm making every evening as I wait for the six o'clock news? What would she think of my story, *For Algeria, for the Mules, and for the Others?* I can hear her now, *Caro, you're incorrigible, you claim to admonish literature and here you are admonished by literature.* **Verdict:** Guilty. **Incriminating Motive:** Overdose of literature, contraband of literature of all kinds, smuggling of literature! Tracts, political libel, pamphlets, criticism of the League of Nations, criticism of the United Nations, criticism of democracy, criticism of *Literary Moralities*, criticism of literary immorality, criticism of literary im*lk*ortality, *no rectifications!* criticism of literary cynicism, criticism of literary *genre*, criticism of literary *religiosity!* **Sentence:** *Exile for life!*

---

[9]Kierkegaard? *Wrong!* Kant in his *Essay on the Introduction of the Concept of Negative Grandeur.*

So you claim that you enjoy literature? that you believe in literature? Go and practice it somewhere else! Take your *crape* [sic] somewhere else! As if we still had to be meddling with literature! A *crass* ignorance of spolioligature! You are *envisioning* the dead end! Can you see it before your eyes? *To see tragic literature sink and be able to laugh it off, it's all the more divine in view of the respect and esteem that are owed to it!*

I am *halted* in front of page 132, the master's most redoubtable page, which has crushed me flat as a pancake. I presently know and hear it by heart, I can recite it without stumbling, I think I can begin to understand it, I can thus begin to stuff the fireplace with the manuscripts of the first campaigns I led against myself, I can stuff the fireplace with the disorder of my thoughts, I'm in the chaos left by Macha in my life of a failed musician, I am somewhere on the wasteland left by the assassination of the *Pharaoh*.

<*Algeria in stagnation!*>

The first box burns with an ease that makes me shiver with delight, look how they burn so high, look how they crackle, *the pages, the pages*, that were so hard to engender, so easy to annihilate, so lovely to conceive, so ugly to conserve! At least they'll have warmed my body! For months on end! A heap of hopes! A semitrailer of ideas! I currently have written enough to heat the house for the cold winter predicted to come, I think my body is warm and my heart is cold, yes, the body heated and the heart frozen in the desert of the trees of Algiers, the heart frozen on the Avenue Daumesnil <*impossible to open the window! impossible to see the sky! impossible to see the daylight, it's utterly impossible!*> the cold heart in the desert of Minneapolis streets, the cold heart in Golden Valley. Therefore I can *remain seated in front of a fire in the most protected room of the house and suddenly feel the clutches of death. It reaches out of the fire, all the sharp angles of the objects in the room are pointing their fingers at me, in weights in the mass of the roof and walls above and around, it's in the water, in the snow, in the heat, and in my blood,* **<sure, sure, our need to consolidate is <decidedly> impossible to satisfy, Mr. Dagerman!>** *a ream of paper consumes a Sequoia sempervirens, Monsieur Writer (in plain English), better watch what you're doing! Acres of shit! Better to plant a tree than let this bunch blacken reams of paper with their logorrhea and literary dysentery!*

She was frightened when she saw the liberty I had taken with the *facts: you state that in 1966 you were a student in the College of Liberal Arts at Algiers, but at that time you were enrolled in a UEC at the Château of Morgues-les-Gonesses, you say that you majored in theology when you never even stuck your nose in any serious book of theology; a Schleiermacher never reached the heavens of theology and Schelling even less! You say that in*

1985 you and Macha were separated when at that time you were moving into your apartment at 21 Avenue Daumesnil, the avenue of depression! A flagrant delight of invention, enough to revoke your poetic license! You say that on August 1, 1979, you spent a whole night dressing the corpse of the neighbor's husband on the Rue Roulegon in Aix-en-Provence when in reality you were on your way to San Francisco by way of Bangor . . . !

I utter in paraphrasing the master: *my book is what is important, it's not the Algerian Evening News,* **Le Monde,** *or* **Le Débat!**

She replies: Your head is stuffed to the gills with references and pseudohistorical facts that have nothing to do with *national realities,* you're nothing more than a little compiler that renegades are made of Law *<and more sternly>*: *critics* like you are what they use to make all our ideological molasses and political confusion! Where do you *place yourself* in all that? What *area* are you talking about? These are the ingredients that are used to make (in plain English) *cop-outs! <Why do you torture me with* **English words?***>*

I said: *no heresy is hard pressed for justifying dates!* And I was telling you thus that one day, *in the heart of the Broceliande forest,* there was a little mule, *no rectification,* who was living *fi rayet ma yakoun,*[10] he loved to *sine,* he love to *doze,* he loved to *kane* with the other mules of the very large and very mysterious forest of his ancestors *<Hum! Mum! Good Lord!>,* when he met a mule from Mount Chenoua he did not fail to wave and say hello to him and ask about Old Keblout, when he met a mule from the Kalââ of the Beni-Hammed, he never failed to make a curtsy according to the Aklide rite and puff his cheeks up with the good air of the sulfurs of Nadhor and, beating his clogs like cymbals, expressing to him the formula of the four fraternal salutes in the double Akla language:

Remôr! Mortiuri! Kalôr and Râni! Ya 'Abdelghani!
And 'Abdelghani to play him the old refrain of villainies!
And 'Abdelmoumen to sing him the old sommelier's song!
And 'Abdelmoutalleb to tell him the old secret of secretions!
And 'Abdelkhalid to offer him the old scepter of skepticism!
And 'Abdelkader to reveal to him the old doctrinaires' doctrine!
And 'Abdelhamid to invite him to the old castle of the enchanted souls!

Djams was enchanted. The *repetition* of the formula sent him into the greatest joy!
—Eh Pops? What did Habel do with the scepter? What do you do with a scepter of skepticism?
—My son, you defend yourself from doctrines and doctrinaires!

---

[10]*I.e., as happy as a lark!*

—So what about the old song?
—Armed with the scepter, you can do it all over again!
—Armed with the violin of villainies, you can do an elegy or a drama! Sometimes even an Opera!
—What about the castle? and the secret?
—My son, I'm not a big bagful of explanations! After all, this is only a story! But you're learning quickly, and that brings great joy to me!

<*The spirit that lives in him snoozes often and for long periods of time, it curls up, woozy, under the covers of the* dead letter; *but he always wakes up over and over again when the unpredictable weather of the spiritual world favors his return to life and gets his sap moving, something that will happen again*> (extract of the reading that Macha interrupted when she came into the room. The little book of the *Maker* of discourse on religion *for those who hold him in contempt who comprise cultivated minds* that I had in my hands placed it *outside of herself!* The *Macher* in question was stuck in her throat! The *Maker* in question was weighing on her heart!
—What do you mean, Chlayer how?
—Schleiermacher! Schleiermacher!
—My friend, since when have you gotten interested in Christian theology?
—Since Salman Rushdie's condemnation, my dear lady!
—Now really, what's the connection?
—Immanent! Tragic!
—Imminent! Tragic! <*in her anger she wears a Medusa's mask!*>
—I said: <*Immanent*> *and tragic! Tragic because of immanence! For once we're not going to look for a foreign element in the enemy's bazaar! The worm is in the fruit!*
She was confusing the *Maker* with the Dragon Slayer)!

There we were paralyzed: I'm sorry for what I said, I should have shut up, I should have drowned my head under water, she's sorry for what she said, but *even more sternly, she fires away:* and besides, the masters you've chosen are a bunch of nerds! and phallocrats! faschocrats too! They've got nothing to do with *reality!* Wake up, dear, the world's not going to stop and wait for you forever! And let me tell you: *you're not the only one in the world who has been afraid! you're not the only one!*

At the other end of memory, over there, in the blue Country. In N*'s prolonged gaze, in the depths of her chestnut and hazel eyes, at the other end of time, *no rectifications!*, I can see the roof of a mosque painted in green and white lime and four white minarets, four missiles carrying warheads of hate and fear, four missiles that will never be fired, four missiles carrying payloads of violence and ignorance that are ready to fire off, but that remain planted there, immobile for the rest of time, the minarets go off, Madame, the minarets, no, but we, we are the ones who go off, *Cape Catastrophe!*

If everything is so desperately closed, then why so many ridiculous curtsies? If everything is so desperately dismal, then why are you so calm and collected? If you think they're treating you like a dog, then why do you act and look like a dog?

Swan Cemetery: I hang suspended, as if *arrested* over the grave that was freshly dug, all around it a large carpet of astroturf, with four flowerpots, azaleas, I think, azaleas and chrysanthemums, with four armchairs in the first row, for the deceased's nearest of kin, then four armchairs in a second row, for the friends of the defunct and his family, there is the winch and pulley that will *effortlessly* lower the coffin to its final destination, because if there are any squeaks or jolts during the final descent, there's also a chrome railing erected up to the level of my knees.
The Crank-man: Do you think there will be any jolts or squeaks, *Mister Professor?* Do you think it'll be hard to get the coffin down without a squeak? Think of what a *faux-pas* or a *false movement* would cause during the descent! The dead have to be lowered into the netherworld in calm and serenity, the dead have to reach their final resting place *without a jolt*, states the political sacristan, our specialty is burial *with ease;* we have counted more than two thousand, three hundred descents *ad patrem* without the slightest hitch, and the dead are grateful to us! To die in silence is to die in beauty! To die in beauty is to die without leaving a trace and without uttering a word! That's what's beautiful in the funerals that we make!
There is the high surrounding wall of the cemetery, the wall that hides the cemetery from the environs where I live, and there is a real lawn in between. *What's the difference?* In the *real* cemetery, there is astroturf, but in the *fake* environs, there is a real lawn whose green won't fool you, my lawn in no way *looks like* the cemetery lawn, there are too many dandelions that give it the color of the lawn of a fake cemetery *even on rainy days*, but one thing is sure for now: *I'll be sent packing, bashed with insults, chased out of the cemetery! Already my father didn't make it*, no rectification, at *Sidi M'hamed, our Père-Lachaise, my dear! They erased his Turkish name, they vaporized his name in Algeria in its prayers, our father Destouches who art in heaven, please write for us! He was still a good Muslim!*

No matter what you're doing, your soul is unraveling,
no matter what you're doing, your head is cracking, so go take a walk in the ceme-

tery on a rainy day, that'll get me back to my wits, I'm reduced to this extreme pain, limited to this *expedient,*

give a cemetery for my thoughts! the seed from the weed! *le bon grain et l'ivresse!* At the rate things are going, my thoughts will soon be turned inside out! The little book is going, it's rolling along! *Thot, Thot! Tchoufa!* It's rolling at your expense! *Thot! Thot et Tchoufa!*

Dico: *A cemetery for your thoughts!*

I don't have any ancestors in this cemetery, no friends in this cemetery, but here's where I drag my thoughts to get them out of their torpor, to get them out of their *apathy.*

My thoughts are killing me, I drag them over to the cemetery, my thoughts scoff at me, I stick their nose down into the grave, my thoughts escape me, I make them take a trip around the dead, my thoughts stop when I begin to slow down, at the slightest hesitation I agonize, *an empty pumpkin! a fat and squat pumpkin that rings hollow!*

We go back home on a bicycle, my thoughts and I, and they weigh as much as all the stones of the containing wall.

Along our way we meet <the great Lady in black> she disdains us, she doesn't even wave to acknowledge us, the dead bitch! She won't have anything to do with us, she doesn't even *desire* us anymore, and we would even be led to believe she didn't even see us! (in plain English) *She doesn't even seem to have noticed our presence!* We must be her ghosts! It's not she who is haunting us! It is we who are dancing a *pow-wow* around the learned goddess! We would be led to believe *that she couldn't care less* about our being! <*There's a sentence that ought to enrage the envious and the professional linguists!*> We leave her in her *indifference* behind the containing wall, behind the wall where we are all *buried alive,* but today I know that Minneapolis-U.S.A. is the great cemetery of the modern living dead, I know that Charlottesville-U.S.A. is the great dormitory of moderns in exile, I know that Washington-*DCeased* is the great mortuary of the modern living dead, and for that reason I have been sent here, they sent me here to bury *me* alive, in Minneapolis, Minnehaha, *the river that goes haha! the river that laughs at death! The city that commits Harakiri! No rectifications!*

For mules and for others, this debris of old castles, for mules, the bits and pieces of old stone, these memories of a person in agony of death,
for the moment, **I am nothing, I know nothing,**

but I will not be perpetually cornered,
thrown to the bottom of the wall,
there is neither wall nor corner;
I don't believe it.
There is myself,
the builder of thick coffins of life! <unheimlich, isn't it?>
and for the others, these stammerings of a mule skinned alive, and for the others,
these shards of old clothing and to Algeria all the chaos of my thoughts,

e agony
a Agon
i 'Agoun
o 'franconia
u agôgôs!

His mumbling woke him up with a start, **do I really have to attain the Norm?** *Will I ever get to the Norm? Then upon his lips that were* **stuttering** *were delicately placed a pair of cool hands. Monsieur Mrad, I beg of you, please be calm, collect yourself, everyone is sleeping here, Nora happened to be kneeling next to him, her chestnut and hazel eyes, no rectifications! wide open, bloodshot for lack of sleep. She caressed his face, you're beautiful, melancholic, and pale; when you recover from this horrible fever we'll go off together, we'll leave this awful city and we'll go to Spain, yes, we'll go to Valencia, to Jenaro's, and when you're better, then we'll go on from there, but for now let your burning head rest in my hands and try to sleep a little.*

Every one of his daydreams that followed was as lousy as the one before, for as long as he never left Algiers, he would always be sick, that was it, he knew well, it was this accursed city, Algiers, Algiers, his bête noire, he now knew, he knew that the city had provoked his migraines, the terrible headaches that clenched his temples in a vise every time he tried to open his eyes to the surrounding reality, he knew that this city had turned him into this hybrid creature, half-dog and half-goat, this creature so hard of thinking that it thirsted for death and dark tobacco! *Cut!*

Macha: What are you doing over there, right when you're piling up your boxes, c'mon, get your sentences together! Pack up your precious quotations! Your precious words! When you construct them, when you take them out, when you suck them through your teeth, I can imagine what's going on inside! *<she plants her index finger on the narrator's forehead!>* For once could you *simply* tell me what's going on?
—It's not normal, it's not aesthetic, it's not even political! I am trying to pay homage!

Yes, *with humility,* to pay homage to Antonin the Mômo, my companion in exile! My clandestine *paredre!* The aborted fetus of French ligature! And if you continue to badger me like that, *I'm going to go crazy! I'll chimneysweep the consortium of hybrid beings that bridle my thinking!*
ra la vèze
katedu
kaledun!

Plain Text, no one could ever imagine a night so black, a street so empty, a soul so solitary, a shriek so terrifying, a death rattle so poignant, a word so disordered, a body so tortured. The city is giving birth to my cerebral death, I feel my head airing out its atoms of the great state, I feel my head airing out its atoms of literary opium, and I expose my bare skull to the healing rain, I expose the skin of my wounded soul to the raindrops of oblivion, every passing hour, and *why did I continue to count in hours?* Why, my son, why count in hours and months since I don't *need* to exist anymore? since I'm not *supposed* to exist any more?! since I am *deprived of time!* since I have *no right to time!* I give my bare hands to the rage of the past, and we are decimated, we are a nation in mourning, but no one is yet aware, and that is why, my son, that is the only reason why I would like to tell to you once more the story of Algeria, the story of its mule and of others, that is why it is my duty to tell you, before I die and disappear forever, I must tell you the story of the mules that were sold at the marketplace of the sacred story, and the history of these Algerians who were sold at the marketplace of the *storybook slum! The time is ripe to collect them as monuments remaining from the primitive world, and to deposit them in the warehouses of history; their life has ended and will never begin again*
(who, meanwhile, has *made off* with time? who has claimed time as private property? the exclusive property of a *limited* mind?)
(who, meanwhile, has *made off* with Islam? who has claimed Islam as private property, the private property of a *stillborn* mind?)
(who, meanwhile, has *made off* with history? who has claimed history as private property, the private property of an *enslaved* mind?) *<Very pleasing, don't you think? In plain English I could go on doing this for more than a hundred pages! All modern vanity would pass through the grinder!>*

They were reproached for *loving* disorder and strong odors, they were reproached for having a taste for stinking things <all the same, it's thanks to them that on a bright day in July 1988 they didn't like garlic! Gee!> So what were they really reproached for? For dressing like slobs? For being faggots? For being *mal fagotés?* For being listless and lazy, for not working like the rest of the world, is that why they were being reproached? For being *the bad consciences* of oblivion: *as long as they keep prowling around we'll never be able to forget what they did to our cities and our women! I thought we could make a pact with them, but since I've seen the state of their teeth, I know it would be impossible! Impossible to cut a deal with them! Impossible to fraternize with them! They're not enough like us, my dear lady! Their teeth completely rotted by hash and Mary Jane! They're all assassins! Look what they've done with Algiers! Look at what they've done with their country! I'd like to forget the Vel d'Hiv once and for all! Their presence alone makes it impossible to get them out of my mind!*

<Hashish at noon: the shadows are a bridge over the river of light flowing in the street> W.B.   (Mo, 6, 850)
@ *the art of getting to the bottom when one reads and writes. Those who know how to draft things in the most superficial ways are the best writers*   (Ibid., 8, 850)>

At present everything has to be rescued from disaster, everything has to be consigned to disaster in my house-and-coffin: the consul is a worthy man and his compassion is ostensibly sincere: we understand full well the nature of your *predicament:* a very harsh climate, a foreign language, belligerent or indifferent neighbors, an inhuman solitude, et cetera, but we are currently unable to change the scenery of your situation: but why are you so obstinately refusing our offer to provide you with a domesticated animal? You are, as they say, stubborn as a mule. All the same, grass is not what is lacking in that country!

Scholium # 6: *While we watch the grass is growing! Seren K.K.K. Serein Kierkegaard! Serein Kierkegaard! Serein Kiergegaard! Ever seen that in the history of fifisophy! And there we are in a pretty pickle!*

And in boring me, the editor: in your last piece of writing you use too many *scatological* terms, *too many exclamation points! too many ellipses!* I could have torn my hair out when, *not once, your honor, not once, I made sure it wouldn't happen!,* he insists: then how do you explain why the *Guardian* and, oh! yes! well! well! For the *New York Times Book Review* you take the cake! *The most scatological writer since Rabelais!* and the narrator chuckles: kiki, cacke, cocoa, culcul, cacomanie, Your Honor, but never caca, only capital letters! SNCF! Et cetera! *What do you have to say for yourself! The most blasphemous book of the past decade! One blasphemy per page!* But it's in the *dreams and nightmares* of my character, Your Honor! Don't these scribbling mutthounds know how to *read between the lines!* They can't catch what's really going on! Their way of burying me, their way of sociologizing me, their satrap way of *intertextualizing is aberrant, Your Honor,* their underhanded way of frightening the widows and orphans of French and Maghrebian literature! Their way of turning everything to mush! Aphasia makers! Mind fornicators! Francophone pimps! They whore around with concepts! Fancifiers of sensible ideas! Asskissers! Fomenters of mental stress! They scorn all thinking! The mind under the influence, this pure surface of anal mental projection, the *anxiety of influence,* that's what they call it, Your Honor, to end up in the critichism, yes, the *écritchure* of state monopolies and private property! It's a mix of Chombard de Lowe and Rémy de Gourmont! Céline stuffed with pralines! Some Kateb Yacine stirred into Arab crude! Some Mômo with Chocolindon! The mad Elsa with a little Bassani! Some Saint-Bernhard with garlic and onions! Some Rushdie and cauliflower à la merdre! Some couscous sprinkled with Apollinaire, some kémia with Musil sauce, tahini with Aragon, some Rûmi over head cheese! Meddeb à l'américaine! Jebran Khalil Jebran with henna! Lobster with Jean-Sole Tartar sauce, pepper stuffed with Farès and rice, Sollers with turpentine, *in other words, a little Rimbaud à l'armoricanine, say wha'cha wanna say, Your Honor, you tell me whatever you want and a whole lot more!*

Scholium # 7: *What was it that motivated the author of the Study of Mores when he put into living print, in his work of imagination, all the notable characters of his time? First of all for his pleasure, clearly ... that explains his descriptions. We need to find another reason in the* direct quotations *and evidence shows that publicity was camouflaged in the writing. Balzac was one of the first to have fathomed the power of hidden advertising. In our day ... newspapers were unaware of its force ... Midnight had hardly chimed when the workers finished the layout; the headline people were just slipping a few lines at the bottom of a column for Regnault noodles or the Brazilian Mixture. Echo advertising was unknown. Even less known was the ingenious procedure of quotation within a novel ...* (H. Clouzot and R.-H. Valensi, *Le Paris de la "Comédie humaine"* [Paris 1926]).

And no sooner: the clergy, the clerical class: *it became a mania:* every time a representative of the official clergy of state came to visit him it was for the purpose of launching a little sermon about the *insane* nature of his refusal to keep a domesticated animal! The consul was persuaded that the neighbors had become suspicious because the narrator never invited company over to the house, and that a furry animal would be sufficient enough for all of his needs! <while you're at it why not a

parakeet, Monsieur le Consul? Or a goat?> The answer of the triple Consul: *You can't be serious! You're not a good militant! You're not a good patriot! You're not a good Muslim! If you owned a small domesticated animal there would be a lot more compassion in your writings! Just a little animal! For example, a little dog!*
<Conclusion (in plain English): *Too coarse to be tamed!* Too *hardened* to be domesticated. This dog can't be taught new tricks!>

The Messiah <*a coded message originating from the Nerve-zone*> was stopped on page 132 of the single book, an unsurpassable page, a page whose immobility makes me suffocate! *Return of the migraines!* I've been writing in my blue notebook for months on end, for months I've been making my hen scratches, *no rectification*, scribbling and dribbling in the blue notebook, and the Automaton always marks *page 132*, as if the Kriss of my thoughts found in this number a Voirol column of his dereliction, <*near the Voirol-Algiers column more than three hundred dead were discovered last night. All were Maghrebians*> as if this bitchy watchdog <my thoughts> had been paralyzed by the strident curve of this fickle number, the gauge of distorting tendencies, the *Dow Jones* of my thoughts, *heavy trading today:* 1,320,000 cerebral operations, 1,320,000 shares exchanged? or 132 years of getting one's brains stuffed with idealist Christian garbage? 132,000,000 neurons reborn or 132 years of servitude? 132,000,000,000 enervated thoughts about *criticism* or 132 years of blind colonialism? 132,000,000,000,000 deaths caused by mental obnubilation? I saw you in an Iraq wrecked and ruined! *You saw nothing under the skies of Baghdad!* I saw you in an Iraq in agony of death! I saw you in an Iraq undone and defeated! *You saw nothing under the skies of Baghdad!* Ah! oh yeah! sure, my dear, I saw you in ecstasy over the telegenic sidewalks of the modern world! I saw that you were fascinated by the electronic graffiti writers in front of an Iraq in flames! *You saw nothing, nothing!* And I see you enervated by seeing me insist on this little defeat (in plain English) *of yours!* I saw the squadrons of aircraft of the sick Armada turn you into mental marmalade! *Smart bombs and Ecology! You realize your train of life is derailing! Tomahawks and the Rain Forest!* You lowered your arms and you're in bliss! I saw it happen! *You couldn't say anything, you're lying!* You lowered your underwear and you were in bliss! *Prout! Prouste!* Cum in your hand! *Prout! Prouste! in your panties of pleasure! Are you finished, my angel dear? Do you want Mommie to come and wipe you, or do you want to wipe yourself all on your own? Ya'got my message on the shortwave Sony that Mommie said she would? My eyes were closed while I was getting it all down, I wasn't watching TV, I came without even jerkin' off! Hey! Besides, my back was turned! Ya didn't see everything? (in Plain English) Amazing, how strong it was. First time in my life!* I saw well the little party you held for your overstimulated neurons! The more your blood was flowing the more you wanted! What thirst! You said, for the first time in my life I can finally rejoice in the death of others *without remorse!* You said coldly, *they only get what they deserve! All these jerks had to do was hold on!* You said your *ejacacultio praecox* is a function of your *televisual distraction*, but all that means is that you're *distracted*, Oh my God! What sinister distraction and what sad ejaculation at five o'clock in the evening! In awaiting *victory* you put a string of little yellow ribbons around the trees, you tied them to telephone poles, you tied them to the doors of your houses, <Merzak: What? It's already Christmas? Or Halloween?> and then you tied them to your pecker, you wrapped them around your family jewels, you afforded yourself a ton of good tribal conscience and you liberated the innocent soul of the old tribes, *no rectification*, for the most abject ruin of reasons, you got rid of Indians and for good measure you named your helicopters *Apache* and your smart bombs *Tomahawk. Your head is still burning*, but you've already done *tchoufa*, you did tchoufa and now you're etchoufing, your Dicky Do did Tchoufa! *Tchoufa of the southern area of Dien Bien Phu, Tchoufa! Algeria, Tchoufa! The Malvinas, retchoufa! Allende, Tchoufa! Sarajevo, Tchoufa! Nagorno Karabakh, Tchoufa! What a terrible spurt of five o'clock news! Let us screw in peace!*

I am at the Waldorf Astoria, my luggage is open on the folding rack, the curtains are closed off from a neon light, my eyes are open on the void that awaits me, *no rectifications!* I'm only a few hours from my departure. Good-bye family, pigs, chicks, *Good-bye my mules and others* and while waiting for the breakfast, I scratch into my blue notebook some childhood memories, some youthful worries, *stupidities of my youth!* I unroll the parchment of all my trials and tribulations, I calculate all the bad luck, I say the rosary of all my mistakes, I enumerate the hecatomb, I write in bold letters, *for since this morning, Tuesday, November 12, 1989, my brains, my marrow, and my guts are ground to **shreds***! *fadeout in black to the white crystal screen, the **Power Book 140** has become *my thought-treatment machine!* <only requirement: automatism: it goes on its own!>

No center, especially *no center*, not even several, just a few points, some *proliferating points*, you push on a key and the machine begins to purr, the Automaton, that's it, *it goes on its own*, it's the *practical* confirmation of the spiritual automaton, another one of Baruch's inventions, *the old dead dog of philosophy:* when you reach the knowledge of the third genre you push a button and the machine begins to spout forth the seven wonders of the world! a force and a will of steel! Nothing is said for your distraction! You're sovereign! Sovereignty is for you! The only thing I have to decide is *when* to stop it, *where* to stop it, *how* to stop it. The sentences line up on their own power, they're crazy about living: there's a problem of stopping, *don't turn it on since it goes all by itself,* that's what I'm explaining to R. B., *they turn his existence over to modern folly,* but he doesn't understand me very well, he doesn't get it, he's baffled by what I say about a text that engenders itself, it bothers him, he, the guy who is so wrapped up in his *love stories and gossip,* this history of the text that gets along without its author, this text that doesn't give a damn, *well, well,* about its progenitor, about its troublemaker! That, R. B., he can't comprehend, that, R. B., he can't swallow! the negator, the argonaut, R. B., he cherishes it!, *no rectification!* R. B. is ready to concede anything and everything to modernity, but he holds *mordicus* to his idea that the *authentic* novel needs an argonaut, *the writer is a boatsman who passes, my dear friend, not a computer programmer, come on! A ferryman of the Styx and not a common ferry driver,* I explain, I explain, I fill my lungs, but it's all for nothing, it doesn't get him anywhere, it doesn't say anything to him, *it doesn't ring a bell!* My explanation is worthless, it's all the same, *no rectification,* there I apply the rights of seniority, my tribe was there before everyone else, it's the colon that took it out of our hands with *Fissah, Toubib, Algèbre, Amiral, Récif, and Couscous.* It does add up to a mass, but it's not quantity that counts for us, we prefer that they borrow simple things like that! We, well, we prefer to give the little that we have! It's all the same to us if others *stammer* in our language, in a word, the friend doesn't understand me, and it's not a matter of time or pedagogy. I think I really *summed things up,* I believe I respected the contract, I even gave it to the *tester,* I even had a few good pages examined by the *taste text,* the best pages to try, the best *passages,* but he still displays the sign that reads *Daily Break from eight o'clock p.m. to two o'clock a.m., he sweats too much over his thing to accept something similar!* He has a hell of a time trying to get a *hard-on* with his thing! I said in vain that it had nothing to do with getting our dicks hard, he gets stubborn, he knocks his head against the wall, he wants it at any price, he *holds* to his erection! He affirms that it's *essential* for the proper maintenance of literary business. While he meditates and takes his breaks, I aim my cursor at the *Save* key and don't stop. The Automaton wakes up *illico* and begins to record the debate, it swallows the debacle, no problem digesting the scum I serve up to it, it knows I can always trash the good stuff. *But you're missing the essential, my dear friend, the essential, you're not taking any risks, you want it to flow smoothly, but that's not what the modern reader,* well, well, *expects of literature, it's not what he expects of a novel, a* real *novel,* while he catches his breath and lights up another cigarette,

the Automaton goes into the sleep mode, *zerrrrrrrrrr!* You might think it's swooning, a *mental collapse!* The conversation takes a bad turn, he doesn't feel *concerned* anymore, the obscurity *shuts him up,* I aim my little arrow toward the *Format* region and, a matter of delaying my move a little, I italicize quickly, *well, well* and *zerrrrrrrrrr!* The Automaton is always on the sleep mode, but in fact it's sleeping with only one eye closed, our conversation frankly doesn't interest him anymore, a literature without suspicion, a terrolature without suction, a sexoligature without egological mucus, he can't conceive, for him *it's pure automatism, it's the return to zurrealismus! in short the misunderstanding par excellence!* and while he's afraid, I'm still italicizing, he needs to feel that his reader *to come* will have the feeling that *it's the very Thing he holds between his hands!* He believes the *future of literature will be as hard as iron!* What *counts* is literature! Hors literature will be horror! Ur-literature! *Horror literature!* Let him say (paternalistically): *She was led astray, the poor soul! That's all! She'll get over it, she's healthy, indispensable, vital, just like our good Christian religion! But she's a woman above all!* Beforehand *you've got to pay her a little lip service!* You've got to seduce her, reassure her! Be reassuring with her! That's what she's looking for! That's what she wants! Everything else aside, that's what the modern reader is looking for! Do you understand, my dear, what I am writing is **me,** my experience, my memory, my sex, my philosophy! Ma, Mon, mine, mou, Moi, muck and mire, miasma! For R. B. it's because of must that the modern reader is ready to sacrifice his $21.95! Don't sing in my ear about the tax you've got to pay for your drives, don't give me a song and dance about how you've got to pay the tab for expulsion, <*to cash in on life, you must make a deposit! let me insist on this!*>, useless to replay my tirade on repulsion, useless to roar that people *don't give a damn about* impulsion alone! useless to insist that *our payments are due!* He stiffens up, he gets erect, his face goes gray, he gets yellow, he thinks my story of the Automaton, my little story about the *depopulator is the night when all the cows are gray!* A well of obscurantism! *You'll be thrown out of the party if you defend an idea like that before the central committee! That's all part of the past! Today you've got to be young and dynamic! Give body and soul to beings and things! Throw a slap in the face of disenchantment! Recover the subject! Give our readers the additional soul that they lacked! Give them seconds and even thirds!* Return of the ready-made intellectual! Free delivery! Domino's Pizza! Ah! Plain Text, again! Plain Text, *vite!*
It's the plan of the entire world's egoism leveled against me.
That's quite serious!

Sync # 4: *"Therefore, salutations to the son of my loins, who comes in his hour as an inter-*
preter and discovers the passage: You are the One who Crosses the Horizons of Glass and
the Saintly Constellation of Sahou.
Pass, you are pure."

Hard for me to understand in these conditions what I discovered as if by *magic* on
the Rue de la grande Truanderie, I run down it quickly, I happen onto the Rue
Saint-Denis where something strange, very strange, takes place. All the women seem
to know me, they all look as if they want to *celebrate my coming; they are wearing long*
skirts, they have rainbow-colored scarves, and they are all ready to let themselves go.
One says hello to me, another winks at me, as if we had slept together the night
before, another extends her arms like an old friend, a fourth invites me to come up
and look at her etchings, a fifth treats me like a good little boy with green eyes, a
sixth tells me that it would be good for me to come and have a nap with her, a sev-
enth that I'm the first man of her life, an eighth blows me a lusciously infinite kiss,
no rectifications! I continue hustling down the street, at the summit of the Rue des
Prêcheurs, and I become even more popular. All these women are standing in front
of the entry to the apartment buildings, in a glimpse they jump over to the side-
walk to *block my passage* <accordingly> and beg me to choose which one I'd prefer
to have next to me during my evening prayers. There's the one who thinks I'm gay
because I lowered my eyes when I crossed her path and the one who thinks I'm
Adonis because of my blond hair, there's the one who asks if I am a celibate husband with kids and the one who thinks I'm *cute*, the twelfth offers me a cup of hot
chocolate and invites me over with her sisters who live on the third floor. A pair of
twins ask me if I want to be married to them for an evening, there's also the little
fat one whom I find sweet and friendly, who didn't ask me for a thing, the thir-
teenth wants to know my name and tells me that I look sad, the fourteenth informs
me that I need a faithful and loving wife. *Your wife left you, don't be upset, I can be a*
better replacement, take me for your wife for one night, O young writer! you won't be sorry!
But please, don't be in the dumps, an adulterous wife isn't worth a poet's tear! The fifteenth
asks me if I've had sex since the last Ramadan, the sixteenth if I'm circumcised, the
seventeenth if I've ever been afraid in my life, if I'm afraid of women, if I'm afraid
of death, the eighteenth, if I'm a *foreigner*, if I love life, the nineteenth, if I like
blow-jobs and that she'd really *do a good job!* The twentieth treats me like a Sultan,
Come with your Sultane, O my handsome Sultan. The twenty-first looks like my mother,
the twenty-second like somebody in one of my nightmares, the twenty-third like

one of my dreams. When I get down to the Rue de la Cossonerie, the women are more discreet, they watch me furtively, but they don't dare to talk to me. I think they're a little frigid, that they're a little scared, a little bitter about life, they look like wax mannequins that somebody had forgotten to take out of a display in an empty storefront, a store that went bankrupt. I saw their high heels and in the eyes of these women I saw a whole bankrupt city, in their eyes, I saw an entire city turn into a mass of bankrupt stores, in their eyes, I saw entire lives go bankrupt, I saw an entire civilization *go* bankrupt! *Tchoufa!* Rue des Innocents, I felt a very strong fever shiver through my body, Rue du Plat d'Etain, an immense feeling of disgust rippled through my body, a tidal wave of giddiness tossed my soul into upheaval, a great pain clinched my chest, *no rectification!* I must have bifurcated, I must have left the galley, left the Rue des Morts, and I got lost, North, South, *North-West, North by Northwest*, it was impossible to tell, I was calmed a little on the Rue de Palestro when I climbed up the stair of oblivion, Rue de Racy, Rue Lemoine, Rue Blondel, Rue Saint Apolline, sorry for having treated these women so inhumanly, angry at myself for not having accepted to go and see the Guadeloupean woman's etchings, sorry for having turned down the offer to have tea with the Marseillaise, a blow-job by the nineteenth, shared the funereal bed with the twins. I found it monstrous not to have married the poetess, thinking that I had behaved in a *vile* manner with these women who had welcomed me with warmth and generosity, but it was *too late. Poor loquacious warblers who were emigrating from one desert to another, sad warblers who had lost their springtime.* I had to leave these damned streets immediately, immediately evacuate these haunted places before I went crazy. It was on the Rue de l'Echiquier that the checkerboard of destiny changed *abruptly*, I thought I had aimed myself in the direction of the Latin Quarter all the time I continued to walk away from it, I was at my wit's end on the Rue des Ecuries, <DUR, *red-black!*> slipping toward despair on the Rue de Conservatoire, in delirium on Rue Bergère, shivering with fear on the Rue de l'Echiquier, hopelessly lost, screaming, Rue d'Hauteville, an abandoned child, in tatters, Rue de l'Echiquier again, *yes, yes, I was going around in circles, I was incapable of reading a map, incapable of asking anyone where I was!* Hallucinating Rue de Mazagran, the shadow of a shadow Boulevard Bonne Nouvelle, and back on the Rue Saint-Denis, returning like a madman, my soul torn and struggling, my body in shards, *without nerves! ready to marry them all, drink their tea, their beer, admire their etchings, be their Sultan for a day, be the job of their blows, ready for anything, and behind me, behind me, the wind blew away all the marks of my footprints, and this song of Narcissus, handsome Narcissus <!> hauntingly returned:*

In the Passage Vivienne
She tells me: I'm from Vienna
And She wanted to add:
I live with my uncle,
He's the bro of my dad
And I wash his furuncle,
A good fate for my lad,
I looked for the wench, o'well,
In the Passage Bonne-Nouvelle,
In vain I await the lady
In the Passage Brady.

...

Well there they are, my loves in a passage!

Céline in an icebox, Proust in cotton, Kafka in the carapace of a cockroach, Pound in an insane asylum, Burroughs in a typewriter that slobbers and vomits, Mômo in a cancer, none of it *moves* R. B. He prefers to moo with the cows, to baa with the sheep, to howl with the wolves, hoot with the owls of Minerva, but with the cries of Francis Bacon he finds it all so *exaggerated,* he says that it's *excessive* and even *outrageous,* and *with a voice of authority, whenever you have one, you've seen them all! El bordomo, my friend! And ya wanna know, it's not even pretty! Gimme a break! C'mon buddy, I know ya didn't get your phud!*

The world of pee aitch dees knocks us awry, like concrete mortar boards! kata-lanbaneien, the world of peons and squares calls out to us, their cry cuts through the polluted atmosphere, through all the mental breeze, and it sounds like a metered poem, a lettered poem, almost a spectacle, a *tantric* poem, *a real parade of styles, parades of Societies.*
The aggregated Society for disaggregated Ph.D.s, the disaggregated philosophical Society, the disaggregated literary Society, the disaggregated historical Society, the disaggregated Society of Romance Languages, the disaggregated Society of Urdu, the disaggregated Society of economists, the disaggregated Society of puericulture, the disaggregated Society of physicists, the disaggregated Society of the Fourth World, the disaggregated Society of North Korea, the disaggregated Society of the League of Nations, the disaggregated Society of United Nations, the disaggregated Society of the living dead, the disaggregated Society of North Africa, the disaggre-gated Society of the Friends of Montaigne, the disaggregated Society of Francophony,

the disaggregated Societies of the eastern bloc, the disaggregated Societies of North America, the disaggregated Societies of South America. *You, the living dead of all nations of the world, get aggregated!*

"Pass, You are pure!"

The 1990s, *in plain text.*

I return, I go out, but it's all the same thing because in every event I'm not playing the same anymore, I'm out of bounds, *Penalty!* In bounds I'm just as much out of bounds, with a little more interiority, that's all, more *interiority*, because interiority has deteriorated, that's what, that's why interiority stinks, there's too much mental gas in their interiority, they all want to have their interiority made over in the meantime! Merzak: *What's going on in their heads? What's passing through their brains! Is it a new sect or what?* Too much flatulence and not enough nerve, even if I play, I'm still out of bounds, so I play all the same, but I'm out of bounds all the same, I play all the same, I'm in bounds, I'm in the shit, because there's no out of bounds, *no exit!* without knowing what they're talking about they'll tell you *no exit,* all the while they're sipping a stinging coffee at the Rostand, and under the pretext that I'm seated, right there, next to them, they think that we *share* the same world, they think that we *live in* the same world, they think that we *believe* in the *same world,* because nothing's out of bounds, because there's no place to retire, even if I'm in retirement! *early retirement!* even if I anticipated it all with a *golden parachute!* With anticipated disgust! By the anticipation of disgust! But also by the disgust of anticipation! This idea, yes, this idea, that's what they can't understand! But I'm not out of bounds! I'm in and out of bounds, I'm a fence sitter, a grandstand player, and you know, *that's no small business!* Outside of this melodrama, outside of this videodrama, *out of the game! Fin de partie!* That's how I'd like to have called my *pensum,* but the name was already taken, everything was taken in advance! Everything was *reserved!* Everything was polluted, everything was fucked from the start! So I fucked myself over and again, I fucked up retirement! If only I didn't have to write the story for my son, *the surgeon, he exists!,* I would never have found the strength to write my *Dead Letters,* I would have given it all up! I should have said *thumbs down!* I wouldn't even have had the idea, *because it's an idea, you can be sure of that!,* to write this homage to a dead writer, to *someone who really died for literature,* for once, *not a living-dead species,* but a *real* corpse, a writer who really died for literature! Not a zombie like me, I would never have found the strength to write *without correcting, without rewriting,* without the little story, without this fable that had been bestowed upon me one fine spring evening at the foot of Lovecraft's tomb, Prospect Street in Providence, Rhode Island, whispering in my ear the first words about the impending disaster, I wouldn't have had the courage to get myself wrapped up in this adventure, I'd have been incapable of *understanding* why Sadeg had died, I'd have been incapable of unveiling his assassins, finding the *real* assassins! I would have chalked it up to literature! I would have accused literature for being the whore you made of her! I would have been hoodwinked into believing that she was the guilty party! The bitch! The sleazebag! That dirty little liar! That cocksucker! the cockamaniphagiac! the anthropophagiac! the scriptophagiac! I would have been my own assassin! I would have sucked hash and waited for literary grace! I would have waited for the effects of addiction! That's why I say *presentissimally* that I'm not *out of bounds!* that there's no out of bounds! Nor homeland! nor familyland! at the limit, no orphanage! Mega! *Oh! mega orphanage!* Not even, not even adieu, fatherland! adieu, Motherland, adieu familyland! adieu, orphantofairyland! I return, I go out, I'm outside of the vilodrama, outside of the orphanofamily romance! out of this romance of orphan bandits and wreckers, these olivertwisteries, but I'm not *out of bounds.* To the contrary, it would be my way of still playing the game of being *in-and-out-of-bounds*, but out of the bounds of the games you play in your bars, in your cafés, out of the bounds of the game you play in your symposia, your colloquies. *In symposia there's sin and posing, in colloquies there's the cloacal cloak*, and it's not even etymological! nor philological! *Jic, jic, jic!* out of the boundaries of the ga*me*s you play in your journals! out of the bounds of the ga*me*s you play in the caca*dem*ies! *no rectification!* out of the bounds of the ga*me*s you play in your uni-adversities! out of the jimmies of the gimmes you play with zee-editors! no ga*me* for what you play with the indebted editors of journals! out of play, out of bounds, you'll fall flat on your face with all your literary loony tunes *if you really play by its rules!* It'll break your spine *if you really rub it hard!* So then, don't you see, dear Madame the Inspectrice, the early retirement was a ruse of my own! I had to reject all the pomp because I didn't need any more *distractions!* I didn't need any more of your deleterious distractions! *Early retirement,* beginning by putting me out to pasture, to fallow pasture that had first of all *intrigued, amused* you, almost made you laugh, because all the same you couldn't avoid asking me where I had got-ten such an *ingenious* idea, *no rectification,* be honest, girlfriend, it wouldn't have penetrated your thick skull that a ballpoint would roll out a nifty idea like that! Where did you find a golden jewel like that in such a puny little body? Where'd this madrepore come from? <look how sickening it is to hear yourself talking! don't you see that it doesn't mean a thing?> *Hands off my Jansenism! hands off my fascism!*

Boy, you really went into reverse! You really found my idea both *improper* and a tiny bit *untimely!* God only knows why, on that very day, the tone and groan of your voice were that of a Destiny, your voice intoned like that of the Kommandantur! *Literatchure,* my dear friend, *what you are saying,* it is verily true, is in zish Momente, in a cryzish! Sho what vee vish to try ish to firsht analysh sha shocial, politichal, and economichal caushes of zhish cryzish and, shecond, it ish to try to proposh perhapsh shome sholushuns, or shome remadies, but perch-pectivshs, zhorishuns of shthoughtsh shat will permit ush, perhapsh, to get ush out of zhish cryzish, *make it short please! In plain English!* Deo volente, let's see the light at the end of the tunnel, and *amen!*

<don't forget the little black heater;
citri-nore,
there is nothing,
no beings,
and it's hard to inspire life,
you have to take everything out of yourself, and it doesn't come on its own!>

The 1980s, *in plain rage.*

At the time, I was still delegated by the university to send an invitation to the master, he responded, I only now can comprehend, saying, *what I need, my good friend, is a pillbox that will block out all the street noise, that will be blocked off from the sight of the Street of the Dead, <death is murmuring!> a little molehole to avoid seeing or hearing the din, so that I won't be a servant to the public and so that I can sort myself out,* and here I hadn't understood a thing, me, the asshole, *<Me, I, myself, the man nailed, crucified, out of it, ligatured!>* I didn't grasp a thing about the master's *worry* for a moment, I, me, myself took pity on the master, I, me, myself, I allowed myself to believe that he was out of it, he was acting like an old fart! that he was beginning to babble! I had the disgusting thought that right where he had put his feet for the last time, myself and other assholes of the same species, we would be able to set our zombie feet in his footsteps and *take the baton, take up where he leaves off, step forward,* without losing a beat, *Entrez! Entrez! Step in! Please step in! Don't be shy! The place is empty! Come in and relax! Make yourself at home! Faites comme chez vous! Don't worry about the lice!* I, me, myself, I made it look as if there was a seat to be taken, a warm cushion just waiting for me! The only thing that shook me out of my dogmatic sleep, *<read, read that, read it correctly if you can!>* is that the master *hooked right on,* he immediately *plugged into* what I tried to tell you about the music of the sentence, the parabolic sentence and parataxis, into the time that was needed to write this damned sentence, into the energy that you need to get even the slightest sentence out of nothing, into the courage you need to have, the suffering you need to endure if your sentences aren't going to turn to shit, and while he was talking about all that, I nonetheless understood that his own kraft paper was made of our brains, I understood that he had discovered the road that passes directly to our brains.

I don't admit that ignorant fools,
because I don't have the time to think about a problem and cast it aside,
take advantage by ripping off another layer of my skin under the pretext
of driving me into a corner.
So what I am is never the elixir of some mental distillation
and in reality I am inaccessible, but they still get me
ALTHOUGH
since my work here
less and less in depth!

I left the apartment that he was living in at the time, with one eye on the street, another on the sky, a street where I had never felt so afraid, not because *<pa ... pa ... papa! pas de rectifications! no ... no ... nono ... no rectifications!>* I had understood I was alone, not because, *<parce <papa! papa!> que>* I had understood, O banality of banalities, that all humans of today stand alone, are faceless faces in the crowd, solitary in the multitude, alone in the great anthill of the world, but *mais <mama! mama!>* because I could go, *heading where? North? South? West? East? Northwest? North by Northwest! Southwest, South by Southwest? North-South?* Every exit was closed! everywhere the same thing! No exit, no direction! You think that you're living and that you're headed toward death, *<Wrong way! Wrong guess! Try again!>* you think you're living aging maturing wizening and soon *reposing* in the mausoleum of oblivion when *you're already* dead and when you pay your monthly bills to Ms. D.! *Hello, hello, my friend, how are you, Ms. D.!* the stubborn bitch! *The* mortgage hound! she won't spare you a dime! no *second mortgage! pay it all up at once! survival on the installment plan! Ms. D. as a moneylender! 840 monthly payments! 25,550 days! 613,200 hours! 36,792,000 minutes! 22,075,200,000 seconds! That's what you reap if you ask for a seventy-year mortgage!* Astronomical! Hardly! Not a bit! A mere trifle when you think about it! A real massacre! When everything has been mortgaged for aeons! I had gone three times in every direction, I made a hole nine hundred and ninety-nine times at each end of the suffocating planet, Afric, Amerfric, Eurofric, Asifric, fric, fric, fric! money, money, money! but then, that time, I dug in my heels, I'd neither go, come, leave, come back, go up, go down, nor go out, *Stuck!* I was cooked,

I would only yell or jab at people, anyone would do, young and strong and strapping, but *icy*, cold as a corpse, paralyzed! shivering! terrorized! And with only one thought in my head: hole up! build a barricade! get back into my chicken coop, close the curtains and wait, *no rectification*, until it was all over, until *everything was all over!*

:A blind fall back to earth:
The theory of the blind that the new city is mapping out, they're not afraid of anything and what they want is not a good enough indication of tendency: for them the earth turns on its axis as usual: Would I have been less fearful had I been born blind? Can a blind person be afraid? What is it that will frighten a blind person? *Something appears different from what it is. The best way to see is therefore to close your eyes and to touch it!*

Merzak: *I don't know what they daubed over their eyes, but it looks like they can't see anything, their eyes are opened wide like a walleye, but they don't seem to see anything at all, they come to be engulfed in this Museum to buy postcards and take pictures of the Mona Lisa behind her sarcophagus of glass! They come to see what they've already been shown in effigy! That's normal! An originary interdiction has to correspond to a postnatal scotoma! Conclusion: in order to see, one must be blind! You've got to rip your eyes out if you want to see a little more clearly! I tore my eyes out before the production of my first film! For my next film I'll have to crush my ears! The number of people with red-tipped canes in the theater of the Cinemathèque is disquieting! Every time I try to get lost in the basement of the Trocadero I leave with my head ablaze! Outside, on the Place Troca, at the exit from the movie, a horde of movie victims runs their hands over the cold bare flesh of the golden statues! Under the great pyramid the sky is brighter than a blind man's eyes!*

The *Mandarin* is filled to the gills: better say that it's the end of Ramadan, you can smoke, everything you say is smoky, everything you think is destructive, soon no one will see anything anymore, soon the moon will have totally disappeared from the horizon, soon the last glimmer of hope for the day will be hidden in the clouds, *for my next book I'd better tear my eyes out*
(return of the migraines).
Cephalou Anis
And gave
Alkaselsis!
Evidently, given the circumstances and the conditions in which I am presently living and working, it is not to be hoped that, toward the end of this story in free

verse, things will abruptly improve, that would go against the grain of what ought to happen! For the sake of *convergence*, it would probably be advisable to put off reading the little story that I had promised to write for my son's *edification*, for *convergence*, it would be in one's best interest to turn one's attention to the little fable that I concocted at the cost of my most fragile, most delicate, and most serene health, to *educate* my son, to give him an exact idea not of *what is waiting for him*, as the diviners and distillers of mendacious booze always say, *for there is nothing worth waiting for*, but what most *presently* makes him fret! *At this hour and for eternity!* For don't you see, dear Lady Literary Customs Inspector, it is not in this tale of a man pursued, it is not in this tale of a man exiled, that you will find the moral of this story, *this story is immoral from one end to the other!* this story is un*worldly!* but in what makes it *stand in suspension*, i.e., in the little tale, the little fabliau about the end of Brotherhood, the end of Motherhood, about the end of Familyhood and the end of Orphanhood (Ugh!)! A little story where I can flatter myself for having invented a new category for the *periodization* of modern history, *Orphanhood!* and a new temporal category of modern history, *the eternity of the totally present!* Where I demonstrate that, having mortgaged the present of your past, *mortgaged* the present of your future, and auctioned off the present of your present, *O Nihilism! O Families! O Castles in Spain!* there remains for you only the *eternity of your present!* as you can well observe, Madame Inspector, think nothing at all of making a *story!* there's nothing *exciting* enough, nothing worth the hubbub! Nothing *exalting* enough to write a story! not enough *nerve* to do another love story about the world, in which I demonstrate that, what? the *present of eternity* is lost! It's bitterness bound with the sun! nerve bound with the present! *It's gone, gone forever! Gone! like the snow in the sun!* <*Jupiter: "To be avenged of this theft I will send them a deadly gift that will charm them to the bottom of their souls, and they will cherish their own scourge!" Hesiod? Hesiod!*>

(Plain Text) Eternal present! Eternal health! Eternal happiness! Eternal youth! Eternal culture! Eternal reason! Eternal love! Eternal hope! and their *pendant ornament:* Eternal stupidity! Eternal sadness! Eternal unconsciousness! Eternal despair! Eternal hate! Eternal ignorance! Eternal senescence! Eternal literary boredom! Eternal consumption! Eternal consummation! Eternal bullshit! *O grievous present!*

Let me explain: You've got *to begin by being dead,* you've first got to die, you've got to pay your debt by dying honorably: the Mummy! <*"I died during the crusade for having consumed too many raisins on the beach of Syria."* Gustave? did he spit that out!> *(In plain English) I give up!* you can take everything! *Please, help yourself, it's free, Gratis!* Make yourself at home! Didn't you see the announcement? Let me inform you right off: *Due to his imminent retirement/the imminent doubling of his boredom/,* Professor

Mourad Ben Kda, the son of a businesswoman and a businessman, himself a businessman of modern letters, an amateur theologian from time to time, and author of iconoclastic and pornographic novels, is leaving the teaching of literature essentially to dedicate himself to yachting. He will leave the port of Duluth in a ketch that he acquired by virtue of the outrageous profits he drew from his notorious *Dead Letters.* Consequently all of the books and *goods* <?> that he acquired over the course of his long career in research and teaching <*nonsense*> will soon be auctioned off. The proceeds from this sale will be donated for the creation of a Sadeg Hedayet Foundation! The goal of this foundation will be to attempt to save, to encourage, and to defray the costs of publishing all of the writings that will allow people to better understand the nature of the great Iranian writer's death, born in Teheran on February 17, 1903, died in Paris on April 10, 1951, in a maid's room on the Rue Championnet. The remains of the body are still at rest in the *Moslem Chapel* of the Père-Lachaise Cemetery. *Dear Sadeg, you knew how to deliver yourself from this abominable world, would you be able to come to the annual Meeting on Contemporary Literature of Despair to be held this year? We await your response. Hope is a chain forged through ignorance . . .*

Sync # 5 (in plain text):
In the right tone, he arrived as the interpreter in his hour to defend his mother's heart, in front of the smiling god. In the right tone, he made Bennou, the phoenix of his spirit, surge forth. He had discovered the passage. *He had entered into wisdom in the sanctuary of the serene life . . .*

Algiers, *disaster*

What did the Mollahssons do during the Seven Furies?
Along their way, in passage, the women ran back
home and closed their windows,
closed the store,
Thus is the path of the dead in my country/
Cosi vanno via i morti, al mio paese!
From the stupid to the same! They appear as if they finally understood, that they could no longer be done with Mother Courage, that they would make some room for their *moitiés,* they adore her, for her they gather piles of arms and of tracts in their hands, they idealize her, cultivate her, virginize her, saint-martyrize her! transform her into a stealth bomb, *the "flamme" of the revolution!* her torch! *the woman is the future*

of man <boy, they really aragonize at a clip!> get going so that I can adore, get going so that I can push you ahead, get going so that I can promise you a radiant future, and now that I'm celebrating you, now that I'm erecting commemorative monuments for you, now that I'm immatriculating your posterity, and when the new peace comes, then the homunculus goes back in, the comedy's over! the tragedy's over! everybody goes back home, women and children first! *coitus interruptus!* the love story's over! comedy for a day! give way to the Mollahssons, the roaches and bugs! *No rectification!* make way for the snails and slugs! *Just kidding!* That's what they proffer, *it was only in fun, Mamyia, gimme a break! We nev'new wha'wewas doin'! The violence of the war went to our heads! Without wanting to vex you Mamyia, it would be preferable if you quietly stayed at home!* We just lost our bearings! *And from now to the time there will be another revolution,* the Mollahssons' thing, *it won't be tomorrow evening! Congratulations, Madame Algeria, for the fat imbecile baby you gave us! And thanks for all your help! Seven years, nuff said!*

Nono: *the terrible adventure ended in a lamentable rout! What had begun in exaltation is ending in nausea. The country? What country? <then, in rectifying>: But I'm confident, I'm confident in the future, dear Mrad! This state of things won't last; our new, active, modern administration will change all that!*

Ammeyar *<Lampedusian!>: The Algerians will never want to improve their lot for the simple reason that they're so conceited: their vanity is greater than their misery, the Nif, my brother <he sinks a stiffly pointed index finger into the tip of his nose!> the Nose, the mortally boasting pride of the Khorotol, any intervention of foreign persons in Algerian affairs —* **and our writers are these foreign persons, our accursed poets, our accursed artists!** *— all intromission of foreign persons in Algerian* **affairs**, *be it by their origin, be it by their ideology, is disrupting our dream of accomplished perfection, is deranging our complacent expectation of* **nothing***; trampled over by a dozen different nations, Algerians believe that* **a glorious past of enervated niggers** *gives them the right to sumptuous funeral celebrations! O my old comrades, do you think that you are the first in hoping you will lead Algeria into the great flow of universal history? Do you think you are the first to wish to derail this nation from the tracks of modern history? How many Muslim imams, how many Knights of the Order of the King of France, how many barons of Anjou, how many legists of the Great Catholic King have conceived the same admirable folly? And how many Spanish viceroys, how many reformed functionaries of Charles III? How many mamelukes and imperial dukes? Who's still in a position to remember their names? Algeria has chosen sleep, despite their invocations, why then would she have listened to them if she believed she is*

*rich and wise? If she is admired and envied by all other countries of Araby, and if, in a word,
she is* **perfect?**

The narrator felt discouraged, but he had drive enough to stammer <*beginning of
dialogue*>: *All that ought not to last; yet it will last forever; the human* **forever** *(all too
human, surely): a century, two centuries! We've already consumed the first two-thirds! After
which all this will be different! Different, but worse! History called us* <the Lions of the
Maghreb>: *those who follow us will be the Jackals, the Hyenas. As long as we are Lions,
Jackals, Sheep, the mules and the others, we will continue to believe ourselves to be the*
damned of the earth!

Siphi <*Celino-Esteràzic*>: Thus end our secrets as soon as they are broadcast in public! there is nothing terrible in us or on the earth and in the sky other than perhaps
what has not yet been said, we'll be calm only when everything has been said, once
and for all. ***Then silence can reign and no one will be afraid to speak;*** that's how it
will be!

At present, *damn it*, nothing that's worth living is within my reach! Macha jumped
ship, *boo! hoo!* under the pretext that we had no future together! She had to move
on with her life! <*Your* **Dead Letters** *was the straw that broke the camel's back!, she
chimes on, you sacrificed our happiness for your ambitions and your love of literature! Nonsense! Total nonsense!*> She put up with all these goings and comings! She couldn't
stand any more of these moves on the fly! And Geoff's presence was just too trying! She understood that he found my *Dead Letters* both *amusing and inoffensive!*
[Νουχ! Νουχ!] Her absence left a black hole in my life, *Sssssss! Svoooooop!*
I'm left with nothing! *Mrad Blackhole!*
<*Now that I'm this lover who is nothing without the one he loves, in this estrangement
that comes to him only from her. Without her eyes, without her voice. The power that novels wield over me! What is said in novels is what is shouted over the rooftops!*>
Djams and Hams, my sons, *are estranged from me,* under the pretext that their life
was in danger! Satellized!
My friends are *estranged from me,* under the pretext that I ought to stew in my own
juice! Satanized! *Boo! Hoo!*
The soldierlike journalists and the soldered critics, sticking together, *have lost all
interest* in me, under the pretext that their readers couldn't *care* about what happens to me! Satyrized! Now what can I do? Shut up? Retract what I've said? About
what? Continue to bury myself? *Zeus! Zeus! O Zeus! Have pity on your flock!*
Haven't I turned into what I was trying to fight when I wrote my *Dead Letters?* Am

I not a *man buried alive?* What my contemporaries fail to understand is that the *Fatwality* that condemns me is not limited to me alone! Behind the smokescreen of my condemnation there are thousands of writers, translators, typographers, journalists, and readers who *expect* to be condemned in their turn! Who are already condemned! Infibulated! Yesterday, Wabanate, the Japanese translator of my *Dead Letters,* was attacked on his way home: he was slashed across his eye as a *warning* to other translators <80 stitches! That's friendly advice!>. *Yesterday* Emilio was *mysteriously* assassinated in Milan: strangely, he had just accepted the task of translating the accursed book! Intimidated! Why are the Democrats waiting so long to do something about it? What are the media waiting for? What are the mediacrats waiting for? *Boo Hoo! 'Ala Souad Sa'dnah!*[11]

For a moment of pause: Did I deserve as much? If so, then how?
"An animal deprived of reason cannot be virtuous; but this omission doesn't constitute a demerit (demeritum), as there can be no infraction of an inner law. The animal has not been determined to be a consequence of an opposition to the moral law or the force of a counter-measure. Here the consequence is not a privation, but a negation for lack of positive reason. Inversely, imagine a man who abandons another of his kin, whose distress he witnesses, and to whom he could easily bring assistance. In his heart of hearts he hears the positive law of the love of one's next of kin; but then, he smothers this law that supposes an inner, real action committed by motives that make the omission possible. This zero is the consequence of a real opposition. Certain men feel first of all real grief in not executing goodness toward those to whom they naturally tend; force of habit relieves all, and this painful difficulty finally passes almost unperceived. Consequently, the sins of commission are not in any way morally *different from sins of omission, but solely in respect to* magnitude. *Physically,* in other words according to outer consequence, they are as well of a different species. Whoever receives nothing suffers from a lack, and the one who is deprived has lost something. But in respect to the moral condition of whoever sins by omission, it is sufficient that the sin of commission be of a higher degree of action."*[12]
—Here I am. Proven innocent? Or the beneficiary of royal grace? I can't tell which; I only know that I am here, seated, and am not at all moving about. *In sum, under house arrest!* Here I am, standing at the summit, or am I at the foot? I can't tell which, I only know that here I am, standing in, *suspenso gradu,* my legs <and my work>

---

[11] O ill fate! Sad be our black Destiny!

[12] Kant? Evidently! *Essay on the Introduction of the Concept of Negative Grandeur.*

have been under arrest for several months, without my raising a foot and without my making the slightest movement.

I am still waiting for a storm—*so I can burn my piles of paper*—and repetition. If only the storm would come! This waiting is already giving me an unspoken sense of joy and felicity, even if my judgment bears that repetition is not at all possible <But is it for sure? Hedayet perhaps? … >.

What will produce this storm? It will give me the chance to light a blaze in my chimney in the middle of summer. I will reduce my *identity* to ashes, but I'm ready; it will make me almost unrecognizable, even to my own eyes, but I shall not waver, even though I'm standing on one leg <the leg I didn't run over when I was in a bicycle race against death!> If the storm does not pass, I'll act surreptitiously; without in the least dying, I'll make out as if I were dead so that the family <?> and my friends <?> will bury me. When they wrap a shroud around me, I'll secretly conceal my waiting inside of me. No one *will want to know a thing about it!* Otherwise they would make sure they weren't burying a man who was still living.

Besides, for some time now I've been doing everything that depends upon me to avoid turning into the scapegoat they wanted to me to be. I'm amputating myself, I'm getting rid of all incommensurable material so that I can be reduced to a common measure. Every morning I strip away from my soul all remains of impatience and its endless effort; a lost cause, *the next moment, Geoff or his double (Rick?) reappears to remind me of what I have to do.* Every morning I shave all the stubble of ridicule off my face; in vain, for the next morning, my beard is just as long as it was before. I revoke myself the way banks revoke old bills in order to put new ones into circulation; but the operation never succeeds. *I change all the currency* of ideas and the paper hypotheses in my wallet into ideological pocket money—Aha! in that currency my fortune is reduced to next to nothing.

I stop; my position <writer in exile> and my situation <in "clan-destiny"> do not warrant being broadcast in words.[13]

Omar: *really hallucinating to see somebody lose his marbles so casually in the great avenues of thought! Hey! Mourad! Your line of sight is making you lose track of the certain in view of the uncertain! You're really taking a long shot! You're about to play double or nothing! You're tossing out the baby with the bath water! You're tossing your grandmother into the nettlepatch! If I were you that's not the way I'd bet on making my success!*

Mourad (after Beroalde): *Righte, then, tell me chap, ye really want to succeede? Prithee reade*

---

[13]Sam Beckett? *Wrong!* Kierkegaard, *Repetition:* C'est moi qui souligne, dear companion of exile!

*this volume from its true bias; 'tis composed like these paintings that showe thee one & then t'other; nay, be naught distraught, **my dear Omar**; if I have chaunced to say something that regards; or strikes thy eares from aside; and stinks a bit to thy tongue: 'tis a perspective of eares that is wronged & nay who might ever know in earnest what I mean if his soul happened naught to have seen and read the whole, & not inquired o'er the true sense of my busynesse!*

—Sapeva che il clero islamico avrebbe potuto esserne urtato?
—Certo che lo sapevo. Ho passato la maggior parte della mia esistenza a provocare i reli-giosi di svariate fedi. Sono cresciuto in Nord Africa, e ne ho visti tanti di fanatici sconvolti. Ma i musulmani dell'Algeria del Marocco e dell Tunisia, dove vive la mia famiglia, non osererbbero molestare nessuno. Capiscono che religione e società sono due entità diverse. Per-tanto sono riusciti ad acquistare una certa tolleranza. Anche in Grand Bretagna sono molti i musulmani contrari alla mia persecuzione. Recentamente, il 90 per cento degli ascoltatori di una stazione radio musulmana, a Bradford nell sostanza erano contrari alla fatwah. Ma nessuno ha osato di chiarlo pubblicamente, perché tenmono per la propria vita.

Voice-over, then

—Do you know that the Islamic clergy might have been damaged by this?
—I know it for sure. I have spent the greater part of my existence in provoking religious orders of many faiths and credos. I grew up in North Africa, and since then I have never seen so many religious fanatics overthrown. But the Muslims of Alge-ria and Morocco and Tunisia, I would never dare to touch anyone where my family lives. We understand that religion and society are two diverse entities. Therefore I have succeeded in keeping a certain tolerance. And too, in Great Britain there are many Muslims who live contrary to my convictions. Recently 90 percent of those polled through a Muslim radio station, at Bradford, were of views substantially contrary to the fatwah. But no one dared to state the point in public, for fear of their own lives,

voice-fadeout, Siphilus, voice-on: *God only knows how many valiant teeth we will have in our jaws when we return to earth the next time! Will we really ever see each other again? Riverrun? Riverrun! And au revoir!*

The time when I used to hold receptions is over, over is the time when I had little *fêtes* for my students, when in the cafés of the Via Benvenuto Cellini I used to discuss the fate of francophone literature, the time of my eccentric little acrobatic feats is over, my *intellectual overtures* are over, my door-to-door Jehovah Witness sales of slandered, riffled, emptied, strewn, washed-out *pensée* is over. Night has fallen, there are no more enchanted evenings, no more evening walks along the avenues of the dying city, no more tales to tattle to the kids before putting them to bed, no more ceremonies, no more rituals, *no more founding myths, no more "'master narratives'"* <nonsense!> the young woman sits with her legs crossed at the foot of the fireplace of the meeting hall, she throws little logs on the fire to make the flames rise, she tells Mourad about her day with the Oglala, *my lynx-like eye tells me that I used to look like an Oglala Indian woman, he told me without my saying a word, I think he's a little enamored of me. Might it be because you will have finally gleaned what I meant in what I told you about your work?* <in uttering this last word, she lays stress on what is neurotic in my writing and appears as if she broke an egg over the open book of the Law, *no rectifications, or you're dead!*> You wake up in the middle of the night in a sweat and you say you're afraid, I ask you what it is that causes your fright, and you start laughing, you think you can be done with your fears by taking refuge in all the seaweed and kelp of your slavish thought, you're insomniac, you wait for daybreak, you ruin your eyes, you drink one cup of coffee after the other, you make like you're somebody who doesn't fear a thing, from afar you look like a bird of prey, up close you remind me of a *baby*, and there's all this disorder, the disorder of the city, there's all this tobacco smoke you inhale while the men of the city are sleeping, you cough and hack a little, you try to lick your wounds, all the rats of the city get up at the same time as you, you say hello to them, you write for them, there are the storefronts, they sadden you, they've been empty for such a long time, emptied of their merchandise, sure, pass on, keep passing, but they been emptied of all *attractions!* and from time to time you'd better get out of your prison to breathe the human air of distress, *no rectifications!*, you see the sun rise, you're alone in your sleepy city, sure, sure, but still your neighbor is getting ready to *go to work*, he too has to tear himself away from his dreams to go off and dig his own grave in the debased and vile city, *no rectification!*, he too has to abandon his rage and spite to go off and play his role in the urban jungle, *no rectifications!*, he isn't the only one who doesn't realize, every morning, that he's waking up the entire neighborhood with his rusty muffler, one day a neighbor who doesn't care in the slightest about literature told you, yes, he was the one who told you, *literature doesn't interest me, it does nothing for me, it doesn't change a thing in my life, about literature I could give a good goddamn!*

Thank God, winter is coming and will seal all these human hordes into their houses. It'll close the windows, muffle all the clatter, slacken it, silence the song of death, the time of a season: no more howling, no more *modern* music! no more information, no more popular evening outings, no more *Music Festival!* no more *fraternizing!* No more Ray, no more ribbing and railing! *no rectifications!*, but if it continues the way it does this text will start to look more and more like the notebook of someone who is mentally handicapped: with his puns and conundrums, his vituperations, his transmissions of thought, his uncalled-for associations, his depraved ways, his unpaved streets, his jagged sidewalks, his toothless sarcasms, his untimely stories, his ready-made quotations, his deboned idiom, his undigested philosophy, his remorse and its hellish aftermath. *Can I still take pleasure in the time? Can I still play with time like a child?* Geoff, my bodyguard during the day, tells that he just finished reading my *Dead Letters*. I didn't dare to ask him what he thought. But at our usual teatime accompanied by *muffins* that we snack on every afternoon, he mustered all his intellectual courage and started in plain English, *I see no wrong in it, Mr. Mrad, no wrong at all! What's wrong with your folks, Sir? It's incomprehensible, totally incomprehensible to me! Beats me!* To reassure him I began to read aloud the refrain of the little story I was writing in English for Djams and Hams: *Once upon a time there was a man who wrote a book that a billion people didn't like because they thought it was blasphemy. They tried to kill him for it, and they ended up killing each other. Few of these people had even seen the book, yet everyone, friend and foe alike, found that it revealed their own worst natures.*

Geoff: *Which nature? What have they discovered about themselves that is supposed to be in your book?*

Mrad: *May be hyenas, may be wolves! Or just hatred!* Human fear and hatred! *Deep down! Very deep!*

Geoff: *Good grief! There is no hope then, no hope at all?*

Mrad: (serenely? sadly?) *Nope! Don't think so! Really don't!*

(again the night was black at my window from the attic where I could see the autobiography of the present time being written in the fluttering branches of the deflowered lilacs).

Sync # 6: *There used to be a passage of Desire.* [A6a, 4, 77]

Djams, *Plain text*, wants me to tell him once again the story of the mule from Mount Chenoua, Macha tells me, *sereine*, that she's busy writing a nice love story and won't stop beginning over and over again, she asks me what I did with my *Self*, and I'll write her back to explain to her that in order to extirpate it from my nervous system I had to be rid of my *fat Self soup*, in order to be delivered from you, my dear Macha, I had to get dissolved, I tossed myself into a three-ton vat of pensic acid, three tons of anti-selfic acid, three tons of mental acid, three cartloads of opium to get back to health, and there I am banished, there I am the prey of the little clever raging opinions in the middle of an America in free-trade agreements with Japan and Mexico and with a searing pain in my mercantile heart, she'll tell me that Djams has sprouted a fourth tooth and Hams has whooping cough, she'll tell me they're pining for Pops, she'll tell me they've grown to forget their name, and that on rainy days she still likes to eat the salad from the garden, just the way she did when she was pregnant, she'll tell me that they have learned a new language, a language that resembles that of their ancestors, but that this idiom doesn't quite yet resemble any language because *this tongue doesn't have any bone*, a tongue more dangerous than a rattlesnake, a tongue that can't be trained, <*Thus the dog frantically unearthed the stolen bone—and on the spot—was forgotten!*> she will tell me the three disasters that struck Alger-la-Blanche, <Her letter would begin thus: *what is happening in Algeria at this time is absolutely perplexing!*> and she'll make fun of me, she'll make fun of me on a fine morning in July, far, very far from the road that leads to *Corps* (Alpes-Maritimes?), far, very far from the road that leads to her body, to her thoughts, to her dreams, far from the dead end that leads to her soul, far from the teeth of the old dragon that was biting her neck before the big auction, before the Halles were destroyed, before my hole was dug, before she began *herself* to dig the hole of my grave. On my side, I will write a letter that will show her that I've lost the taste to summarize, a letter that will allow her to understand why I'm no longer afraid to forget the *big bowl of mush* she made of me, <My letter might begin thus: *What is happening in the United States at this time is absolutely perplexing!*> I'll tell her the story of my meeting with the palm reader, my trip to Skye and Harris, my trips to watch migratory birds in the Lofoten, <*monk puffins, mad bassans, black backs, tridactyl gulls, goldeneyes, penguins, Foerhh! Foerhh! Foerhh! Arctic Sterns! Labes' Terns <for the rhyme>! Tchiu! Tchiu! it's fa-fa-flying*> my night in Rorbu near Bergen, and oblivion, the slow progression of oblivion, the slow disaffection of the nerve factory. I'll also tell my story about the night I spent with the musk oxen, the closing of the doors of time, the barricades of Golden Valley, the peregrination to Duluth, the cutter that took me to Jerusalem, the fear that threw me *like a stray dog without a collar* on the great wall of China, *no rectifications!*, and then after that I'll go outside, I'll get out of my asylum, I'll leave my writing studio in order to start yelling, and then? I won't go and complain to the Pope, no, he wouldn't have pity on me, he wouldn't renounce me either, *who then would hear me if I yelled out among the hierarchy of Angels?! The Algerians? The others? The mules?*

The *last* critique: Master! Honorable Friend! May I ask a last question if you allow: what's happening to the French in all this? What are you doing to our fine French language?
—*As for French, everyone knows right now, it's enough to make one sick*
French is what is really sick
from an illness, a fatigue, that makes one believe one is French,
in other words at the end,
                    finished off!
so, yeah, what about *me? you've got to know from the start that I'm not French, and from then on, no rectifications!, that I am unfinished, the Unfinished! The Big Unfinished! The Great Unfinished Interior! I mustn't forget that I have* **my** *language and that I must* **speak** *it at all cost under the threat of death! Forever!*
—*But, Massster, cried the bewildered critic who had meanwhile finished his glass of bourbon, Massster, you're talking like a child!*
—*Everything, everything, my child, is bound up with kids! Get it, son!*
—*Gotcha, Master!*
Class dismissed!

Sunday, August 15, 1992: Once again I took refuge in the attic. No noise. No woman's voice, no kids crying on the second floor. The neighbors have deserted the area. There's absolutely no one around. This time I'm alone. *Totally.* I sent Geoff packing. The old man who I was has gotten weak and innocent like a child. That's me. This evening I take a walk downtown. Without a mask or a wig! Without dark glasses! Once again I am *myself* <risky, isn't it?> I recognized myself. Let *them* recognize me! *I don't give a damn!* Silence prevails. *Was I dreaming? Hallucinating? Sleepwalking? Stuttering? <Runaround of mechanical feelings, new idiocies, legendary concretions, little long-term cretinizing machines>* In truth, that's enough … 133 pages … Whew! enough? … enough! Got to get back to the notes scribbled for the *Spiritual Automaton.* Get these notes *finished.*
                    Current state of the *Geiger-Geist* counter: **Narrative impulsion:** 5. **Compulsion to write:** 5. **Theoretical repulsion:** 5. **Rhetorical expulsion:** 5. You pass. A grade of high pass. *I award you 5 on a scale of 5!*

From here on no more surprises; no more surprises, no more
decomposition, no more
shadows!
I'm prospering, I'm prospering!
Excellent, excellent!

"Pass, you are pure."
<dance, suffering, whirling dervish dance, idiotic dance!>.
It's Fini.[14]

Providence–Paris–Providence
June–August 1992

---

[14]*Post-scriptum.*
Current anatomy and physiology are such that they have blocked entry to what life is made for:
  an element
  that was left outside
  and replaced by
  society, family, army, police, administration, science, religion, love, hate, arithmetic, geometry, trigonometry, differential calculus, quantum theory, the failure of science, music, philosophy, metaphysics, psychoanalysis, metapsychology, Logos, Plato, above and beyond Plato Yoga, god, nonbeing, pure spirit, the cosmos, nothingness, the universe, being, the arcane idiocy of initiations, contingentility, Taylorism, rationing, the black market, war, epidemics, television, star wars, Baudrillard, commercial cinema, malls, social security, AIDS, Le Pen, deconstruction, and above all the stupidity and pretension of everyone who can't hold a candle to Derrida, and above all the stupidity of the new adepts of bad faith, and above that the bad faith of disinformation, and above disinformation, conservatism, and below fear in the guts, and cowardice besides, and underground all the cynicism, and on the ground Somalia, and in the sky the Ayatollahs, and on Haiti, and on the island of Haiti the hate #2 and on the hate #2 the hate #3, and under the tongue envy, and in the ear Radio-France, and in every neuron a CNN and in this hatred-hatred a disaster, and in the heart of the disaster Russia ready for salvage and in the heart hope, this little *something that thus was left in the sky beyond us, and what makes life live in the world beyond but that has nothing to do with us, I mean the intrinsic, archaic physical being of our anatomy.*
  That world beyond, like something between black humor and the cock-and-bull who cry, and that we call out for,
  but Salman Rushdie will tell it to you, because I believe that Salman Rushdie's book was written and that he grieves for the prenatal assassination of poetry!

Antonin, the Mômo, *Cahiers due Retour à Paris, October-November 1946.* Revised and rescribbled December 16, 1992, in Providence-Of-Every-Church!

Afterword

A Novel Machine

Algeria is no longer a Mediterranean paradise. It is neither the homosocial utopia André Gide celebrated at the turn of the century in *Les nourritures terrestres* nor the never-never land of what Club Med made of the North African coast sixty years later. Gutted and drained by violence aimed at everyone by every kind of warring faction, the nation no longer stands as the emblem of self-determination or successful decolonization. In any event we can be sure that Algeria never stood for the timeless landscape of metaphysical intensity that Albert Camus concocted for his readers at Editions Gallimard in Paris in the postwar years. However messy it may have become, Algeria remains a rich and varied terrain for the study of what Edward Said has lately called "a comparative literature of colonialism" with many "intertwined and overlapping histories."[1] Algeria, we can recall, is the repository of some of the most loathsome effects of the French mission of civilization. As of 1830 it was the site for the erasure of many cultures through direct and indirect means, including military intervention and the imposition of postrevolutionary missionary institutions.

The history is familiar and is being rehearsed everywhere and over again. But Algeria gives rise, for complicated and perplexing reasons, to bodies of writing that contend with the awesome burden of the colonial experience. Some works, like Frantz Fanon's *The Wretched of the Earth*, analyze the struggle that colonized populations must lead both against Western models of occupation and against the very nationalisms being used to inspire the production of energies directed toward liberation. Others, marked differently by their relation with the language and culture imposed on them, variously act out their plight by writing novels and fiction. As Françoise Lionnet, Winifred Woodhull, Isaac Yetif, and others have shown us, a considerable body of writing of French expression emerged from Algeria and the Maghreb in general over the past three decades.[2] Some writers invert the great tradition of realism to hold up a mirror before the abject conditions of life in the colonies. Others produce ironic and perversely drawn self-portraits of subjects mutilating themselves in view of their French masters. Others still look to myth to nuance many of the black-and-white views of crisis being purveyed in newspapers. Above all, most of these writers share a common pleasure and predicament: they move in and out of one idiom and another; they engage dialogue with the occupant in discourses whose very grammar conveys the values of the colonizers.[3] When the Maghrebian writer decides to write in the tongue of the enemy, already the illusion of a one-on-one confrontation is shattered. The writer begins to circulate *between* different registers of experience, and thus to gain access to undecidable areas of political expression, of creation, and of resistance, to areas where geographical and subjective positions cannot be easily fixed.

Réda Bensmaïa's novel intervenes in these traditions. It displays all the ironies and paradoxes that fall under the rubric of "Maghrebian literature of French expression" or "francophone writing" at the same time it throws them into a compelling geopolitical arena. For unlike many novelists who merely write of the horrors of postcolonial Algeria, Bensmaïa is not a neo-Balzacian champion of reality but an ironist. In *The Year of Passages* nowhere is found the slightest trace of those sententious truths that would make us feel proud, in colonial matters, to have chosen antireligious, anti-French, anti-Ayatollah, or pro-traditional points of view. Bensmaïa's writing gives us a hilarious, almost self-destructive portrait of a figure shuttling between different continents, cultures, and idioms just after the collapse of Franco-Algerian relations in 1992. The plight of the narrator, an Algerian, concerns the fate of French, Arabic, and English writing — generally speaking, of literature *tout court* — in a postelectronic age, that is, at a moment when space and time are so compressed that gaps or feedback loops required for critical assessment, for perspective, or space of constructive doubt, analysis, reflection, etc., are passed, or rather, *passé*. Bensmaïa shows us that there exists no eminence on which anyone can stand to look dispassionately at the questions of postnationalism, literature, and cultural politics. The reader of *The Year of Passages* will immediately ponder the limits of "agency" of literature or the "geopolitical aesthetic" of Algerian or francophone creation.

A new force is found in the very *passages* Bensmaïa follows from within the condition of a writer who is presented as a displaced North African subject, a philosopher, and a traveler torn asunder by the current conditions of Algeria. Like a riddle or extended conundrum, the novel is a self-deprecating expression of disbelief over what has happened to the author's motherland. A formerly beautiful country is now bathed in blood and senseless terror. The novel, a hilariously picaresque voyage to deadlands — to cemeteries in Europe and America, to Minnesota, to and from Algiers and Paris, to French and American academies — sets the native country in a funny and cruel perspective of an ingenuous wanderer. The protagonist of the novel is a nomad in a literal sense, an African who lives according to the seasons — except that, trained not as a hunter-gatherer, he is apprenticed instead in intellectual matters. He resembles a bungling trickster, a teacher and writer of things philosophical, literary, French, and francophone. He must subsist on whatever convenient political and aesthetic material he can fabricate from trends imposed on him by the American academy.

The story tells about how to stay alive and not be killed either by one's brethren or by the war machine of capital institutions. The novel transposes the energies expended in the gassy debates of our midst — let's say, about political correctness, about Lacan and the phallus, postmodernism versus poststructuralism, about Camille Paglia's rivalries with Madonna — onto *real* issues: about what it is to be expatriated against one's will, about why it is impossible to gain a pluricultural identity, about terrorism and literature, about what it means to be unable to do anything about bloodshed that goes virtually unnoticed in the world at large and, no less, from the standpoint of an individual who refuses to abandon a deeply enracinated commitment to literature — about the stakes of crafting a fiction that will address and embody all of these.

The Year of Passages tells of displacement and of the experience of deterritorialization and individual encounters in travels between Algeria, France, and North America. Although American readers will not fail to delight in the satirical representations that recall the traits of Montesquieu's sketch of prerevolutionary France in the *Lettres persanes*, they will quickly note that the novel grows out of a profoundly Algerian experience. The strength of the irony that drives *The Year of Passages* cannot be felt without a perspective of historical data that inform and inspire its writing. Written in French and originally entitled *L'année des passages*, the novel was finished in the fall of 1992. At that time events were indicating that Algeria was following a path descending toward total civil suicide. According to Mohammed Harbi, when the nation declared a state of emergency on February 9, 1992, the

announcement was a predictable outcome of two events, namely, the formal disso-
lution of the redoubtable Front Islamique du Salut (the FIS, organized and legal-
ized in Algeria in September 1989), and the assassination of the newly elected president Mohammed Boudiaf, on June 29 of the same year.[4]

Both events were symptoms of a deeper crisis that plagues every
Algerian citizen. According to Harbi, foreigners cannot easily understand the tumult
of the nation's culture because of its deep roots in Islam. Contrary to Western divi-
sions between church and state, in Algeria religion envelops and determines *all*
areas of secular life. When, in 1962, the new state liberated itself from French colonial dictate, it could not entirely reject European and Mediterranean economic
standards of production, first imposed in the nineteenth century, that had recently
been intensified in the Cold War. Any simple or draconian solution to the economic
and cultural hiatus between Algeria and industrial societies to the North risked opening the floodgates of social chaos. The gap between secular and religious cultures
was insurmountable. Quick shifts in the economy could unravel an Algerian cultural
fabric weaving together strands of many different religious and ethnic origins. The
menace of change or collapse was marked no less predictably by an intensification
of religious fervor. But the new Islamicism that was witnessed with the creation of
an independent Algeria in 1962 reached back to currents, forged in the 1930s, that
had also come in reaction to the sense of an erosion of deep-seated values. Thus in
the 1960s, the period in which Bensmaïa came of age, it could be said that in both
political and diplomatic spheres Algeria strove to impose on its citizens a single
national identity. *Ulemas*, reformist movements, sought a "return to roots" and a
means of purifying Islam, by removing the magma the religion felt it had accumulated from contact with rural worlds beyond the thin border stretching between
the Mediterranean and the hinterland to the south. At the same time, populist organi-
zations rallied support for Algeria without heeding the many contradictions coexist-
ing in a nation comprised of so many different cultures. These two movements—
reform and a return to fundamentals—grew in a context from which the newer,
francophone elites were attempting to find ways of extricating themselves. National
populism that carried the day in 1962 was fraught with "a congenital weakness"
resulting from an inner combination, first, of a voluntaristic project that envisioned
a strict administration of the country and, second, of another that would aim at
cultural restoration by appeal to the "myth of an 'authenticity.'"

The Algerian nation was thus defined by exclusively Muslim
traits. After 1962 secondary education returned to the compulsory teaching of religion; Arabization constituted a "demagogic instrument of social control"; social

space was redrawn to exclude women from much of its greater area; extensive networks of mosques were established to produce the uncanny impression of absolute unity. Religion became so closely identified with the state that Berber and mixed colonial elements that grew out of Algerian history were eliminated from educational programs. There soon resulted a citizenry divided between *francophones*, who directed the economy and occupied strategic positions that included government and the military ranks, and the *arabophones*, who administered education, culture, and justice. The "state revolution" that the FLN (Front de Libération Nationale) had heralded so proudly splintered after President Houari Boumédiane's death on December 27, 1978. Younger generations—including that of Bensmaïa—began to press for Berber and arabophone presence, for pluralism, and for dialogue. But no sanctions for mediation were ever established. In a knee-jerk reaction, members of the "socialist ideology" amplified speeches about a future "Algerian model" that would rid itself of all bourgeois and imperial forces residing in the country. A resonant "official" discourse, which hardly represented the complexities of the Algerian population in general, emerged. Islam was therefore staged to perpetuate itself at the cost of destroying the differences that had given to the culture so much of its wealth.

As of 1982, then, Islam was marshaled to silence Berbers and lay groups that had been visible long before the revolution. The conservative ulemas were not allowed to voice themselves independently of state channels: a hyperreactionary Islam grew within Islam, giving rise to a divided–united Algeria that drew allegiance from arabophone subjects who had been attempting to emerge into the ranks being vacated by the francophone elite. Soon born was the Front Islamique du Salut, an extremist group affiliated with the military forces that inspired many of the proclamations for a new and exclusively Islamic Algeria. The movement also appealed to urban middle classes that had felt threatened by the popular movements favoring the expression of extreme nationalism. As many elements of the Algerian bourgeoisie were obliged to identify with the FIS, the military ranks concurrently accrued power and, in the end, reduced the range of ideological options open to the population. In Harbi's words, the result today is that "society is simplified. Two forces oppose one another in a battle that tears the country to shreds: Islamicism and the army."

In the tally of elections at the end of 1991 the Front Islamique de Salut gained 188 seats; the timed-honored FLN, 19; the Socialist Front, 25; and independent candidates, only 3. The FIS succeeded because of widespread distrust and hate for the reigning system. As in the bloody years of the Algerian war, paramilitary groups were formed and led to a military coup on January 11, 1992. Conditions are now such that "the force of the FIS resides first of all in the hate that the majority of populations vows to the system set in place; a hate so great and of such cruelty and intolerance, of which the armed Islamicist elements are evidence, that it cannot be eradicated, as witnessed by the multiplication of various *maquis* [local resistance groups]." The army, already riddled with factions of different French and Islamic sympathies, profits from the middle classes and secular groups. It cannot cope with the differences in the society at large.

Some voices seek linguistic pluralism to include Arabic, Berber, and French, and others plead for sexual equality. Since the relations of force are so powerful and so nuanced, the impossibility of finding middle-of-the-road positions inspires inflexible behavior, intolerance, and improvised solutions to deeply seated conflicts scattered over a vast and varied geography. Who would ever want to be an Algerian citizen when "the confrontation between the army and the Islamicists contains all the ingredients to throw the nation into a filthy war: deadly and punctual raids on sea and in the air, use of napalm, reprisals, tortures, psychological warfare, the mix of blood and tears"? As Bensmaïa's novel shows in its initial episodes, when the narrator decides to forsake his Algerian identity, his only way out of the dilemma is to leave the country. Implying that no individual or group can aspire to dialogue or to a pluralization that would make the nation cohere, the action shows that in Algeria whoever is blessed with armed force reigns for the current moment. Reductive solutions are set in the place of complex social interactions. A *mimicry* of reasoned exchange or consensus results. In Algeria one witnesses an utter silencing of a world composed of principally minoritarian voices. The story of "passage" in Bensmaïa's novel seems to emerge from these harrowing conditions of life.

Recent events make the point even more salient. On May 9 and 10, 1994, four clerics were murdered, two French and two nationals (one an imam and the other a muezzin) in Algiers. Between September 1993 and May 1994, thirty-four foreigners were killed in the nation at large. On May 10, in Algiers a march was organized "for reconciliation and national peace." The 20,000 participants who took to the streets fell well below the predicted number of 100,000, to some degree because the FIS refused to participate in a demonstration favoring dialogue. In the words of Paul Cambon, the horror of such terrorism "only adds to the abundant list of French, foreign, and Algerian victims whose only wrongdoing was to attest to a shard of liberty and dialogue in a country where radical Islamicists want to impose a cope of lead and blood because they know that, hereafter, without recourse to violence and terror, they cannot impose their law."[5]

These traumatic events appear not only to set the narrative of
The Year of Passages in motion but also, in a complicated way, to aggravate and inspire
the author's very decision to write. Abandonment of an identity obtained through
the protagonist's origins is mirrored by the new affiliations that come with his passage from Algeria to North America. The movement to and from North Africa,
France, and North America also marks a shift away from necrofilial relations with
a dead father, a paternal cadaver of "French literature," in the direction of a decision
to *write* a piece of literature, neither French nor francophone, having no simple
generic status nor any recognizable place of destination or readership. The text that
results is nomadic. The very event of its writing shows us that those who dare to
practice literature of French expression in Algeria face dilemmas far more complex
than those that pertain to the literary tradition of the colonizer. Out of any context
or debate that would anchor the work, the novelist writes a fiction in America, within
a department of literature, in which the practice of writing often leads to dismissal.
In these departments professors speak the *lingua franca* of literary analysis, deconstruction, history, poetics, etc., but rarely do they dare to practice what they extol
(following Bensmaïa's style, mimicking the fabled protestor of good sense, we would
exclaim, "Bensmaïa is a teacher of literature, he's a film scholar, but he's not a writer!
Goddamn it, he's an imposter! He thinks he's a poet! He's a self-involved mandarin!
He's gone off the deep end!"). The writer commits critical treason by doing what
the academy generally sends to the pastures of what it deems to be an ineffectual
but necessary subculture called "creative writing."

In a vein that runs through the canon of French studies much
of *The Year of Passages* betrays not only the author's bitterness and sorrow over the
Algerian condition, but also the joys and fears that a scholar experiences in breaking
oedipal ties with the great masters—Rimbaud, Gide, Barthes—who colonized Algeria in polymorphous ways. At the same time, however, Bensmaïa incorporates
them into a narrative and style of his own signature. In roughly psychoanalytic
terms, the motherland and the father figures are "introjected" into the oral flow of
the narrator's exclamations. Literature, the *raison d'être* of the narrator's professional life, is given new urgency through the concrete risks that, as a subject raised
in Algerian and French cultures, he runs by satirizing his different physical and spiritual origins. Bensmaïa's many parodic allusions to Salman Rushdie constitute a defen-
sive strategy and a measure for comparison with the political violence of Algerian
fundamentalism. Were an extremist to read what Bensmaïa says about the deadly
silence of Algiers during Ramadan, the author would indeed, as the "plot" of the

novel suggests, become a target for assassination. A simplistic reading—and Bensmaïa suggests that the current climate in Algeria invites disastrous reduction of all
complex ethical and political dilemmas—would make the author an "enemy of the
people."

Early on in the story a cultural dignitary confronts the narra-
tor, who is rumored to be the author of a text entitled *Dead Letters* (apparently a
variant of the *Satanic Verses* or the *Lettres persanes*). The cultural attaché warns him
that if he publishes the text—and we know that it could well resemble *The Year of
Passages*—he is going to get "bumped off." Extremist hit squads, terrorists or fanatics of the kind that bombed the World Trade Center, might track him down. As
the placards announce near metal-detection devices in every international airport,
any antic in areas where terrorism is practiced is "no laughing matter." For his own
sanity the narrator is deported to the culturally pure, vapid, sanitary, walleyed world
of Minnesota. The passage from the urban setting to Middle America recalls what
another North African novelist of French expression, Albert Camus, in *L'homme
révolté* once conceived as a form of "intellectual suicide." But in the context of contemporary Algeria it is also a temporary escape from frightful political and historical realities.

No matter where he goes, be it Algiers or Minneapolis, the nar-
rator confronts death. At least two ironies are visible in the relation that the novel
holds with oblivion and the specter of an Algeria awash in the blood of civil chaos.
First, as the French title suggests, *L'année des passages* is both a year of "passages,"
"travels," "crossings," rites of "passage" (from academic to creative realms), as well
as of many deaths, of unlikely transmogrifications, that give new cause and purpose
to the lives of the author, his readers, and his translator. Each episode avers to be a
comic encounter with everything that resists language, be it the dark aura of the
Algerian Museum of Art, in which local artists are hidden behind those of the French
elite; an afternoon wasted with a real estate agent who drones on about her dead
husband and the solid construction of houses in Golden Valley, Minnesota; reflections on Chagall's paintings of homeland and exile; a crazed descent down the Rue
Saint-Denis in Paris; or, no less, an uncanny encounter with a grave digger in a
cemetery in Providence.

The narrator, however much he persists in denying his passion
for literature, no matter how often he decides to abandon it once and for all, nonetheless rehearses its beginnings, its movement, and its demise in order, inescapably, to
renew and displace it into different worlds. He does so by the tactile "experience"
of death through a physical encounter of language. Bensmaïa works in tandem with

Montaigne and Roland Barthes, two past masters who continually "tasted" the effects of death in their essays on literature and popular culture. Beyond the half-risible, half-real expression of paranoia over conspiracies that might be launched by the FIS, the novel deals with a continuous death that is enacted through creative writing. The forms of death mimed in the novel remain sacrificial insofar as they inspire creative reaction on the part of the reader: they prompt us to ask why we too are not writing novels. Why does a public weaned on Proust and Gide live the subservient lives of teachers of French fiction, as adherents of French alliances or members in associations of professors of French? Why not defy Jean-Paul Sartre by mobilizing the teaching and writing of literature to deal with political dilemmas? Why not use the heritage to reinvent and rearticulate the horizons of real and imaginary experience? *The Year of Passages* responds to these questions by working through the fact of death by means of a deliciously brute experience of language. The narrator's apprenticeship with oblivion takes place "out of bounds," out of a canon or an origin that would inspire him (but all the while within the bounds of a series of critical works in a collection labeled "out of bounds"). The chronicle leads the implied author back through his nation and culture of origin.

Several consequences result. For those who know Bensmaïa's other writings the shape of the text hardly resembles a memoir. It is more like a Vertovian montage of rushes or "dailies" of an autobiography shown being spliced together in a cutting room. Shards of life are cut and pasted (according to the code-*x* and code-*v* functions of Microsoft Word) into an open-ended structure that has no consequence or outcome. A comparison of the novel to his other work is illustrative. In 1985 Bensmaïa had completed *The Barthes Effect*, a translation of a thesis defended at the Ecole Pratique des Hautes Etudes (rewritten from a French version titled *Barthes à l'essai*), in which he stresses how the fragmentary form, Montaigne's personal essay, gets further atomized under the thrust of contemporary experience. At the same time Bensmaïa had written a number of pathfinding essays on sublimation in classical and modern cinema (including Chris Marker's *La jetée* and Albert Lewin's *The Picture of Dorian Gray*), as well as on film theory, for journals such as *Iris* and *Hors cadre*. He had also published pivotal essays on twentieth century literature of the Maghreb in Harvard's *New History of French Literature* and in *Yale French Studies*. In all of the work Bensmaïa argues that the transitional areas of film and writing—montages, special effects, lap-dissolves—bristle with expressive combinations of languages and images betraying signs of murderous force at work not just in narrative or in idea but all over the *surface*, be it that of a screen or a page of printed text. He locates where and how we get lost, spaced-out, or deterritorialized by the heterogeneous operations of writing that is not restricted to a single genre, tradition, or national style. At the same time, however, we know that our critical relation to literature and cinema is often determined by codes of production imposed by academic economies.

In *The Year of Passages* it is important to note how the text accounts for the author's commodification in the form of an institutional object. A crucial moment in the plot turns on the narrator's encounter with francophone studies. The narrator decides to leave his country *against* his will and discovers that he has been participating in a sham of those "expanded curricula" of "cultural" studies that embrace francophone literatures, not for the sake of broadening horizons, as he erroneously believed, but for serving institutional reasons or filling quotas dictated by administrators producing the sham of "equal opportunity." He is who he is because of a perceived institutional need to deflect attention away from the ineffectiveness of French literature on the horizon of multicultural studies. In a regional city of France, while sitting at a café (a site where many of the "events" of the novel explode into consciousness), the narrator discovers he was shanghaied into speaking at a francophone literature conference attended by partisans of good sense and first-world standing. From that moment the fiction moves toward and away from the image of the narrator — a sort of latter-day Roquentin — who discovers bad faith everywhere, but especially in the phony motivations that give rise to an American francophone "canon," or the fake sanctification that comes when a "minority" status is ascribed to fellow travelers and friends who inspire *The Year of Passages*: Kateb Yacine, Nabile Farès, and Abdelkebir Khatibi. The narrator's rejection of the ideology of francophone studies becomes the mettle and drive that produce in the physical object of the novel a real and variegated piece of francophone writing. Born of its resistance to itself, the novel is actualized when it "passes" its own limit and returns to a fictive Algerian heaven in its final sentences.

Bensmaïa patterns his text in accord with some of the precepts of Gilles Deleuze, who contends, first, that a minority literature never quite seeks an identity through a dialectical relation with a dominant culture and, second, that any writing worth its salt always emits *other* languages within its own idiom. In order to mobilize and animate the novel Bensmaïa finds two of his "other" voices in the tempo of Louis-Ferdinand Céline and in the glyphic, explosively self-contained, but also self-eradicating form of Antonin Artaud's poetry. Céline, the writer who crowns his sentences with exclamation points, uses puncatuation and spacing to yield a music of fear, desperation, irony, comic helplessness, and wit. For Bensmaïa Céline's style and rhythm are not merely vehicles of ideology, but energies that can be used for effractive *operations*, creative praxes, that shred every kind of received belief. Artaud, who is omnipresent in the poetic fragments that stud the narrative picture—and the text is composed as a storyboard or a script with autonomous sound and image tracks—is used to project single "takes," photographic shots, that turn the representation of speech into something that might be called a "becoming-image," an indeterminate, half-jelled, half-frozen picture of a writing self getting lost in the blitz of the passage of time.

The writers who inspire the narrator become the hidden agents, the real "conspirators" behind and within the writing. They allow Bensmaïa to parody many sacrosanct authors of different vanguards. Here and there we hear echoes of Thomas Bernhardt, Louis Althusser ("Louis the Strangler," as he is allusively named), Julia Kristeva, Jean-François Lyotard, and others, all of whom are turned into clichés of themselves. The painter he idolizes at the beginning, named Francesco (the toponym of San Francisco), refers of course to "Saint" Francis Bacon, who is taken literally and with an animality of the type that Deleuze brings forth in his famous essay on the painter. Almost every canonical author of twentieth-century France is parodied. But above all, it is Céline who offers a mechanism that sets language and the social drive into motion; his work envelops and even impugns Bensmaïa himself, making the first-person narrator the object of his own ridicule.

The overall effect is one of a continuous self-questioning and fragmentation. Many of the effects are obtained through a polyglot register. The text is written in several languages at once, which often translates into one idiom what it hears in another. Puns abound. The French of the original is stippled with English, Arabic, German and Latin. The narrator has the childish trait of writers—like a Maria Tsvetaeva—who listen and look to language for its multiple, confusing, wondrously generative, nonmimetic traits that expand and explode form within its own confines. The narrator is thus always *rewriting* what he hears (an inner voice, Aely, constantly informs him of anagrams that flicker on the surface of the words he sees and hears). His consciousness, a clownlike personification of one of his many alter egos, always intervenes between brackets or arrows to mock the serious tenor that pervades discourses that are being heard.

The movement that passes between idioms and nations takes place within a metaphor of writing. In the classical canon the latter takes the form of pen and ink ("as I long as I have enough ink and paper," Montaigne wrote at the beginning of his essay on vanity, "I can travel forever and endlessly"); modern writers such as Burroughs let the typewriter become the machine that takes over their affective lives; for Godard and his followers the camera becomes an autonomous writing instrument. Adhering to the same tradition Bensmaïa patterns *The Year of Passages* according to an electronic machine, a Macintosh Power Book 140. The "characters" of the novel function identically, as the novel of the author's other, "Macha," refers not at all to a real female but to a sort of macho-machine, a machination, a *machin*-truck, that drives the discourse. Both in proper names and in the syntax the reader will note abrupt shifts signaled by "plain text," "italic," "bold," or other commands set in 12-point Chicago type along the top of the Microsoft menu. These ruptures of thought, action, and deliberation that turn between expression and word processing bring us back to the kernal of creation, to an object-self that is *outside* of the writer's psyche or consciousness. The electronic apparatus dictates the pattern of experience being recounted, and it gives shape and movement to a language that can never be fixed in print. *The Year of Passages* becomes a novel-machine. It overtakes the author, the translator, and, best of all, the reader.

The translation has been crafted to reproduce wherever possible the rhythm of Bensmaïa's expression. Many of the tensions of *The Year of Passages* are visible on the surfaces of words and even characters. Meanings are produced from interferences that inhere in the almost unconscious montages of letters passing through different idioms. At the same time a mix of slang and philosophy makes the writing skitter from street-smart wit to the sublimities of Spinoza and Kant. Everywhere the styles of *others* are incorporated into Bensmaïa's diction, such that the English version is required to locate much of the meaning of the text in a perpetual clash of tones. Time and again the reader will note different inflections, in italic and roman font, in English and French, or between various types of parentheses, that all dislocate and redirect the movement of meaning. In order to reproduce these effects without laboring over a *mot juste*, in order to approximate the speed of transcription that passes over Bensmaïa's page as if it were a liquid-crystal screen, I have sometimes appealed to "plain French" or "plain English" to demarcate exactly where the narrator jumps between different idioms. In matters of slang I have attempted to obtain effects that skitter between a certain appropriateness (where clichés and, in the style of Céline, exclamations say things better than descriptive abstraction) and the contained explosions of irony. The task that Réda Bensmaïa has imposed upon the translator amounts to an invitation to follow the lead of a gifted writer. To him is owed the pleasure of the labor, but to the translator the burden of being responsible for what falls out of the bounds of Bensmaïa's magnificent creation.

Notes

1. *Culture and Imperialism* (New York: Alfred A. Knopf, 1993), 18.

2. Françoise Lionnet, *Autobiographical Voices: Race, Gender, Self-Portraiture* (Ithaca, N.Y.: Cornell University Press, 1989); Winifred Woodhull, *Transfigurations of the Maghreb: Feminism, Decolonization, and Literatures* (Minneapolis: University of Minnesota Press, 1993); Isaac Yetif, *Le Thème de l'aliénation dans le roman maghrébin d'expression française* (Sherbrook, Canada, 1972). Soraya Mékerta has authored a lively recent study: "Mektoub; or, *Written in the Sand:* Une poétique nomade de l'effacement" (Ph.D. dissertation, University of Minnesota, 1994).

3. Readers of postcolonial literature will welcome John and Jean Comaroff's work on the relation of dialogical principles (an essential literary condition) to colonization; see *Ethnography and the Historical Imagination* (Boulder, Colo.: Westview Press, 1992), especially 235–62.

4. The events are reported in Harbi's "L'Algérie prise au piège de son histoire," *Le Monde diplomatique* 41, no. 482 (May 1994), 3. His arguments are fleshed out in the four paragraphs that follow the citation of this note.

5. Paul Cambon, editorial, *Le Quotidien*, May 10, 1994.

Réda Bensmaïa is currently professor of French at Brown University. He is the author of *The Barthes Effect: The Essay as a Reflective Text* (Minnesota, 1987) and the editor of *Gilles Deleuze* (1989). He has written numerous articles on the readership of literary production to cinema, ideology and colonial history, the plastic arts, desire, and aesthetics, as well as issues surrounding linguistic alienation and bilingualism in Magrebian literature.

Tom Conley is professor of French and Italian at the University of Minnesota. He is the author of *The Graphic Unconscious in Early Modern French Literature* (1992) and *Film Hieroglyphs* (Minnesota, 1991). He has translated Michel de Certeau, *The Writing of History* (1992); Gilles Deleuze, *The Fold* (Minnesota, 1993); and Jean Louis Scheder, *The Deluge, the Plague: Paolo Uccello* (1994). His latest work, *The Self-Made Map: Cartographical Writing in Early Modern France*, is forthcoming from the University of Minnesota Press.